THE FIRST THING I REMEMBERED AFTER WAKING UP AS A REBOOT was a shrill yell bouncing off the walls and ringing in my ears. I had thought, *What idiot is making that noise?*

It was me.

I screamed as they branded my wrist with my bar code. I screamed as they locked me in a cell. I screamed until I arrived at HARC, and they told me screaming meant death. Acting like I was still a human child meant death. Disobeying orders meant death.

And then I was silent.

Also by Amy Tintera

Rebel

REBOOT

AMY TINTERA

HarperTeen is an imprint of HarperCollins Publishers.

Reboot

www.epicreads.com

Library of Congress Cataloging-in-Publication Data
Tintera, Amy.
Reboot / Amy Tintera. — First edition.
pages cm
Summary: "Seventeen-year-old Wren rises from the dead as a Reboot and is trained as an elite crime-fighting soldier until she is given an order she refuses to follow."—Provided by publisher.
ISBN 978-0-06-221708-0
[1. Adventure and adventurers—Fiction. 2. Soldiers—Fiction. 3. Dead—Fiction. 4. Science fiction.] I. Title.
PZ7.T493Reb 2013 2012051741
[Fic]—dc23 CIP
AC

Typography by Torborg Davern
14 15 16 17 18 CG/RRDH 10 9 8 7 6 5 4 3 2 1
❖
First paperback edition, 2014

For my sister, Laura

REBOOT

ONE

THEY ALWAYS SCREAMED.

My assignment wailed as she slipped in the mud, whipping her head around to see if I was gaining on her.

I was.

Her feet hit solid pavement and she broke into a full sprint. My feet grazed the ground as I chased her, my short legs easily overtaking her panicked attempt at running.

I yanked her arm. She hit the ground. The sound that escaped her mouth was more animal than human as she desperately tried to stand.

I hated the screaming.

I pulled two sets of cuffs off my belt and secured them

around her wrists and feet.

"No, no, no, no," she choked out as I attached the leash to her handcuffs. "I didn't do it."

I wrapped the leash around my hand and ignored her protests as I hauled her to her feet and dragged her down the street past the crumbling wooden shacks.

"It wasn't me! I didn't kill nobody!" Her movements became wild, almost convulsive, and I turned to glare at her.

"There's some human left in you, ain't there?" she asked, craning her neck to look at the number above the bar code on my wrist.

She froze. Her eyes flew from the *178* printed on my skin to my face and she let out another shrick.

No. There was no human left in me.

The screaming continued as I led her to the shuttle and threw her inside with the other members of her gang. The metal bars clanged down as soon as I stepped aside, but she didn't try to make a run for it. She dove behind two bloodied humans in back.

Away from me.

I turned around, my eyes flicking over the slums. The deserted dirt road stretched out in front of me, dotted with poorly constructed wooden homes. One of them was leaning so heavily to the left I thought it might tip over at the slightest gust of wind.

"Wren One-seventy-eight," I said, adjusting the camera on

my helmet so it pointed straight out. "Assignment secure."

"Assist Tom Forty-five," a voice on the other end of my com ordered. "In pursuit on Dallas Street. Coming up on the corner of Main."

I took off down the dirt road and turned into an alley, the stench of rotten trash hanging in the humid air so thick I wanted to bat it away from my face. I sucked in a deep breath and held it in my lungs, trying to block out the smell of the slums.

Forty-five whizzed past the alleyway on the paved road in front of me, his black pants torn and flapping against his skinny legs. He left a liquid trail behind him I assumed was blood.

I darted onto the street and flew past him, the sound of my boots causing the human ahead of us to turn. This one didn't scream.

Yet.

He stumbled on the uneven road and a knife fell from his hand and skidded across the pavement. I was close enough to hear his panicked breathing as he dove for it. I reached for him, but he shot to his feet, whirling around and slicing the blade across my stomach.

I jumped back as the blood trickled down my midsection and the human's lips turned up in a triumphant smile, like this was a victory.

I resisted the urge to roll my eyes.

Forty-five hurled himself at the beefy human, taking them both down. I hadn't trained Forty-five, and it was obvious.

Sloppy and impulsive, he was barely faster than the human.

Before I could intercede, Beefy took hold of Forty-five's neck, gave his helmet a shove with his palm, and jammed the knife straight through the boy's forehead. I winced as Forty-five gurgled and slid off him, his bright, gold eyes vacant as he hit the dirt.

The human scrambled to his feet, doing a few celebratory jumps and making whooping sounds. "Yeah! What you got, Blondie?"

I adjusted my com, ignoring the human's annoying attempt to bait me. "Wren One-seventy-eight. Forty-five down." Beefy's smile slid off his face at the mention of my number.

"Continue." The voice coming through my com was flat, uninterested.

I locked eyes with Beefy. I wanted him to run. I wanted to kick his legs out from under him and smash that triumphant look on his face into the dirt.

I took a quick glance down at Forty-five.

I wanted it to hurt.

Beefy whirled around and raced away from me, pumping his flabby arms as fast as he could. I bit back a smile as I watched him go. I'd let him have a tiny head start.

The chase was my favorite part.

I leaped over Forty-five's body and the human looked back as I gained on him. I grabbed his shirt and he stumbled with a grunt, his face smacking against the ground. He clawed desperately at the gravel, but it was too late. I jammed my foot into his back as I pulled out my cuffs. I snapped them around his ankles.

He screamed, of course.

"Wren One-seventy-eight. Forty-five's assignment is now secure."

"Report to the shuttle," the voice in my ear said.

I attached a leash to Beefy's wrists, jerking it tighter until he yelped in pain, and tugged him over to Tom Forty-five's body. He was a young kid, maybe fourteen or so, just out of training. I avoided his vacant eyes as I roped the leash around his wrists.

I lugged them past the sad little wooden houses of the slums and back to the shuttle, the blood crusting on my stomach as my wound closed. I shoved Beefy into the black box with the other humans, who cringed at the mere sight of me.

I turned away and headed for the other shuttle, pausing to pull the knife out of Tom Forty-five's head. The door opened and the Reboots looked up from their seats, their eyes immediately skipping over me to rest on Forty-five.

I pushed aside the nagging voice that said I should have been able to save him, and carefully placed him on the floor. I took a quick glance around the shuttle and found my most recent trainee, Marie One-thirty-five, strapped into her seat. I scanned her for signs of injury, but didn't see any. She'd survived her first solo mission. Not that I'd expected otherwise.

She looked from me to Forty-five and back again. She'd

been silent through most of our training, so I barely knew her any better then I had her first day as a newbie, but I thought the expression on her face was gratitude. My trainees had the best survival rate.

I handed the knife to the shuttle officer, who gave me a sympathetic look. Leb was the only officer I could tolerate. The only human I could tolerate, for that matter.

I took one of the small seats lined up inside the black windowless shuttle, pulling the straps down my chest as I leaned back. I stole a glance up at the other Reboots, but they were all looking at Forty-five sadly. One even wiped at tears on her face, smearing blood and dirt across her cheek in the process.

The lower numbers often cried. Forty-five probably cried. He was only dead forty-five minutes before he rose. The less time dead before the Reboot, the more humanity retained.

I was dead for 178 minutes.

I didn't cry.

Leb walked to the front of the shuttle and gripped the edge of the open door as he peered inside.

"Ready," he said to the officer piloting the shuttle. He pulled the door closed and I heard the locks snap into place. We lifted off the ground as Leb slid into his seat.

I shut my eyes until I felt the shuttle land with a jerk. The Reboots silently filed out onto the rooftop, and I resisted the urge to look back at Forty-five one more time as I brought up the rear.

I joined the line, pulling my long-sleeved black shirt off to reveal a thin white undershirt. The cool air tickled my skin as I tossed the shirt over my shoulder, spread my legs, and held my arms out like I was trying to fly.

I saw a Reboot fly once. He jumped off the top of a fifteen-story building with his arms spread, hit the ground, and tried to drag his broken body to freedom. He made it maybe two feet before they put a bullet in his head.

A guard, a human who smelled like sweat and smoke, quickly patted me down. He could barely keep the grimace off his face and I turned to look at the squat little buildings of the slums instead. The guards hated touching me. I think they flipped for it.

He jerked his head toward the door, wiping his hands on his pants like he could wash the dead off.

Nope. I'd tried.

A guard held the door open for me and I slipped through. The top floors of the facility were all staff offices, and I ran down several flights of dark stairs and stopped at the eighth floor, Reboot quarters. Below were two more floors Reboots were allowed to access on a regular basis, but under that it was mostly medical research labs I rarely visited. They liked to examine us occasionally, but they mostly used the space to research human diseases. Reboots don't get sick.

I held my bar code out to the guard at the door and he scanned it and nodded. My boots made little noise on the concrete floor as I made my way down the hall. The girls in my wing were all asleep, or pretending to be. I could see into every room through the glass walls. Privacy was a human right, not a Reboot one. Two girls per room, one in each of the twin beds pushed against either wall. A dresser at the end of both beds and one wardrobe at the back of the room to share—that's what we called home.

I stopped in front of my quarters and waited for the guard to call in the order for someone upstairs to open my door. Only the humans could open the doors once they were locked at night.

The door slid open and Ever rolled over in her bed as I stepped inside. She hadn't been sleeping much the last few weeks. It seemed she was always awake when I came in after an assignment.

Her big, green Reboot eyes glowed in the darkness and she lifted her eyebrows, asking silently how the mission went. Talking after lights-out was prohibited.

I held up four fingers on one hand, five on the other, and she let out a little sigh. Her face scrunched up with an emotion I could no longer stir up in myself, and I turned away to loosen the strap of my helmet. I put it on my dresser with my camera and com and peeled off my clothes. I quickly pulled on sweats—I was cold, always cold—and climbed into my tiny bed.

Ever's pretty Fifty-six face was still crumpled in sadness, and I rolled to stare at the wall, uncomfortable. We'd been roommates four years, since we were thirteen, but I'd never gotten used to the way emotion poured out of her like a human.

I closed my eyes, but the sounds of human screams pulsed against my head.

I hated the screaming. Their screaming was my screaming. The first thing I remembered after waking up as a Reboot was a shrill yell bouncing off the walls and ringing in my ears. I had thought, *What idiot is making that noise?*

It was me. Me, shrieking like a crack addict two days out from a fix.

Rather embarrassing. I'd always prided myself on being the quiet stoic one in every situation. The one standing there calmly while the adults lost it.

But at the age of twelve, when I woke up in the Dead Room of the hospital 178 minutes after taking three bullets to the chest, I screamed.

I screamed as they branded my wrist with my bar code, my number, and my human name, Wren Connolly. I screamed as they locked me in a cell, as they escorted me to the shuttle, as they put me in line with the other newly undead former children. I screamed until I arrived at the Human Advancement and Repopulation Corporation, or HARC, facility, and they told me screaming meant death. Acting like I was still a human child meant death. Disobeying orders meant death.

And then I was silent.

TWO

"DO YOU THINK THERE WILL BE A HOT ONE THIS TIME?" Ever asked as I smoothed my black shirt down to my pants.

"Didn't you think Seventy-two was hot?" I asked, turning around to give her an amused look. She liked it when I looked amused.

"Kind of a jerk," she said.

"Agreed."

"I feel like we've had a real dry spell."

I laced up my boots, genuine amusement sparking inside me. New Reboots arrived about every six weeks, a time many saw as an opportunity to replenish the dating pool.

We weren't allowed to date, but the birth-control chip they

shot into the females' arms the first day suggested they knew that was one rule they couldn't actually enforce.

For me, new Reboots meant only the start of a new training cycle. I didn't date.

The lock on the door to our room clicked, like it did every morning at seven, and the clear door slid open. Ever stepped out, looping her long brown hair into a knot as she waited. She often waited for me in the morning so we could walk to the cafeteria together. I guessed this was a friend thing. I saw the other girls doing it, so I went along with it.

I joined her in the hallway and the pasty human standing just outside our door shrank back at the sight of me. She pulled the stack of clothes she was carrying closer to her chest, waiting for us to leave so she could drop them on our beds. No human working at HARC wanted to enter a small, enclosed space with me.

Ever and I headed down the hallway, eyes straight forward. The humans built glass walls so they could see our every movement. Reboots tried to afford one another a smidgen of privacy. The halls were quiet in the mornings, the only sounds the occasional murmur of voices and the soft hum of the air-conditioning.

The cafeteria was one floor down, through a pair of big red doors that warned of the dangers inside. We stepped into the room, which was blindingly white except for the clear glass that lined the upper portion of one wall. HARC officers were stationed on the other side, behind the guns mounted to the glass.

Most of the Reboots were already there, hundreds of them sitting on little round plastic seats at long tables. The rows of bright eyes shining out against pale skin looked like a string of lights down every table. The smell of death hung in the air, causing most humans who entered to wrinkle their noses. I rarely noticed anymore.

Ever and I didn't eat together. Once we got our food, she split off to the table for the Under-sixties with her tray and I sat down at the table for One-twenties and higher. The only one who came close to my number was Hugo, at One-fifty.

Marie One-thirty-five nodded at me as I sat down, as did a few others, but Reboots over 120 minutes dead were not known for their social skills. There was rarely much talking. The rest of the room was noisy, though; the chatter of Reboots filled the cafeteria.

I bit into a piece of bacon as the red doors at the end of the room opened and a guard marched in, followed by the newbies. I counted fourteen. I'd heard a rumor the humans were working on a vaccine to prevent Rebooting. It didn't look like they'd succeeded yet.

There were no adults among them. Reboots over the age of twenty were killed as soon as they Rebooted. *If* they Rebooted. It was uncommon.

"They ain't right," a teacher once told me when I asked why

they shot the adults. "The kids ain't all there anymore, but the adults . . . they ain't right."

Even from a distance, I could see some of the newbies shaking. They ranged in age from about eleven or twelve to older teenagers, but the terror that radiated from them was the same. It would have been less than a month since they Rebooted, and it took most much longer to accept what had happened to them. They were placed in a holding facility at the hospital in their hometown for a few weeks to adjust until HARC assigned them to a city. We continued to age like normal humans, so Reboots under the age of eleven were held at the facility until they reached a useful age.

I'd had to spend only a few days at the holding facility, but it was one of the worst parts of Rebooting. The actual building where they kept us wasn't bad, simply a smaller version of where I lived now, but the panic was constant, all consuming. We all knew there was a good possibility we would Reboot if we died (it was almost certain in the slums), but the reality of it was still horrifying. At first, anyway. Once the shock wore off and I made it through training, I realized I was much better off as a Reboot than I'd ever been as a human.

Rebooting itself was simply a different reaction to the KDH virus. KDH killed most people, but for some—the young, the strong—the virus worked differently. Even those who died of something other than KDH could Reboot, if they'd had the KDH virus even once in their lifetime. It Rebooted the body after death, bringing it back stronger, more powerful.

But also colder, emotionless. An evil copy of what we used to be, the humans said. Most would rather die completely than be one of the "lucky" ones who Rebooted.

The guards ordered the newbies to sit. They all did so quickly, already informed that they followed orders or got a bullet in the brain.

The guards left, letting the doors slam as they hurried out. Not even our hardened guards liked to be in the presence of so many Reboots at once.

The laughter and scuffling started right away, but I turned my attention back to my breakfast. The only newbie I had any interest in was my next trainee, but we wouldn't be paired up until tomorrow. The Nineties liked to break 'em all in right away. Considering the speed at which we healed, I saw no problem with the newbies being roughed up a little. Might as well start toughening them up now.

The Nineties were rowdier than usual today. I shoved the last piece of bacon in my mouth as the hollering rose to an annoying level. I dropped my tray on top of the trash can and headed for the exit.

A flash of color streaked across the white floor, coming to a stop at my feet with a squeak. It was a newbie, shot down the slick tile like a toy. I just missed stepping on his head and planted my boot on the floor.

Blood trickled from his nose and a bruise had formed under

one eye. His long, lanky legs were sprawled across the floor, his thin white T-shirt clinging to the frame of an underfed former human.

His close-cropped black hair matched his eyes, so dark I couldn't find his pupils. They probably used to be brown. Brown eyes usually took on a golden sort of glow after death, but I liked his blackness. It was in stark contrast to the white of the cafeteria, to the glow of the other Reboots' eyes.

No one came near him now that he was in my space, but someone yelled, "Twenty-two!" and laughed.

Twenty-two? That couldn't be his number. I hadn't seen anyone under forty in a few years. Well, there was a Thirty-seven last year, but she died within a month.

I nudged at his arm with my boot so I could see his bar code. Callum Reyes. Twenty-two.

I raised my eyebrows. He was only dead twenty-two minutes before he Rebooted. He was practically still human. My eyes shifted back to his face to see a smile spreading across his lips. Why was he smiling? This didn't seem like an appropriate time to be smiling.

"Hi," he said, propping himself up on his elbows. "Apparently they call me Twenty-two."

"It's your number," I replied.

He smiled bigger. I wanted to tell him to stop it.

"I know. And yours?"

I pulled up my sleeve and turned my arm to reveal the *178*.

His eyes widened and I felt a surge of satisfaction when his grin faltered.

"You're One-seventy-eight?" he asked, hopping to his feet.

Even humans had heard of me.

"Yes," I said.

"Really?" His eyes flicked over me quickly. His smile had returned.

I frowned at his doubt, and he laughed.

"Sorry. I thought you'd be . . . I don't know. Bigger?"

"I can't control my height," I said, trying to pull myself up an extra inch or two. Not that it would help. He towered over me and I had to lift my chin to look him in the eye.

He laughed, although I had no idea at what. Was my height funny? His laugh was big, genuine, echoing across the now-silent cafeteria. It didn't belong here, that laugh. He didn't belong here, with those full lips curving up with actual happiness.

I sidestepped him to walk away, but he grabbed my wrist. A few Reboots gasped. No one touched me. They didn't even come near me, except for Ever.

"I didn't catch your name," he said, turning my arm so he could see, oblivious to the fact that this was a weird thing to do. "Wren," he read, releasing me. "I'm Callum. Nice to meet you."

I frowned at him over my shoulder as I headed for the door. I didn't know what it was to meet him, but *nice* was not the word I would have picked.

* * *

Newbie day was my favorite. As I headed into the gym later that morning with the other trainers, excitement rippled through my chest. I almost smiled.

Almost.

The newbies were sitting on the shiny wood floor in the center of the large room, next to several black mats. They turned away from the instructor to look at us, their faces tight with fear. It looked like no one had puked yet.

"Don't look at them," Manny One-nineteen barked. He was in charge of wrangling the newbies their first few days here. He'd been doing it for longer than I'd been here, and I figured it was because he was bitter about missing the opportunity to be a trainer by one minute.

All the newbies focused their attention on Manny except Twenty-two, who gave me that weird smile before turning around.

HARC medical personnel were lined up against the wall behind Manny, holding their clipboards and some tech equipment I couldn't begin to understand. There were four of them today, three men and a woman, all dressed in their usual white lab coats. The doctors and scientists always came out to observe the newbies. Later, they would take them down to one of the medical floors to be poked and prodded.

"Welcome to Rosa," Manny said, arms crossed over his chest, eyebrows low likc he was trying to be scary. Didn't fool me. Not now, and not when I was a twelve-year-old newbie.

"Your trainers will pick you tomorrow. Today they will

observe you," Manny continued. His voice echoed across the gym. It was a giant empty room with dingy white walls that had been stained with blood many times.

Manny began listing off their numbers and pointing for our benefit. The highest was One-twenty-one, a well-built older teenager who probably looked intimidating even as a human.

HARC coveted the higher numbers. Me, above all. My body had had more time than most to adapt to the change, so I regenerated and healed faster than anyone at the facility. Rebooting only occurred after every bodily function shut down. The brain, the heart, the lungs—everything had to go before the process could start. I'd heard the number of minutes dead referred to as a "rest," a time for the body to regroup and refresh and prepare for what was next. The longer the rest, the better the Reboot.

Today was no different. Manny paired off newbies and ordered them to go at it, giving them a chance to impress us. One-twenty-one picked up the fighting quickly, his partner a bloody mess within minutes.

Callum Twenty-two spent more time on the floor than standing in front of his shorter, younger partner. He was clumsy and his long limbs went everywhere except where he wanted. He moved like a human—as though he'd never Rebooted at all. The lower numbers didn't heal as fast and they had too much leftover human emotion.

When humans first began rising from the dead they called it a "miracle." Reboots were a cure for the virus that had wiped out most of the population. They were stronger and faster and almost invincible.

Then, as it became apparent a Reboot wasn't the human they'd known, but a sort of cold, altered copy, they called us monsters. The humans shut out the Reboots, banished them from their homes, and eventually decided the only course of action was to execute every one of them.

The Reboots retaliated, but they were outnumbered and lost the war. Now we are slaves. The Reboot project began almost twenty years ago, a few years after the end of the war, when HARC realized putting us to work was far more useful than simply executing every human who rose. We didn't get sick; we could survive with less food and water than a human; we had a higher threshold for pain. We might have been monsters, but we were still stronger and faster and far more useful than any human army. Well, most of us anyway. The lower numbers were more likely to die in the field, making training them a waste of my time. I always picked the highest number.

"I give Twenty-two six months," Ross One-forty-nine said from beside me. He rarely said much, but I got the feeling he enjoyed training as much as I did. It was exciting, the possibility of shaping a scared, useless Reboot into something much better.

"Three," Hugo countered.

"Wonderful," Lissy muttered under her breath. At One-twenty-four, she was the lowest of the trainers, and therefore got last pick of newbies. Twenty-two would be her problem.

"Maybe if you trained them better all your newbies wouldn't

get their heads chopped off," Hugo said. Hugo had been my trainee two years ago, and he was just ending his first year as a trainer. He already had an excellent track record of keeping his newbies alive.

"Only one got his head chopped off," Lissy said, pressing her hands against the messy curls that sprang from her head.

"The others were shot," I said. "And Forty-five got a knife through the head."

"Forty-five was hopeless," Lissy spat. She glared at the floor, most likely lacking the courage to turn that glare on me.

"One-seventy-eight!" Manny called, motioning me over.

I walked across the gym floor into the center of the circle the newbies had made on the ground. Most avoided eye contact.

"Volunteer?" Manny asked them.

Twenty-two's hand shot up. The only one. I doubt he would have volunteered if he had known what was coming.

"Up," Manny said.

Twenty-two bounced to his feet, a smile of ignorance plastered on his face.

"Your broken bones will take five to ten minutes to heal, depending on your personal recovery time," Manny said. He nodded at me.

I grabbed Twenty-two's arm, twisted it behind his back, and cracked it with one quick thrust. He let out a yell and jerked the arm away, cradling it against his chest. The newbies' eyes were wide, watching me with a mixture of horror and fascination.

"Try and punch her," Manny said.

Twenty-two looked up at him, the pain etched all over his face. "What?"

"Punch her," Manny repeated.

Twenty-two took a hesitant step toward me. He swung at me weakly, and I leaned back to miss it. He doubled over in pain, a tiny whimper escaping from his throat.

"You're not invincible," Manny said. "I don't care what you heard as a human. You feel pain; you can get hurt. And in the field five to ten minutes is too long to be incapacitated." He gestured at the other trainers, and the newbies' faces fell as they realized what was coming.

The cracks reverberated through the gym as the trainers broke each of their arms.

I never liked this exercise much. Too much screaming.

The point was to learn to push aside the pain and fight through it. Each broken bone hurt just as much as the last; the difference was how a Reboot learned to work through it. A human would lie on the ground sobbing. A Reboot didn't acknowledge pain.

I looked down at Twenty-two, who had slumped to the ground, his face scrunched up in agony. He looked up at me and I thought he might yell. They usually yelled at me after I broke their arms.

"You're not going to break anything else, are you?" he asked.

"No. Not right now."

"Oh, so later, then? Great. I'll look forward to that." He winced as he looked down at his arm.

Manny pointed for the trainers to go back to the wall and gestured for the newbies to come to him.

"You should get up," I said to Twenty-two.

Oblivious to Manny's glare, Twenty-two slowly got to his feet, raising an eyebrow at me.

"Are we doing my leg next?" he asked. "Can I get some warning next time? A quick 'Hey, I'm going to snap your bone with my bare hands right now. Brace yourself.'"

One of the trainers behind me snorted, and Manny snapped his fingers impatiently. "Get over here, Twenty-two, and sit. Quietly."

I joined the trainers, taking a quick glance at Twenty-two as he plopped down in the circle. He was still watching me, his eyes sparkling, and I quickly looked away. What a strange newbie.

THREE

I SNUCK ANOTHER GLANCE AT THE END OF THE LINE AS I PICKED up my tray for lunch. Twenty-two was there, scanning the cafeteria. His eyes rested on me and I quickly turned away as he began to wave.

I focused my attention on the human behind the counter as she plunked the steak on my tray. There were three of them lined up behind the glass counter, two women and a man. Reboots used to do the service jobs at HARC as well, until the humans began to get restless about the lack of employment and HARC created a few more jobs to keep them happy. Still, they often looked less than enthused about serving Reboots.

I let them fill my tray, and then I headed across the cafeteria to take my usual seat next to Hugo. I stuck my fork into the perfectly cooked steak and popped a bite in my mouth. HARC gave a line to parents of Reboots about how we were so much better off in their care (not that the parents had a choice). We would be useful, they said. We could have something resembling a life. I didn't know if we were better off, but we were certainly better fed. A Reboot could survive on less food, but we performed at our best when we were fed regularly, and well. We became weak and useless, like a human, if we were denied food.

"Can I sit here?"

I looked up to see Twenty-two standing in front of me, tray in hand. His white shirt was bloodied, probably from one of the Nineties taking a second opportunity to break him in. It would often go on for a couple days, until the guards got tired of the commotion.

"The Under-sixties are over there," I said, pointing to Ever's table. They were talking and laughing, one boy gesturing wildly with his arms.

He looked back at them. "Is that a rule?"

I paused. Was it? No, we started that one ourselves. "No," I replied.

"Then can I sit here?"

I couldn't think of a reason why not, although it still struck me as a bad idea.

"Okay," I said hesitantly.

He plopped down in the seat across from me. Several of the One-twenties turned to me, a combination of confusion and annoyance on their faces. Marie One-thirty-five squinted, her head swinging from me to Twenty-two. I ignored it.

"Why do you do that if it's not a rule?" he asked, gesturing around the cafeteria.

"The closer numbers have more in common," I said, taking a bite of steak.

"That's stupid."

I frowned. It wasn't stupid. It was the truth.

"I don't see how the minutes you were dead affect your personality," he said.

"That's because you're a Twenty-two."

He raised an eyebrow before returning his attention to his meat. He poked it like he was afraid it might jump up and return the favor if he bit into it. He wrinkled his nose and watched as I popped a chunk in my mouth.

"Is it good?" he asked. "It looks funny."

"Yeah, it's good."

He looked down at it doubtfully. "What is it?"

"Steak."

"Cow, then?"

"Yes. Never had meat, huh?" All types of meat were hard to come by in the slums, unless a human took a job with HARC. They controlled the farms, and hunting was often a fruitless effort. Overhunting had stripped the land of most wild animals years ago. A rabbit or squirrel would pop up on occasion, but I didn't see them often. Reboots ate better than most humans, which only made them hate us more.

"No," Twenty-two replied. His expression suggested he had no interest in changing that.

"Try it; you'll like it."

He raised a bite to his lips and shoved it in quickly. He chewed slowly and swallowed with a grimace. He looked down at the hunk of steak left on his plate.

"I don't know. It's weird."

"Just eat it and quit bitching about it," Lissy snapped from a few seats down. She had little patience for her newbies. Twenty-two would be no exception.

He glanced over at her briefly, then back to me. Lissy frowned at his total disregard for her.

"She's kinda grouchy, huh?" he said quietly to me.

Always. I almost smiled when I looked over to see Lissy stabbing her meat like it was trying to get away. Hugo raised his knife over his steak with a grimace, imitating her. Ross One-forty-nine blinked twice at him, which I was pretty sure was his version of a smile.

"Everyone's saying she'll be my trainer," Twenty-two said.

Lissy's head popped up and she pointed her knife at him as she spoke. "Everyone is right. So shut it and eat that."

Twenty-two's defiant face was different from any other I'd seen. His smile didn't disappear; it merely changed to a mocking, challenging grin. He dropped his fork and leaned back in his chair. He didn't have to say *make me*. It was clear.

Lissy shoveled her remaining food in her mouth and jumped to her feet, muttering to herself. She shot a look at Twenty-two as she stomped past.

"I hope you get yourself killed quickly so I don't have to put up with you for long," she growled.

"I think that's the strategy she takes with all her newbies," Hugo said with a chuckle, watching as she pushed Fifty-one out of her way and flew through the exit doors.

"She's supposed to make them good Reboots," I said, the memory of pulling the knife out of Forty-five's head flashing through my mind.

"Then maybe you should do it," Twenty-two said, perking up. "You get to pick, don't you?"

"Yes. And I don't train such low numbers."

"Why not?"

"Because they're no good."

Marie One-thirty-five let out a short laugh, and Twenty-two cast an amused glance from her back to me.

"Maybe because they don't have you. Also, I'm insulted." His smile suggested he was not.

I poked at my plate with a fork. He could have a point. The lowest of the newbie groups never stood a chance. Was it because of their number? Or because of Lissy, who trained by screaming at them? I looked up at him, at a loss for what to say.

I'd never thought about it.

His smile faded, clearly taking my silence as a rejection. It was not how I meant it, but I kept my mouth shut as he began eating.

I wandered down to the sixth floor after lunch. I was often bored in the days between training cycles, unsure what to do with myself. I couldn't imagine being a lower-number Reboot, one of the many not cut out to be a trainer. They had little to fill their days, especially since HARC considered most forms of entertainment unnecessary for a Reboot.

I peeked into the indoor track room and saw several Reboots running, some racing or chasing after one another. I moved on to the next room, the shooting range, which was full, as usual. It was a favorite pastime. Reboots at every booth pointed their guns at the paper men lined up against the wall. Most hit the intended target—the head—every time. HARC didn't trust us with real bullets, so the ones we used inside the shooting range were made of plastic.

I pushed my hands into the pockets of my black pants as I headed for the last door, the gym. I pulled it open and glanced at the groups of Reboots in various corners. Some were just talking; others were making halfhearted attempts at fighting to avoid yells from the guards.

Ever was in the corner, one of the paper men from the shooting range taped to the wall in front of her. She bounced from foot to foot as she gripped a knife in her hand, studying the target in front of her seriously. A tall girl stood next to her, Mindy Fifty-one, and she watched as the knife flew from Ever's hand and landed in the wall, in the middle of the paper man's head.

Ever stepped closer to Fifty-one and leaned in to talk to her as I headed toward them. Reboots used to play darts in this corner of the gym, but HARC had put a stop to that. The knife throwing was a game, too, just one that looked like practice. I didn't participate, but a few Under-sixties kept a record of how many throws hit the head in a single session. Ever was in the top three, last I'd heard.

Ever started to run her hand down Fifty-one's arm but caught sight of me and quickly stepped away from her, pasting a smile on her face as I approached. "Hey."

"Hi," I said, glancing at Fifty-one. She wiped her eyes with shaky fingers and I wished I hadn't come over. Under-sixty emotion made me uncomfortable. I moved back, ready to make an excuse to leave, when she took a few steps away from us.

"I gotta go," she said. "Ever's at forty-two throws."

I nodded and turned back to Ever, who was pulling the dull knife out of the cork wall. She held it out to me and I shook my head. She went back to her spot on the gym floor and squinted at the target as she turned the knife around in her hands.

"You let Callum sit with you today at lunch," she said, raising an eyebrow at me just before she threw the knife. It landed right in the middle of the forehead.

“He can sit anywhere he wants,” I said, that defiant look he’d given Lissy today flashing in front of my eyes.

Ever laughed as she grabbed the knife out of the wall. “Right. Because you always eat with Under-sixties.”

I shrugged. “He asked. I couldn’t figure out a good reason to say no.”

She laughed again and took her spot a few feet in front of the paper man. “Fair enough.” Her eyes lit up as she glanced over at me. “Do you like him?”

“No.”

“Why not? He’s cute.”

“Everyone here is.”

It was true that all Reboots were attractive, in a way. After death, when the virus took hold and the body Rebooted, the skin cleared, the body sharpened, the eyes glowed. It was like pretty with a hint of deranged.

Although my hint was more like a generous serving.

Ever gave me a look like I was a cute puppy who had wandered over for attention. I never liked that look. “It’s okay to think he’s cute,” she said. “It’s natural.”

Natural for her. I didn’t have feelings like that. They didn’t exist.

I shrugged, avoiding her eyes. She often looked distressed when I told her I didn’t have the same emotions she did. I found it was better to say nothing at all.

She turned away and rocked from foot to foot, letting out a

breath as she prepared to throw again. She stilled as she focused on the target, the knife poised in the air and ready to throw. As she let go one boot came off the ground, her body shifting forward with the effort. She smiled at the knife lodged in the wall.

She threw the knife several more times as I watched, until she hit an even fifty and turned to look at me.

"What did you talk about?" she asked. "I saw him trying to engage you in conversation, that brave soul."

A smile tugged at the edges of my lips. "Food, mostly. He'd never had meat."

"Ah."

"And he asked me to train him."

Ever snorted as she turned away from me. "Poor guy. I can't imagine you training a Twenty-two. You'd probably break the guy in half."

I nodded, watching as the knife sped through the air again. Ever was only a Fifty-six, and she was a good Reboot. Or an adequate one, at least. She'd kept herself alive four years, following orders and successfully completing her assignments.

"Who was your trainer?" I asked. I hadn't paid much attention to Ever as a newbie, even though we lived in the same room. She'd come to HARC almost a year after me, and I hadn't been a trainer myself yet.

"Marcus One-thirty," she said.

I nodded. I vaguely remembered him. He'd died in the field several years ago.

"I was the lowest number in my newbie group, so he got stuck with me." She shrugged. "He was good, though. Thank goodness Lissy wasn't here yet. I probably would have been dead the first week."

Plenty of Lissy's trainees had made it through training perfectly fine, but a string of bad ones had cemented her reputation as a newbie killer. Perhaps it was deserved. Perhaps Twenty-two would be the next victim of her bad luck.

I looked up at Ever as she sank the knife into the wall again.

"How many is that?" she asked.

"Fifty-two."

"Hot damn."

I couldn't help a smile as she grinned at the target. Maybe the Under-sixties weren't all hopeless.

FOUR

MANNY MARCHED THE NEWBIES INTO THE GYM EARLY THE NEXT morning for the choosing. They followed him through the door in a straight line, their faces tight with fear and exhaustion.

They were followed by a few doctors in lab coats. Their tests and X-rays continued into today, which contributed to the newbies' exhaustion. I remembered having to run on a treadmill at a steep incline while attached to all sorts of contraptions. The doctors kept increasing the speed until I finally fell off.

Groups of Reboots stood in clumps behind the trainers, curious to see who got which trainer. Ever was in the corner to my left with several Under-sixties, leaning against the wall as she watched the newbies line up in front of us.

I turned and my eyes went immediately to Twenty-two. His gaze was on Lissy, but when he caught me looking a smile broke out on his face, followed by a pout.

Please? he mouthed.

Pleading didn't work with me. Human targets pleaded with me all the time. "Please don't take me." Or, "Please don't touch me." Or, "Please don't kill me." Didn't work.

That smile, on the other hand . . . I almost let one creep onto my own face.

No. That was ridiculous. I couldn't let this weird smiling boy convince me to do something stupid. I was the best trainer; I only took the best newbies.

Maybe they're the best because you make them that way. The thought had been nagging at me since last night.

The door banged open and the gym quieted as Officer Mayer, commanding officer of the five HARC facilities, strolled across the room. He came to a stop next to the medical personnel and folded his arms over his protruding stomach. Officer Mayer spent the most time in Rosa, the largest of the five facilities, and often showed up to observe the newbies. He watched them throughout the entire six-week process, to keep an eye out for the good ones and weed out any who might be trouble.

"One-seventy-eight," Manny said.

I turned my gaze to One-twenty-one, who nodded at me. He already knew I would choose him. The other Reboots would have told him.

I looked at Twenty-two. How long did he have with Lissy? They'd be out in the field in a couple weeks, and with Lissy's track record, he'd be dead within two months.

His dark eyes held mine. Not many people looked me in the eye. Humans didn't want to look at me at all and Reboots were either scared or felt I was some sort of superior.

And that smile. That smile was strange here. Newbies didn't come in smiling; they came in terrified and miserable.

He was definitely weird.

"One-seventy-eight?" Manny repeated, looking at me expectantly.

"Twenty-two." It was out of my mouth before I could change my mind. A grin spread across his face.

The trainers looked down the line in astonishment. Lissy's mood was already improved.

"Twenty-two?" Manny repeated. "Callum?"

"Yes," I confirmed. I stole a look across the gym to see Officer Mayer rubbing his chin, his mouth twisted in something bordering on disappointment. I thought he might object, make me chose a higher number, but he stayed silent.

"All right," Manny said. "One-fifty?"

Hugo opened his mouth, closed it, and turned to me with a frown. "Are you sure?"

Twenty-two laughed, and Manny motioned for him to be quiet.

No. "Yes," I said.

"I . . . One-twenty-one, then," Hugo said, looking at me like I might protest.

I didn't. I stood there as the other trainers picked their newbies and broke off to start discussing the process. I waited, numb from my decision, until Twenty-two strolled over to me, his hands shoved into the pockets of his black pants.

"You like me after all," he said.

I frowned. I didn't know about that. I was curious. Intrigued. Like? That was pushing it.

"Or maybe not," he said with a laugh.

"I considered what you said. About the lower numbers not having me."

"Ah. So not because of me."

He smiled at me and I got the impression he didn't believe a word that had just come out of my mouth. I shifted from foot to foot uncomfortably. I wanted to fidget, and I never fidgeted.

"Are you a good runner?" I asked quickly.

"I doubt it."

I sighed. "We'll meet at the indoor track every morning at seven."

"Okay."

"Try not to scream when I break your bones. It bothers me. You can cry if you want; that's fine."

He burst out laughing. I didn't realize that was a funny statement.

"Got it," he said, trying unsuccessfully to cover his grin.

"Screaming, no. Crying, yes."

"Have you ever handled any weapons?"

"No."

"Skills?"

"I'm good with tech stuff."

"Tech stuff?" I repeated with a confused frown. "Where did you see computers in the slums?"

"I'm not from the slums." He lowered his voice when he said it.

I blinked. "You're from the *rico*?"

He laughed slightly. "No one calls it that. It's just Austin."

No one from the *rico* called it that. Outside, in the slums, we used the Spanish word for *rich* to refer to the wealthy side of the cities.

I took a quick glance around the gym. There were a few Reboots from the *rico*, but they were certainly in the minority. I'd never trained one. My last trainee, Marie One-thirty-five, had lived on the streets in Richards, and she'd been tougher for it. Slum life made better, stronger Reboots. Twenty-two was doubly screwed. I wasn't sure I would have picked him if I'd known that.

"How'd you die?" I asked.

"KDH."

"I thought they had mostly eradicated the KDH virus in the wealthy parts of town," I said.

"They're close. I'm just one of the lucky few."

I grimaced. KDH was a nasty way to die. They named the virus for the city that had been ground zero of the outbreak, Kill Devil Hills, North Carolina. It was a different strain of a respiratory virus common in children, and killed most humans within a few days.

"My parents took me to a slum hospital because they couldn't afford any medicines," he continued.

"That was dumb." Everyone knew KDH was rampant in the slums. No one was getting treated for it there.

"Yeah, well, they were desperate. And they didn't realize . . ."

"You only go to the hospital in the slums to die and be sorted."

"Yes. How did you die?" he asked.

"I was shot," I said. "Any other skills?"

"I don't think so. Wait, how old were you when you died?"

"Twelve. We're not talking about me."

"Who would shoot a twelve-year-old?" he asked with the innocence that could only come from living his entire life inside walls where nothing bad happened.

"We're not talking about me," I repeated. What was the point, anyway? How would I explain a life of strung-out parents and dirty shacks and the fighting and screaming that came when they went too long without a fix? A rich kid would never understand.

"Newbies!" Manny called, motioning for them to join him by the gym door.

"We're not starting now?" Twenty-two asked.

"No, you have more tests to do," I said, gesturing to the medical personnel. "We'll start tomorrow."

He let out a sigh as he ran a hand down his face. "Seriously? *More* tests?"

"Yes."

He looked from me to the other newbies, who had already joined Manny. "All right. I'll see you tomorrow, then."

"Twenty-two!" Manny yelled. "Move it!"

I gestured for him to go and he jogged across the gym and disappeared out the door. The trainers all stared at me as they filed past. Hugo and Lissy stopped in front of me, wearing matching confused expressions.

"What's wrong with you?" Lissy asked. She had her hands on her hips, her eyebrows lowered.

"Is he special or something?" Hugo asked.

Lissy rolled her eyes. "Yeah. He's real special, Hugo."

I shrugged. "Maybe I can make him better."

"Don't count on it," Lissy muttered. She stalked away. Hugo gave me another befuddled look, then followed her out.

I turned to go, my eyes catching Ever's. She was smiling, her head cocked to the side, then she nodded as if to say, *Good for you.*

FIVE

A SOUND WOKE ME IN THE MIDDLE OF THE NIGHT.

I blinked my eyes until the dream I'd been lost in faded, loosening the death grip I had on the sheets. I'd been in the corner of a tiny apartment, watching my parents yell at the people in the living room. In the dream, they were yelling about me. In reality, I'm not sure they had cared about me enough for that sort of attention.

I rolled over to see Ever crouching on her bed, her teeth bared as she let out a low growl. The noise grew louder as she rocked back and forth on the mattress.

"Ever," I said, sitting up. Violation of the rules, but surely they would want someone to wake her up and stop the racket.

She turned to me. Her bright eyes showed no sign that she recognized me. In fact, she snarled.

"Ever," I said again, tossing off my covers and placing my feet on the cold floor. I reached for her shoulder and her head whipped to me. She opened her mouth and her teeth scraped across the skin of my hand.

I snatched it away. *What the hell was that?*

I held my hand to my chest, my heart beating oddly. I was nervous, I think. I was rarely nervous.

My eyes darted to the hallway. Through the glass wall at the front of our cell I could see a guard approaching, his flashlight aimed in our direction. He stopped in front of our room and peered inside, reaching for his com. He turned away as he spoke into it and I looked back down at Ever, rocking on her bed and growling from deep within her throat. I wanted to press my hand to her mouth to stop the noise, to make the guard go away before Ever got into trouble.

I heard the pounding of footsteps and turned to see a scientist in a white lab coat running down the hall. I took in a sharp breath as I watched the scientist talk frantically to the guard, his bushy eyebrows lowered in worry as he watched Ever.

Humans didn't worry about Reboots. They didn't run to help them.

The scientist pulled a syringe from his pocket and my stomach turned over as I pieced together what was happening.

They'd done something to her, and now they'd realized

they'd messed up. Messed *her* up.

Ever pounced out of bed with a height and speed I had never seen before, smashing her body against the wall. I gasped, stumbling back until my legs hit the bed.

She head butted the glass, a line of blood trickling down her face when she straightened. She bared her teeth at the humans and they both jumped away, the scientist almost dropping his syringe.

"One-seventy-eight."

I turned my eyes to the guard yelling from the other side of the wall.

"Subdue her."

Ever began pounding her hand against the wall, a slow, rhythmic hammering.

Pound.

Pound.

Pound.

Her face determined, she looked at the humans like she would rip their faces off if given half a second.

"I said subdue her, One-seventy-eight. Get her down on the ground." The guard glared at me.

I slowly rose from my bed, clenching my hands into fists when I realized I was shaking.

I'm not scared.

I repeated it in my head. There was no reason to be scared of a Fifty-six. She couldn't hurt me.

Or could she? I'd never seen a Reboot act this way. There wasn't a hint of the Ever I knew in her.

I'm not scared.

I reached for her arm but she was too fast, darting across the room and jumping on top of her bed. She bounced from foot to foot on the mattress, looking at me as if she accepted my challenge.

"Ever, it's fine," I said.

What was wrong with her?

She launched herself off the bed and landed on me. I hit the ground hard, the back of my head knocking against the concrete. I blinked the dots of white out of my eyes as she slammed my wrists to the floor above my head and opened her mouth, bending low as though she wanted to take a chunk out of my neck.

I kicked my legs, knocking her off me, and she flew into the bed with a grunt. I leaped on top of her, pressing my body into her back as she thrashed and snarled.

The door unlocked with a click and slid open, the footsteps of the two humans echoing across the room.

"Keep her down," the guard ordered.

I locked my teeth together, lowering my face closer to Ever's shoulder so he couldn't see the disgusted look I wanted to aim at him.

The scientist knelt down and plunged the syringe into her arm. His fingers shook.

What was that idiot doing? We didn't need medicine.

"It will help her sleep," he said, glancing at me. "She's just having a nightmare."

It wouldn't help her sleep at all. Reboots processed everything too quickly. Her body would metabolize it before it even had a chance to work.

Ever went limp beneath me and I looked down at her in surprise. When I turned to the humans they both gave me their hard expressions, the ones that were supposed to scare me.

Hard to be scared of them when I could break their necks before they realized I was on my feet.

"You're not to tell anyone about this," the scientist said sternly. "Understand?"

No. I didn't understand. *What did they just give her?*

What had they given her before?

What had they done to her?

The humans looked down at me for confirmation that I believed this ridiculous explanation.

Dumb Reboot—her brain doesn't work right.

A guard said that to me once.

I nodded. "I understand."

They left the room and the door closed behind them. I slid off Ever, studying her face. Her eyes were closed, her breathing deep and even.

Asleep. I'd rarely seen her sleep lately.

I gently rolled her over and picked her up under the arms,

hauling her onto the bed. I scooted her legs under the comforter and pulled it over her body.

I climbed into my own bed, unable to stop staring at her.

I didn't sleep. Instead I spent the night alternating between gazing at Ever and the ceiling. When she began to stir I rushed to get into my running clothes and bolted out the door, hiding my face when I thought I saw her roll over to look at me.

Twenty-two was waiting for me at the indoor track, his eyes on the other Reboots speeding around the room.

"Good morning," he said brightly.

I just nodded, because it was not a good morning. I could think of nothing but Ever and her angry, vacant eyes. Would she be back to normal now? Would she even remember?

I was ordered not to say anything.

I had never disobeyed an order.

"Let's go," I said, stepping onto the black rubber. The indoor track was one of my least favorite parts of the HARC facility. It was a 400-meter ring with a guard in the middle, encased in a bulletproof plastic box. The windows could lower quickly to stop a fight with a bullet to the brain.

Destroy the brain. The only way to kill a Reboot.

The ugly lighting gave my pale skin a puke-green hue. Twenty-two's olive skin looked mostly the same, almost nice, under the glow. I looked away, pushing aside thoughts of what my blond hair must look like in here.

Twenty-two could barely run a quarter mile without

stopping, which did not bode well for him escaping angry humans chasing after him. Hopefully we'd avoid those for a while.

A few other Reboots were on the track with us, including Marie One-thirty-five, who looked over her shoulder with a laugh as she blew past us, her dark hair swinging. She was one of the fastest trainees I'd ever had.

"Let's do two minutes of walking and one of running," I said with a sigh as Twenty-two's pace stuttered to an impossibly slow jog.

He nodded, taking in gulps of air. I had to admit, I wasn't in the mood to run this morning. The break was welcome.

"Were you a good runner when you came here?" he asked when he'd caught his breath.

"I was fine. Better than you."

"Well, that's not difficult." He smiled at me. "How old are you?"

"Seventeen."

"Me too. How long do we stay here? Is there an adult facility somewhere? I haven't seen any older Reboots."

"I don't know." I doubted it. As Reboots approached their twenties they stopped coming back from missions. Maybe they did transfer them to some other facility.

Maybe they didn't.

"Where are you from?" he asked.

"Austin."

"Me too." He smiled like we had something in common.

"We're not from the same Austin," I said tightly.

He frowned. "Sorry?"

"You're from the *rico*. I'm from the slums. We're not from the same Austin." I had never seen the Austin *rico* beyond the lights I glimpsed over the wall that divided us from them, but I'd seen some of the other United Cities of Texas. New Dallas. Richards. Bonito (someone was being funny—it was anything but). A few hundred miles in the middle of Texas was all that was left of the large country my parents knew as children. HARC managed to save only Texas from the virus and the Reboot attacks that followed.

"Oh. I've never been to the Austin slums," Twenty-two said. "I mean, except when my parents took me to the hospital. But I was too delusional at that point to remember. Do you think they'll send me on an assignment there? I'd like to see my parents. And my brother. Have you seen your parents since you Rebooted?"

"My parents died when I did."

"Oh, I'm sorry," he said, his face turning serious. "They . . . they got shot, too?"

"Yes," I said tightly, not interested in discussing my parents. "And you don't want to see your parents. They don't send Reboots to their hometown. It confuses people."

"Do Reboots ever take off and go anyway?"

I frowned at him. "Of course not. Even if they wanted to,

you're outfitted with a tracker at the holding facility. They always know where you are."

He held his arms out in front of him. "Where? I don't remember that."

"That's the point. We don't know where it is."

"Oh," he said, a hint of sadness in his voice. "But have you seen the other cities?"

"Yes."

"That's good, right? We'd never get to see anything outside of Austin if we hadn't Rebooted."

"You'll be working," I said. Newbies always had questions about traveling to other cities. It was one of the only perks of becoming a Reboot—the occasional trips elsewhere for special assignments. HARC instituted a "no travel" policy years ago to stop the spread of the KDH virus, and it was still in place today. But his questions were too much this morning. They were making my head spin. "Pick up the pace," I said, breaking into a jog.

He couldn't talk while running, but when we slowed to a walk he opened his mouth with yet more questions.

"Do you believe in the evolution theory?"

Maybe. I gave him a sharp look. "No."

"But it sort of makes sense, doesn't it? That Reboots are just evolved humans? We found an immunity to the virus. A way not to die. I've heard theories the KDH virus is man-made and I think—"

"Twenty-two!" I snapped. HARC was wall-to-wall cameras.

They heard and saw everything we did, and they didn't tolerate that sort of talk. "Enough."

"But—"

"Can you please save the questions?" It came out more tired and sad than I had intended, and he looked at me in concern.

"Oh. Yeah, sure. I'm sorry."

"I'm just tired," I said. I didn't owe him an explanation. I shouldn't have said that.

"Sorry. I'll be quiet." His smile was small and sympathetic and something I couldn't identify tickled my chest. Guilt? Is that what that was?

He was quiet the rest of the run, the only sounds his gasping for air. When we finished I nodded at him and walked away, to my quarters for clothes and then to the showers.

I pressed my clothes and towel to my chest as I shuffled into the steamy room, the sounds of laughter and grunting filling my ears. The showers were often rowdier after the arrival of a new batch of Reboots, and the party was in full swing this morning. Two female Reboots darted past me, one barely holding on to her towel as she screeched in excitement. A male Reboot held open a shower curtain and one of the girls slipped behind it with him.

The showers were for sex first. Bathing second.

They were not technically coed, but the boys' shower was directly next door, and there was nothing but a curtain to separate the two rooms. Occasionally the guards came in and ushered all the boys out, but mostly they didn't care. Reboots did almost everything they were told, except for this.

For a human, sex was connected to love. My mom wasn't much for talking about anything that mattered, but I vaguely remembered the conversation. Sex and love went together.

Not here. The teenage hormones were still there, but the emotions were gone. The general attitude was that none of it mattered anymore. We weren't even human.

The tile was slippery beneath my shoes, and I shuffled carefully past the closed curtains and ducked behind one at the end of the row, still fully clothed. That used to get weird looks, but now everyone knew. I didn't flit around in a towel. I didn't have any interest in sex. I certainly didn't want to be gawked at like some freak.

A few of the girls had scars from their human death, but not like mine. I was dead for so long that by the time they got around to sewing up my three bullet holes, my body thought that's what my skin was supposed to look like. The result was four permanent ugly silver staples holding my skin together in the middle of my chest, and two ragged scars shooting out in either direction. One stretched oddly over my left breast and had become even more misshapen as my breasts grew.

No one needed to see my horribly mangled chest. Not that anyone had ever approached me for sex anyway.

No one wanted to touch a One-seventy-eight. Mangled or not.

SIX

EVER WAS PALE WHEN I RETURNED TO OUR QUARTERS JUST before dinner. I had been avoiding her, but now I found it difficult to tear my gaze away from her pasty skin and shaking hands. If she'd been a human I'd have thought she was sick.

She lifted her eyes to mine as I walked to my dresser to pull on a sweatshirt.

"Hey." She tried to smile at me and I had to look away. She didn't know. *Shouldn't she know?*

They said not to say anything. It was an order.

I stopped in the doorway, pausing when she just sat on the bed, twisting the white sheets around her fingers.

"Are you coming?" I asked.

She looked up at me, a bigger smile on her face. She waited for me; I never waited for her. It appeared she liked it.

Her legs shook as she stood, and I wanted to ask if she was okay. Stupid question. She wasn't. HARC did something to her.

We walked down the stairs to the cafeteria in silence. After we filled our trays I had the wild thought of going to sit with her. But she headed across the cafeteria, shoving a piece of steak in her mouth. I trudged to the One-twenties table.

I watched as Ever plunked down opposite Twenty-two, who looked up and smiled at me. It faded as he watched Ever desperately stuff meat in her mouth. He wrinkled his nose, looking from me to her, like, *What's wrong with her?*

I had no idea.

He motioned for me to come over, but I certainly couldn't do that.

Well, I could. It wasn't a rule. But it would be odd.

Twenty-two patted the seat next to him and I frowned and shook my head. Ever turned to see who he was gesturing to, her eyes skipping down the One-twenties table. She laughed, and I turned to see the trainers all watching me, matching confused expressions on their faces.

Lissy opened her mouth and I stood, picking up my tray. I didn't want more questions or more weird looks. There was no rule that I had to sit with them. I could sit wherever I wanted.

I strode across the cafeteria, dropping my tray on the table next to Ever. Twenty-two looked up at me, dark eyes sparkling.

"Oh, how nice to see you, Wren."

Ever stared at me in amazement as I plopped down in the chair. I glanced over at Twenty-two's tray to see nothing but an untouched piece of bread and a brownie.

"What is that?" I asked. "Did you already eat a real dinner?"

He looked down at the food. "No. I'm not very hungry. At least, I don't think I am. It's hard to tell."

"You'll be able to tell if you starve yourself too long," I said. "It's not fun." Hunger signals for Reboots didn't come as quickly as they did with humans, but when they did come, they were intense. Our bodies could survive without food indefinitely, but it was not appreciated. I'd barely eaten a thing my first few days at the facility and had woken up one day so weak and starving I'd practically had to crawl to the cafeteria.

"Clearly you're hungry," Twenty-two said to Ever with a laugh, pointing to her massive cheeks. It looked as though she'd tried to stuff every piece of meat on her plate in her mouth at once. She managed a weak smile as she swallowed.

I must have looked concerned, because she glanced down at her empty tray and then to me.

"I feel weird," she said quietly, the distress coming through in her voice.

"Weird how?" I asked.

"Like really hungry. And sort of fuzzy." She frowned. "I can't be sick, right?"

She looked at me expectantly and I said nothing. She

returned her gaze to her plate in disappointment.

"The food makes me feel a little better, though. Less shaky," she added.

I felt a pang of something, perhaps that guilt again, and I quickly slid my meat onto her plate. She looked up and smiled at me gratefully.

"You can have my food, too," Twenty-two said, beginning to slide his tray over.

I grabbed the edge of the tray and pushed it back, giving him a warning look. "At least eat a little. You need your strength for training."

"Why do you get to do it?" he asked, pointing to where my meat used to be.

"Because I tell you what to do, not the other way around."

Ever giggled as she popped a giant hunk of beef into her mouth. "I prefer the meat, anyway."

"Do I ever get to tell you what to do?" he asked me.

"I doubt it." I grabbed my tray and got to my feet.

"No, please don't go." It was Ever who spoke, her eyes wide and pleading. She looked like the thirteen-year-old girl I met years ago, sitting on the bed, absolutely terrified to be rooming with One-seventy-eight. She didn't speak a word to me for a month. One day she had simply piped up with, "I'm from New Dallas. You?" and continued talking like we'd been friends all along. She'd had four sisters back home and I think she eventually decided she had to adopt me as a sort of replacement or she would lose her mind.

Still, I never would have guessed I was any sort of comfort to her. I wanted to sit back down and enjoy the sense of being needed, the feeling of someone who liked things about me other than my number and criminal-catching skills.

I sat. It felt like the right decision as soon as I did it. Ever smiled gratefully and I smiled back. Twenty-two looked so delighted suddenly that I dropped my eyes to my plate and concentrated on eating my beans.

A low growl woke me in the middle of the night. I rolled over on my mattress, blinking in the darkness. Ever stood over my bed.

I bolted up to a sitting position, my heart pounding furiously. Her growling stopped and her bright eyes bored into mine.

"Ever?" I whispered.

She lunged at me and I scrambled out of bed and across the room. She bared her teeth as she turned to look for me.

I pressed my back to the wall as she approached, my heart beating faster than the time twenty townspeople had chased after me with lit torches and various kitchen knives. I'd been stabbed multiple times before I managed to outrun them, but somehow a weaponless, growling Ever was scarier.

"Ever!" I said, louder this time, and I ducked below her arm as she lunged at me again.

I ran across her bed and dove for the call button. I pushed

it repeatedly, frantically, until Ever threw herself on top of me. Her fingers closed around my neck and I gasped, pushing her off with all my strength.

She slammed into the glass wall and sprang to her feet, tilting her head to the side as if examining her prey. I balled my fists, the heat of a fight bursting through my body. She charged at me and I dropped to my knees, grabbing one of her ankles.

She smashed to the ground with a yelp and I twisted her leg until it cracked. She let out a scream that must have woken the whole wing. She came for me again, trying to balance on one leg, so I broke that one, too.

She collapsed flat on her back, whimpering slightly. I sat down on my bed, looking at the door. The humans must have been on their way.

But by the time both of Ever's legs had healed they still hadn't come. I broke them again before she could get to her feet, covering my ears with my hands when she began yowling.

They never came.

They must have known. Those human bastards must have known that Ever was losing it, that she attacked me, that I would have to stay up all night, again, to watch her, even after she passed out.

They knew and they didn't care.

I shouldn't have been surprised—Reboots were property, not people—but I felt the anger clenching at my chest anyway. I had always been afforded a little more leeway, a little extra respect because of my number and my track record.

But they didn't care what happened to us.

The people of the slums knew HARC didn't care a lick for them. I'd known it, as a child. HARC might have been a "savior" to the last generation, to the humans they'd helped fight the Reboot war, but not to those of us starving and dying in the slums.

After I became a Reboot, they fed and clothed me and I thought they respected me as the best. I thought maybe they weren't so bad.

Maybe I was wrong.

When morning came I left the room before Ever stirred, but as I walked into the showers after my run I found myself searching for her in the sea of Reboots. A few gave me odd looks, which I ignored. I needed to talk to her and this was the only way.

Ever wouldn't know that I broke her legs four times last night. She wouldn't know what they did to her.

Not unless I told her.

She came out of the changing room wearing only a towel. She stopped and looked at me curiously. I gestured for her to continue and she did, stepping behind a curtain and snapping it closed.

I took a quick glance around to make sure no one was watching and darted behind the curtain with her.

She turned around and arched an eyebrow at me, a little

smile at the edge of her mouth. I blushed as I took a step back, hitting the curtain.

"Hi," she said. It was more of a question, and her smile grew as she hiked her towel farther up her chest.

"There's something wrong with you," I blurted out.

"What do you mean?" Her smile faded.

"You . . . you're having nightmares or something. You've been screaming at night and you attacked me."

A gasp escaped her throat just before she hit the ground. Huge sobs racked her body as I stood there frozen. I didn't know what to think of that response. It seemed a gross overreaction.

Unless she knew what was going on.

I knelt down beside her. "Ever."

She continued to cry, rocking back and forth on her knees with her hands over her face. The sound made me uncomfortable, made my chest tight. I didn't like it.

"Ever," I repeated. "Do you know what's going on?"

She took in desperate gasps of air, lowering her hands from her face.

"It's . . ." She collapsed into sobs again, falling against me.

I almost pushed her off. No one had used me for comfort, perhaps ever (unless I counted the times my mom leaned on me when she was too high to walk). This was an awkward time for me to start, with her being almost naked and all, but I beat down the urge to nudge her away.

Instead I awkwardly patted her back. She pressed her face into my shoulder and cried like a human.

"It's . . . them," she choked out. "They do something to us."

"To who?" I asked.

"To the Under-sixties." She took a deep breath and straightened. Her bright green eyes were tinged with red. "They started giving us shots and it makes us . . ."

She didn't have to say it. I knew what it made them.

"I thought maybe I had slipped by because I was so close to sixty. They must have given me the shot in my sleep while you were on assignment," she sniffled.

"Why would they do this?" I asked.

She shrugged, wiping at her nose. "We don't know. It started a few weeks ago. Some people have said it makes them stronger, but others get all weird and hostile."

Weird and hostile was an understatement.

"Fifty-one was starting to go off the deep end last week," Ever continued. "But she said they gave her another shot and it made her all normal again. Everyone thinks they're doing some sort of experiment on us."

Everyone? Who was everyone? I'd never heard of this.

"We don't talk about it with Over-sixties," she said quietly, obviously noticing the look on my face. "We're not supposed to. They tell the roommates they can't say anything." She tilted her head. "They ordered you not to tell me?"

"Yes."

This brought on a fresh wave of tears, although I wasn't entirely sure why. I thought she choked out a *thank-you*, but it was hard to tell.

I started to get up, but she grabbed my arm. "What did I do? Did I hurt you?"

"No. You screamed a lot. You attacked me. I broke both your legs several times last night. Sorry about that."

She looked down at them. "Oh. That's okay."

"They gave you a shot the night before last, but they never came last night."

"I'm sorry," she whispered. "That's why you look so tired." She wiped at her face with a corner of her towel. "What am I supposed to do?"

I shrugged helplessly. "I don't know."

"What if I hurt you?"

"I'm stronger."

She closed her eyes and nodded slightly, fresh tears running down her cheeks.

Apparently that hadn't been a comforting thing to say.

SEVEN

TWENTY-TWO HIT THE MAT AND DID AS I HAD REQUESTED—he didn't scream.

He pressed his face into the black plastic and his fists clenched the material of his shirt, but he didn't cry. His afternoon had been littered with injuries, but he was doing a decent job of not screaming or crying.

I knelt down and pushed his pants leg up. The bone stuck out from the skin.

"In this case you have to shove it back in," I said.

He moaned and shook his head.

"You have to. You've got to get the bone closer to where it's supposed to be or it won't heal right. Your skin is going to close up around the bone and then I'm going to have to slice the skin open again."

"That is so gross," he mumbled against the mat.

"Sit up."

He slowly pushed himself to a sitting position, grimacing. The training teams around us had turned to stare. Across the room, Hugo was muffling a laugh with his hand.

"Just shove it back in." I focused on Twenty-two again.

"That's it?" he exclaimed. "Shove it in?"

"Give me your hand." I held mine out.

He slipped his hand into mine. It was warm and not as perfect as I had imagined. I thought rich people must have soft hands free of any marks. They didn't have to do hard manual labor like the people in the slums. I was certain Callum had never built a fence or worked a cotton farm in his life.

But his hands were rougher than mine, and when I turned his palm up I saw little scars on his fingers. The scars from human life never fade.

"Like this," I said, placing his palm on the bone. I pushed it in, hard, and he clapped his other hand over his mouth to stop a scream.

He collapsed on the mat again, a soft whimper escaping his throat. I felt a pang of guilt. That guilt again. I didn't know if I liked it.

I hadn't meant to break his leg. It was a good learning experience, one he would have needed eventually anyway, but it had been an unfortunate side effect of him not moving as quickly as I'd told him to.

"You're going to have to learn to move faster." I think I had meant that as an apology. It didn't come out right. "I mean, I didn't—" Wait. I didn't apologize to newbies. I was here to teach him. He needed to know how to pop his own bone back in.

He rolled over onto his back and looked at me in amusement. Well, amusement tinged with searing pain.

"If you apologize every time you hurt me, you won't be doing much of anything else."

A laugh bubbled up in my chest and I quickly turned away so he couldn't see the smile on my face.

"Get up," I said, jumping to my feet.

"My leg's still broken."

"I don't care. Get up. If you just lie there in the field they'll break your other leg and then you're screwed."

He unsteadily got to his feet. "Is it really that bad out there?" he asked, trying to keep all his weight on his good leg.

"It depends," I said.

"On what?"

"Who it is. If you're just extracting a sick person it's fairly easy. If it's a criminal with a big family you might get ambushed getting to them. Depends on how scared they are. If they've gotten cocky and think they can rebel."

"What if they didn't do it?"

"What?"

"Whatever crime we're snatching them for. What if they didn't do it?"

"They always say they didn't do it. It's our job to bring them in. HARC takes care of the rest."

"They let them go if they're innocent?" he asked.

I hesitated. As a Reboot, I was never informed of what happened to the humans I captured. As a girl living in the slums, I knew the truth. Once they took someone, he never came back.

"They're sure of their guilt before they take them," I said.

"How?"

"It's not our concern."

"Why not?" he asked. "We're the ones catching all these people."

"Our job ends there."

"Where do they go?"

I had wondered that myself once. Some sort of prison? I doubted it. "I don't know."

He frowned. "Do they tell anyone? The families?"

It figured the rich boy had no idea how this worked. I did one assignment in the rich area of town for every hundred I did in the slums.

"No. I don't think so, anyway."

"But—"

"How's the leg?" I interrupted.

He looked down, shaking it out. "Getting there."

"Get your arms up, then. Let's keep going."

He met my eyes almost every time I swung at him. I wasn't

sure what to make of the way he looked at me, like he was intrigued by something. The little flutters it caused in my chest were distracting.

"Let's stop for today," I said after his jaw had healed from its second break of the day. Dinner was in ten minutes; everyone else was clearing out of the gym.

I held out my hand to help him off the mat and he took it. As he pulled himself to a standing position, he put his hand lightly on my arm and leaned so close to my ear his breath tickled my cheek.

My first instinct was to jump away. No one came that close to me. Even as a human, I didn't remember anyone being so near I could feel the warmth of their skin. But he began speaking, so softly that I wouldn't be able to hear him if I moved away.

"Do they listen to us all the time in here?" he asked.

"I don't know," I whispered. "I know they do in the field. There are cameras everywhere in here, so probably."

He straightened but didn't step away. I think I meant to put a more appropriate distance between us, but I got distracted by the way he smiled down at me. I'd always lived in a world where I had to look up, but for the first time I wanted to rise up on my toes and bring my face closer to his.

I heard a throat clear and I quickly took a big step back. Whether or not they could hear us, they could most certainly see us. The guard in the corner, the cameras on the wall, the other Reboots passing by—they could see us just fine.

"Good night," I said, turning to quickly walk away.

EIGHT

"YOU'RE JUST OBSERVING THIS TIME," I SAID TO TWENTY-TWO the next night as we stood on the roof of HARC. "Remember that."

He nodded. He kept rubbing his hands up and down his arms and bouncing on his heels. The newbies were always nervous, but I had thought he might stroll onto the roof with his usual smile. He hadn't, and I almost missed it.

Ten Reboots stood on the roof of HARC in the dark, waiting for the shuttle. Five were newbies with their trainers. Lissy cast a scornful glance at Twenty-two as he bounced, then looked at her Forty-three smugly. Forty-three, with his tiny arms and odd facial twitch, didn't seem like much to be smug about.

"Don't speak unless spoken to," I continued, ignoring Lissy. "Do everything the officers tell you to in the field. Otherwise, they will shoot you."

He nodded again as the shuttle landed on the roof with a bang, the gust of wind it brought blowing up my ponytail. The side door slid open and Leb stood there, his black sleeves rolled up to his elbows even though it was a chilly night. He was a tall, well-built guy, and he often looked uncomfortable in the stiff HARC uniform.

He waved his hand, gesturing for us to get on. We stepped inside, the metal clanging underneath our boots. Since there were ten of us going out tonight we were in one of the mid-size shuttles. The small black plastic seats lined the side of the shuttle, facing the one bigger chair for the officer. The door leading to the driver's seat was still open, and I glimpsed the back of a human's head. The drivers never left the shuttle under any circumstance, and didn't interact with the Reboots in back.

Twenty-two stood next to me motionlessly, as I had instructed, and Leb grabbed his arm and turned it over to look at his bar code. He chuckled, the lines on his hard square face more pronounced when he smiled.

"I heard you picked Twenty-two," he said. "Had to see for myself."

I had no idea how to respond to that. I nodded slightly and he smiled, the only guard to smile at any Reboot, much less me. He was a weird human.

"Sit," he said, slamming the driver's door closed and plopping down in his seat. He hadn't even taken his gun out of its holster. He was one of the few officers to leave it on his hip when Reboots entered the shuttle. Most of them stuck it in our faces, trying not to let it wobble.

I sat first and Twenty-two followed, pulling the straps down his chest and fumbling as he tried to snap them. He was shaking now. The newbies were always scared of the shuttle; in their human lives they had never been inside anything that moved so quickly or lifted off the ground. Most hid their fear. It was only Forty-three who let his terror show openly, his breathing heavy and unsteady. Lissy smacked his head.

I stared at Twenty-two as we rose into the air. He closed his eyes. He looked almost human with his black eyes shut. He hadn't developed the speed or agility or predatorlike quality that defined a Reboot yet. He still had so many clumsy human traits. Yet as he stretched his legs out in front of him and ran his hands down his thighs I could see the Reboot in him—the slow, controlled movement, how he seemed to take up every inch of space in a room by the way he held his body. It was a subtle difference, the one between humans and Reboots, but it was unmistakable.

Leb caught me staring and raised his eyebrows. I quickly focused my gaze on my hands.

"You can speak freely," he said.

Twenty-two remained silent as the other newbies whispered

to their trainers, his fingers gripping the bottom of his seat every time we jerked.

"There's no reason to be scared," I said. "Even if we crash, chances are we'd be fine."

"Unless we're decapitated."

"Well, yes. But that seems unlikely."

"Or if the top comes down and crushes our heads in." His eyes flew to the black metal above us.

"Trust me when I say a shuttle crash is the least of your worries tonight."

"Thank you. I feel so much better." He looked at Leb. "How long have you been doing this? Have you ever—"

"Twenty-two," I said sharply. He looked at me and I shook my head. The shuttle had gone silent again.

"What? He said we could speak freely."

"He didn't mean to him."

Twenty-two rolled his eyes and I felt a spark of anger in my chest.

"He could punish you for that," I said, looking at Leb. I glanced at the stick next to his hand. A shuttle officer had never used one on me.

"Do you want me to?" Leb asked, eyeing Twenty-two. He didn't reach for the stick.

I took in a sharp breath. He'd never punished any of my newbies, but he'd never had to. They all did exactly as I said.

Asking permission to hit my newbie was odd, though. I

knew that. The other trainers knew that.

"No," I replied. Every Reboot in the shuttle stared at me. I focused on Twenty-two again.

"Should I be insulted that you hesitated?" he asked with a smile.

"I can still change my mind."

"How will you tell him? He stopped talking. Apparently that means we're only allowed to talk to one another again."

"I will find a stick and beat you myself when we land."

"Promise?"

I heard a sound like laughter from Leb's direction and I looked over in surprise. He ducked his head in an attempt to hide his smile. Twenty-two grinned at me.

"Focus, Twenty-two," I said.

"Can't you call me Callum?"

"Focus, Callum," I said quietly, firmly.

"Sorry," he said, putting on a more serious face.

The shuttle landed and Leb motioned for us to stand. He slid the door open and we marched out into the dark, a soft breeze ruffling my ponytail.

They named the city Rosa after the woman who built it. I had always liked the name, had even been excited to hear I was to be stationed in Rosa.

Twenty-two stared, his lips parted, his neck pulsing strangely. His horror was palpable, but when I turned, I saw nothing unusual.

"What?" I asked.

"What is this? Where are we?"

"Rosa," I said, glancing back as if to make sure. Of course it was Rosa.

"But . . . this is the slums?"

"Yes."

"Are they all like this?" he asked, his voice strained.

"Like what?"

He gestured and I looked again. The slums of Rosa were similar to the slums of Austin, but perhaps a bit worse.

Maybe the very worst. Rosa was a city built by the sick. It was a surprise they survived at all after they were run off from Austin. As I understood it, even the *rico* side of Rosa wasn't much compared to the other cities of Texas.

The buildings were wooden structures erected after the war. The little homes sat close together, one story and two bedrooms and barely standing in some cases. The humans with houses were lucky. The apartments on the other side of town were not as nice.

"We're lucky to have any roof over our head," my mom had said the day we'd been kicked out of yet another apartment. We ended up sleeping in an abandoned building until they got the money together for a shared apartment. We'd never had a house.

I glanced at Twenty-two and was almost tempted to horrify him further with that story, but his eyes were still fixed straight ahead. I followed his gaze.

The roads were mostly dirt, but the two main streets were paved. They were full of holes, though, abandoned after it became clear the slums were nothing but a disease-ridden Reboot breeding ground.

Trash piled up on the side of the street and the stench of rotting food and human waste filled the air. The plumbing system in Rosa was a work in progress.

"They're not all this bad, are they?" he asked.

"Not quite this bad. Similar, though."

"In Austin?" he asked. Silly question, as I could tell he already knew the answer.

"Yes. I've forgotten a lot. But yeah, it was like this."

"And you grew up in . . ."

The sympathetic expression on his face annoyed me. The last thing I needed was pity from a *rico* boy.

"Look at your map," I said sharply. "You need to get familiar with Rosa."

He pulled his map out of his pocket and I couldn't help thinking that he was relieved to be looking anywhere other than at me.

"Which way?" I asked.

He pointed in the wrong direction.

"That's north."

"Is north wrong?"

I sighed. "Yes."

"Sorry." He fumbled with the map, dropping one side as pink spread across his cheeks. A pang of sympathy struck my chest. I hadn't been good at reading maps as a newbie. Humans didn't need maps. Their lives consisted of the same ten-to-fifteen-mile space.

"You're here," I said, pointing to the spot on the map. "We're going here."

He raised his eyes to mine and smiled. "Okay. Thanks."

I took off down the street and he skipped to keep up. He glanced behind him and I turned to see Leb leaning against the shuttle, his eyes on something in the distance.

"He stays there?" he asked.

"Yes. Officers stay with the shuttle unless they lose audio or video feed on a Reboot. Then they will come look for you. But don't expect them to help you with your assignment. They're only here to keep track of us."

We turned a corner and I crept across the patchy dead grass to the door of our target, Thomas Cole. He had killed his son.

They always gave me the child murderers.

I didn't object.

It didn't say so on the assignment slip, but there was a very good chance he had killed his son because the child died and then Rebooted. Once a human became a Reboot, they were property of HARC, and though HARC had no qualms about killing us later, civilians weren't allowed to make that decision. Even if it was their own child. A few parents went the other way, attempting to hide their Reboot children from HARC, but that also led to arrest.

I didn't think most parents minded when their Reboot children were shipped away. They were glad to be rid of us.

"First?" I asked, looking back at Twenty-two.

"Knock."

I nodded. It gave them a chance to come willingly. It rarely worked.

I knocked and held my fist up to Twenty-two, counting out five fingers.

Then I kicked the door in.

Every piece of furniture Thomas Cole owned was piled in front of the door. Not the first time an assignment had blockaded the front door, but definitely one of worst attempts.

I pushed the old, rickety furniture out of the way and hopped over the rest. The people who barricaded themselves in their homes had nowhere else to go. No friends. No family. No human would touch them.

A smile crossed my lips. I quickly wiped it off my face as Twenty-two climbed over the furniture. He would think I was insane, smiling at a time like this.

Two bullets bit at my shoulder as blasts erupted from the hallway. Humans were forbidden to own guns. Many did anyway.

I pointed for Twenty-two to get out of the way. He stumbled over a chair, his eyes fixed on the holes in my shoulder. I ducked as another shot whizzed over my helmet and Twenty-two pressed his body into the rotting wood of the wall.

I ran to the hallway, using my arm to cover my face. Depending on the type of gun he was using, my helmet might offer no protection at all from a direct shot.

But he was a lousy shot. I felt one in my chest and another scrape my neck as the blasts rang in my ears. When I rounded the corner and came face-to-face with him he missed from three feet away.

He was out of bullets with that last shot.

"Twenty-two!" I yelled. Teaching mission.

Cole sent his foot straight into my stomach. A gasp escaped my mouth and my back hit the wall with a loud crack.

He took off at a full sprint to the back door and I hauled myself up to my full height. The pain pinged at me in several places—how many times had he shot me? Four, perhaps. Only two had gone straight through. I was going to have to dig the other two out with a knife when I got home.

"Come on," I called to Twenty-two as I took off after the human.

I only caught a quick glimpse of the terror on his face before I was running at top speed down the dirt road behind Cole. His long legs kicked up dirt as he flew down the street.

I picked up the pace, Twenty-two's footsteps pounding behind me. At least he could keep up now.

I jumped over the trash bin Cole threw in my way and he

disappeared around a corner. He was faster than the average human.

The chase felt good.

I rounded the corner and sidestepped his swing before his fist could make contact with my face.

I loved it when they got cocky and stopped running.

What harm could that little blond girl possibly do to me? No human had ever said it to me, but I'd seen it in their eyes.

I delivered a swift punch to his jaw to answer the question.

He stumbled and I punched him again. Blood on my hands this time.

I took his legs out from under him with one kick and I slapped the handcuffs on his wrists. He let out an angry scream and kicked his feet, frantically trying to make contact with my stomach. I grabbed the foot cuffs and bound his ankles.

I attached the leash and looked up at Twenty-two. His chest rose and fell so quickly I thought something might burst out of it. His face was red, although it seemed more from anger than running.

"Secure the feet if they're runners," I said, pointing. "Especially if they're fast."

Cole spit on my shoes, so I gave him a kick in the mouth. Not necessary. But it felt good.

"Wren One-seventy-eight with Twenty-two," I spoke into my com. "Assignment secure."

"Proceed to shuttle."

I looked up at Twenty-two. "Do you remember how to get back?"

His breathing had slowed. His panic, however, had increased. The smiling Twenty-two, the boy in the shuttle ten minutes ago, was gone, replaced by the terrified Reboot staring at me. His eyes flicked over the bullet wounds still seeping blood all over my body, then to the man I had tied at my feet.

They all looked terrified the first time; I suppose I should have known Twenty-two would be worse.

I pointed in the right direction but he didn't move. I hauled Cole through the dirt and past him, grabbing his arm and giving it a tug.

"Let's go."

He said nothing; I had to glance back to see if he actually followed. He did, trudging along with his face turned to the ground.

"Hey! Hey! Help me!" Cole yelled.

I whirled around to see a human crouched at the side of a building, his arms wrapped around his thin brown pants. Twenty-two stopped and the human fell backward, panicked gasps escaping his mouth. The human's eyes met mine and I saw the flash of recognition. Many humans in Rosa knew me from my five years of assignments. They were never pleased to see me.

Twenty-two drew a shaky breath as he looked from me to the horrified human.

"Curfew violation," I said into my com.

The human let out a yell, scrambling to his feet.

"Leave it," the voice on the other end said.

I jerked my head at Twenty-two, but he was watching the human throw terrified glances over his shoulder as he ran.

"They ordered us to leave it," I said, pulling on Cole's leash again. I turned and Twenty-two followed a few seconds later.

I threw Cole in the human shuttle and we walked to the adjacent one in silence. I felt like I should say something, although I had no idea what. I had a speech I usually made at this point—*toughen up, accept your life, it gets easier*—but I couldn't remember it. His sad little face made me want to say nothing at all.

We entered the Reboot shuttle and Leb gestured for us to sit down. Only Hugo and his newbie were back, so there was nothing to fill the silence as we strapped ourselves in.

The rest of the Reboots trickled in, Lissy and her newbie last. Forty-three had two black eyes and tears streamed down his bloody face. It looked as though they'd had a tough human, and Lissy hadn't done much to get her trainee out of the way. Twenty-two gave me the smallest of grateful smiles. That could have been him. My mouth turned up just slightly.

"Sit," Leb said, turning away as he closed the driver's door.

Forty-three just stood there. Lissy yanked on his shirt and he whirled around, his hand smacking across her face. She gasped and shot to her feet, shoving her hands against his shoulders so hard he stumbled.

Leb strode across the shuttle and grabbed Forty-three by the front of his collar. He roughly shoved him into his seat, gesturing for Lissy to sit as well. She glared at her trainee as she strapped in.

Forty-three's breathing was still heavy, his gold eyes fixed on Leb. The officer didn't notice. Leb sat down and stared at his hands, lost in thought.

Forty-three's mouth twisted, hate spewing from his every pore. I'd seen newbies have similar reactions after their first assignment, although many of them were better at concealing it. The hatred of humans, particularly of HARC officers, was understandable in a new Reboot. They were shoving guns in our faces and yelling and making us do their dirty work. It didn't bother me anymore, but I remembered the feeling as a newbie. I'd understood my trainer didn't have a choice any more than I did. It was the humans who made us do this.

I tried to catch Lissy's eye, to get her to control her trainee before Leb noticed, but she was biting her nails, her gaze on the shuttle wall.

Forty-three thrust his hand into his pocket. I saw only the flash of silver as he jumped up from his seat, but I knew it was a knife. The scream echoed across the shuttle as he ran for Leb, blade aimed at his chest.

I threw off my straps and shot to my feet. The officer's eyes were wide, his hand nowhere near his gun yet. I dove in front of Leb as Forty-three thrust the knife at him. It slid into my stomach like it was a good piece of rare steak.

Forty-three pulled the blade out, red and shaking in his hand. I kicked his leg, easily grabbing the knife as he went down. He rolled onto his knees, sobs shaking his body. He would be eliminated for bringing a weapon onto the shuttle, so I could almost understand the tears.

Some officers might have killed him right away, but Leb was the type to let Officer Mayer deal out the more permanent punishments.

"Great," Lissy muttered under her breath, making no move to help Forty-Three.

I wiped the blood dripping from the blade on my pants and held the knife out to Leb. He still sat there, the poor, slow human. He stared at me and I raised my eyebrows and held the knife a bit closer. He took it.

"Thank you," he said quietly.

I frowned at that response. He lowered his head and I wished I'd nodded or said, "You're welcome." I hadn't been expecting a thank-you. I wasn't even sure why I'd done it. I supposed he was my favorite HARC officer, but that was a bit like having a favorite vegetable. They were all pretty uninteresting.

I went back to my seat, my hand drifting to my stomach. My shirt was soaked through with blood.

Twenty-two's head was in his hands. I focused on the floor, glad I didn't have to meet those panicked, horrified eyes again.

NINE

TWENTY-TWO SAT SLUMPED OVER HIS BREAKFAST, POKING AT the oats with his spoon. His hand rested against his cheek and his eyes drooped. His head was practically on the cafeteria table.

Ever and I sat down across from him, and she gave me a worried glance when she caught sight of his sullen expression. She looked somewhat better today. No growling last night. I actually slept.

"You all right?" Ever asked Twenty-two. I wished she hadn't. He obviously wasn't all right. The newbies rarely were after their first assignment.

"There's no point," he mumbled.

"What do you mean?" Ever asked.

Twenty-two looked up at me. "You're wasting your time with me. You should have picked One-twenty-one. I'll never be able to do this."

Ever glanced from me to him, her eyebrows furrowed in concern. "It gets better," she said. I could tell she was lying.

Twenty-two saw the lie as well. He frowned at her, then turned his head away, his dark eyes hard and angry.

"That guy shot you four times," he said. "You didn't even blink. It's like it didn't register with you."

"I've been shot a lot. You adjust," I said.

"*You* adjust. I can't do that."

"Her trainer shot her over and over," Ever said quietly, and I stiffened. "She was scared, too, so he and the guards shot her until she wasn't scared anymore."

It was true, but I frowned at Ever for sharing. Bullets paralyzed me at first, reminded me of my human death, and my trainer found that unacceptable. He instructed the guards to shoot me until I became desensitized to it.

Some of the anger had fallen off Twenty-two's face as he turned to me. "Who was your trainer?" he asked, disgust in every word. He shouldn't have been disgusted. The only reason I was alive today was because I had a good trainer.

"One-fifty-seven. He died in the field a few months ago." That was what Leb had told me, anyway. He'd been close to twenty years old.

"Shame I couldn't meet that guy," he muttered, crossing his arms over his chest.

"The point is, it got better for her," Ever said, ignoring my frown. "It'll get better for you."

"I don't want it to get better. I don't want to do it at all." He reminded me of a three-year-old with his arms folded and his lips in a bit of a pout. It was almost cute.

"You don't get a choice," I said.

"I should. None of this is my fault. I didn't ask to die and rise from the dead."

My eyes darted around the room. I hoped the humans weren't listening. That was the sort of thing they eliminated Reboots for.

"Pull it together," I said, lowering my voice. "The first time is the hardest. You'll adapt."

"I won't adapt. I don't want to turn into some monster who enjoys hunting people."

And then he gestured at me.

A knife sliced through my chest. I blinked, not sure what to make of the pain. His words echoed in my ears and it was suddenly hard to breathe.

Some monster who enjoys hunting people. I didn't like the words, didn't want him to think of me that way.

Since when did I care what my newbies thought of me?

"Why don't you just piss off?" Ever's voice, harsh and icy, made me look up. She glared at Twenty-two, gripping her fork like she was considering using it as a weapon.

He grabbed his tray and got to his feet. I stole a glance at him and saw confusion and surprise written all over his face. I wasn't sure where either emotion came from. He opened his mouth, looked at Ever, and seemed to think better of it. He spun around and slunk away.

Ever exhaled, relaxing her grip on her fork. "That was crap. You know that, right? Utter crap."

"What?" I was still having trouble gathering air into my lungs. His words kept spinning around my brain, taunting me.

"You're not a monster who enjoys hunting people."

I frowned. That assessment seemed fair. I could see his point.

"Hey. Wren."

I looked up at Ever and she put her hand over mine. "He's wrong. Okay?"

I nodded, slipping my hand out from under hers. Her skin was warm, much warmer than mine, and it made the tightness in my chest worse.

"I still can't believe you picked Callum," she said, taking a bite of her oats.

"It's a challenge, I suppose," I said.

"But you always pick the highest number," she said. "You always do things exactly the same."

I lifted my eyes to hers to find her staring at me intently. She'd been giving me that look since our conversation in the shower. She didn't seem sure what to make of me.

"He asked me to pick him."

"That's it? He asked, so you did it?"

"He needed me more."

Her eyebrows lifted and she slowly smiled at me. "True." She popped a piece of bacon in her mouth. "Plus he's pretty cute when he's not being an ass."

"He's . . ." I didn't know where I was going with that. I couldn't say *not*. That wasn't true. Anyone could see he was cute. Anyone could see those eyes and that smile.

I felt warmth on my face. Was I blushing? I'd never had those kinds of thoughts about a boy.

Ever's mouth dropped open. She'd been kidding about the "cute" thing. She clearly never expected me to agree. She burst out laughing, muffling it with her hand.

I shrugged, embarrassed to have given myself away. Embarrassed to have those feelings at all.

But it clearly pleased Ever. She looked happier than she had in days, and I returned her smile.

"Softie," she teased under her breath.

I entered the gym to see Twenty-two standing in the corner by himself, his back to the other trainers and newbies. He still wore the same miserable expression.

I started at the flash of rage that shot through my body. The sight of him made my heart beat funny, sent prickles of anger rushing over my skin. What right did he have to be miserable, when he was the one calling *me* a monster? I wanted to shake him and scream at him that he had no right to judge me.

I wanted to bash his face in until he took it back.

He looked up as I stomped over, his expression softening just slightly.

"Wren, I—"

"Shut it and get in position."

He didn't get in position. He stood rooted to his spot and reached out to touch me. I quickly stepped away.

"I'm sorry, I didn't mean—"

"Get your arms up!" I yelled so loudly he jumped. I didn't like the tentative smile he was giving me.

He didn't put his arms up, so I threw a hard fast punch straight into his face. He stumbled and fell on his butt.

"Get on your feet and put your arms up," I said tightly. "Block the next one."

He looked dazed, and blood trickled from his nose, but he stood up and stuck his arms in front of his face.

I purposefully threw punches he couldn't block. Hard, fast, angry. My chest burned in a way I had never felt before. My throat ached from the growing lump.

He hit the mat for the tenth time, his face a barely recognizable bloody mess. He didn't get up this time. He collapsed, breathing heavily.

"You're right," I said. "I should have picked One-twenty-one.

But now I'm stuck with you, so I suggest you quit your whining and pull it together. There are no more choices, rich boy. This is it, forever. Get used to it."

I whirled around and stormed out of the gym, the eyes of all the other trainers and newbies on me.

"Nice work, One-seventy-eight," a guard said to me with a nod.

A sick feeling washed over me. I'd heard those words many times in my five years at HARC, but there was no pride or satisfaction on my part this time.

I made a sharp turn into the showers and rushed to a sink. I smeared Twenty-two's blood on the faucet as I clumsily turned the knob.

The water ran red as it dripped from my fingers and I pressed my lips together and turned away. I'd never been squeamish at the sight of blood, but this was different. I saw his face in the red.

I washed my hands four times. When I finished I looked up at my reflection. I couldn't remember the last time I had looked in the mirror. It had been years.

Human memories faded faster the younger a Reboot died. I remembered broad strokes of my life before the age of twelve, but the details were fuzzy. But I remembered my eyes. In my head my eyes were the same light blue they'd been before I died.

My reflection was different. The blue was bright, piercing, unnatural. Inhuman. I would have guessed my eyes would be scarier. Cold and emotionless. But they were . . . pretty? It seemed weird to describe myself that way. But my eyes were big and sad, and the deep blue color was actually kind of nice.

At first glance I was not intimidating. Cute, even. I was the shortest person in most rooms, often shorter than the thirteen- and fourteen-year-old newbies. A tuft of blond hair stuck out the end of my ponytail, hair I'd chopped off to just above my shoulders myself.

I wasn't as scary-looking as I'd imagined. I barely looked scary at all, to be honest.

I certainly didn't look like a monster who enjoyed hunting people.

TEN

THE NIGHT AIR WAS STILL AS I OPENED THE STAIRWELL DOOR and stepped onto the roof of the facility. The humans waited for me near the edge and I headed toward them, adjusting my helmet so it was straight on my head.

"I trust you, One-seventy-eight." Officer Mayer put his hands on his wide hips and gave me a look like I was to respond to that.

"Thank you," I said automatically. Officer Mayer told me he trusted me every time he saw me, as if trying to convince himself. I was the only Reboot to have regular contact with the commanding officer.

I doubted anyone was jealous.

I saw him often, as Rosa was the biggest facility and he kept an office here. I saw the woman standing next to him, Suzanna Palm, very rarely. She was the chairman of HARC, and I had no idea what it was she did, exactly, but her presence tonight couldn't be a good thing.

"I trust you've been told this mission is confidential?" Suzanna asked. She was squinting at me in a way that felt disapproving. Perhaps she was just uncomfortable in her ridiculous heels. Or maybe those wild silver-streaked brown curls blowing all over the place annoyed her. They would have annoyed me.

I nodded as the shuttle landed on the roof. Officer Mayer stepped away as the door opened, giving me a look that was meant to be encouraging. I didn't feel encouraged. The last thing I wanted to do tonight was go on a surprise solo mission. But I did have to admit that I hoped the assignment was a runner. I wouldn't mind smashing a human's face into the ground tonight.

A vision of Twenty-two's bloody face flashed in front of my eyes and I pushed the image back. It wouldn't stay away for long, though. All day I'd seen it and felt the heaviness in my chest. I wanted to tell my brain to stop being dumb. He'd been healed for hours; it wasn't like I'd done any permanent damage.

Leb twisted his hands together as I entered the small shuttle, and he barely glanced at me. His palpable discomfort almost made me nervous. Officer Mayer's solo assignments were rarely good, but Leb was usually the officer on duty for them. They "trusted" him, too, apparently.

We'd take only one shuttle tonight, so the prisoner would come back with us. I took one of the four small seats across from Leb and pulled the straps down my body, trying to ignore the anxious look on his face. I didn't like that look. I focused on my assignment slip instead, which simply said, *Milo, thirties, 5'10"-6', brown hair.* There was no mention of why I was bringing him in. They knew I wouldn't ask.

Twenty-two's comment about how we should know what the human had done to warrant capture ran through my head. I pushed it away. I could wonder about human crimes all I wanted, but HARC never gave out that information on solo missions.

We rode in silence over Rosa until the shuttle descended and settled on the ground. The door slid open to reveal the heart of the slums and I unhooked my straps, getting to my feet. A dirt road curved around tiny wooden houses, every one dark and silent, as it was past curfew.

We'd stopped very close to the assignment's house. Officer Mayer didn't take chances, didn't enjoy the chase the way I did.

The house was just as run-down and sad as all the others, with one notable exception. The windows. Two square windows, at the front of the house, were covered by absolutely nothing. Anyone could walk right by and see everything he owned. Most houses in Rosa didn't have windows, or if they did, they were small and blocked. Theft was rampant. Windows were an invitation.

This human was a total idiot.

I jumped out of the shuttle and jogged through the dirt to the front steps of the house. The boards creaked beneath my feet as I approached the door and stopped, tilting my head toward the house. It was silent, the only noise the rustle of leaves from the tree next door.

Knocking was not required on Officer Mayer's special assignments, so I kicked the door as hard as I could and it swung open to reveal darkness.

I stepped inside, scanning to my left, where I could see the faint outline of a couch and a few chairs. A hallway lay just past the living room, but I saw no sign of life in the other rooms of the house. Perhaps I'd gotten lucky, and the human was a heavy sleeper.

My boots made the slightest sound against the wood as I crept past the couch and down the hallway. The first door on my left was open, a bathroom. The only other door was right across from it, and I pressed the tips of my fingers against it as I gripped the doorknob with my other hand. It squeaked as I turned it, and I winced at the sound.

I pushed the door open and squinted in the darkness at the bed in front of me. It was empty.

I caught a blur of motion out of the corner of my eye and I dug my fingers into either side of the doorframe. No windows in the bedroom. I had him trapped.

The light flipped on and I blinked, surprised. The human—Milo, I assumed—stood next to the bed in nothing but a T-shirt, a pair of boxers, and socks.

He was grinning.

I cocked my head to the side, confused by his reaction. His eyes flicked up and down my body and he smiled wider, gripping something in his hand. It was a metal tube, about two inches long.

"One-seventy-eight, cuff him!" Officer Mayer yelled through my com.

A horrible shrieking sound pierced my ear and I gasped and quickly pulled my com out. I rubbed my ear, frowning at Milo.

"Who's your shuttle officer?" He rushed across the room toward me. I took a step back, lifting my arms to defend myself. He made an exasperated sound. "Would you stop it? I'm on your side."

My side? Which side was that?

I turned at the sound of footsteps and Leb appeared from around the corner, his eyes wide and panicked. He looked from me to Milo and I quickly reached for my cuffs, unable to think of an explanation as to why I hadn't already secured the assignment.

Milo held up a silver device to Leb and the officer's face changed from panic to anger.

"Yours is down, too, right, Leb?" Milo asked.

I froze. The human knew Leb.

Leb opened his mouth, but then snapped it shut and turned

to me. He was worried. Scared. Of me? Leb had never looked scared of me.

He sighed, pinching the bridge of his nose with two fingers. "You took out all video and communications. Even on the shuttle."

"Nice," Milo said, dropping the device on his bed. "I would have appreciated a heads-up, you know."

"I didn't have time," Leb said. "I got the assignment half an hour ago."

Milo sighed. "That is smart of them, I guess. Want to make it up to me by letting me go? You can say I got away."

"She doesn't let people get away," Leb said.

That was true. And why would Leb let him go?

"What the hell were you thinking?" Leb continued angrily. "They're going to know why you shut down their communications. They're going to kill her. And me, maybe."

I blinked, dropping my com, and Leb gave me an apologetic look as I scooped it up. Why would they kill me? I'd followed orders.

"Get in the shuttle," Leb said to Milo. "One-seventy-eight, cuff him."

"What?" Milo exclaimed as I took a step toward him. "Come on, man, you can't give me to them!"

"I don't have a choice," Leb said, gesturing for us to follow him. "If we don't get on that shuttle now and get back to HARC they'll kill me and her, and probably hunt you down in a few days anyway."

"But . . ." Milo looked from me to Leb, his eyes flicking to the cuffs in my hand.

Milo darted into the hallway, pushing Leb out of the way. I grabbed for his waist, catching only a handful of shirt instead. He twisted out of my grasp and shot through the door, slipping on the floor in his socks.

"Oh yes, there's a good idea, Milo," Leb said dryly. "Run from One-seventy-eight."

I raced into the living room and launched myself at Milo. We hit the floor together and he grunted and began squirming beneath me. I reached for my cuffs as he groped for the edge of the couch.

"Would you stop it?" Leb snapped, his boots appearing beside me. "Just let her cuff you."

Milo groaned but stopped squirming long enough for me to snap the cuffs around his wrists. I hauled him up to his feet and he blew a few strands of hair out of his eyes as he twisted around to look at Leb.

"But I think—"

"Just shut up until we get in the shuttle," Leb said, stopping at the doorway with his hand poised over the doorknob. "Got it?"

Milo nodded glumly and Leb pushed his way outside. The pilot was standing next to the shuttle door, his face curious.

"Everything's fine," Leb said to him as he slid open the door of the shuttle. "Let's get back."

The officer nodded and hopped into the driver's seat, and I

pointed for Milo to get inside. The human targets were locked in a separate compartment at the back of the shuttle, a way to safeguard the officer on duty. Milo walked through the small opening and I shut the door behind him.

I settled into my seat, my eyes on Leb. He was pointedly avoiding my gaze.

"Can you help me?" Milo started talking as fast as he could, forehead pressed to the glass compartment. "Maybe during transport. You could let me slip away when they ship me off to Austin, right?"

"Maybe," Leb said.

"Or maybe even tonight. Do you know a way out? Do—"

"Would you give me a minute to think?" Leb frowned at him and leaned forward, resting his elbows on his knees and running his hands into his dark hair.

Silence filled the shuttle, the only sound the hum of the engine. Milo's eyes darted from me to Leb, his face curious.

"Does she talk?" Milo asked after several moments of silence.

Leb didn't reply or make any move to indicate he'd heard him.

"Do you do a lot of solo missions with One-seventy-eight?" Milo asked. "Tony would have appreciated that detail. Have you explained things to her? Maybe she can help me. Or us, eventually."

Leb lifted his head and glared at Milo. "Has there been any progress with Adina?"

"No. They lost three more rebels inside HARC last month in Austin alone and they've stopped getting Reboots out for now."

The rebels. I'd heard whispers of them as a child. Humans in the slums banding together to stand against HARC, tear down the walls between the *rico* and the slums, and bring back a citizen-led government. A girl at school claimed her father was part of a team launching an assault on the Austin HARC facility. The whole family had gone missing a few days later.

My eyes widened and Leb caught sight of my expression. He let out a long sigh, muttering something to himself.

"What does that mean, *they've stopped getting Reboots out for now*?" I asked.

"Oh, come on," Milo said, shooting Leb a look. "You really haven't told her anything?"

"I am not helping you until you get Adina out, so I didn't really see the point," Leb said. "And now you've risked them eliminating her, so it doesn't even matter."

I wished Leb would stop saying that. The sick feeling in my stomach was starting to spread to my throat and I had to swallow the rising lump.

"Please," Milo said, rolling his eyes. "They're not going to do anything to their precious One-seventy-eight. They think she's nothin' but an empty shell anyway." He grimaced. "Sorry, Tiny."

"It's Wren," I said with a frown. Empty shell? I didn't know about that. I wasn't an emotional Under-sixty, but there was something in there.

I was pretty sure there was something in there.

"Listen to me," Milo said, raising his voice so I could hear through the glass. "Reboots escape."

That was ridiculous. I gave him a suspicious look, not sure what kind of game he was playing.

"They escape, and they've formed a reservation in northern Texas, not far from the border. The ones they tell you died in the field? But they mysteriously can't find their bodies? They didn't die."

I hadn't seen a body when my trainer died.

I turned to Leb, my eyes wide. "One-fifty-seven?" I asked.

"Yes. He escaped." Leb shifted uncomfortably.

"How?"

He wouldn't meet my eyes. "I was able to get my hands on a tracker locator and I got him out when he was on assignment."

"Why would you do that?" Why would any human want to help a Reboot? We were mankind's greatest enemy.

"Because they promised to help my daughter," he said. "She's a Reboot at the Austin facility and the rebels said if I helped get out a high number, someone HARC thought would never try to escape, they would break her out in return." His eyes hardened and he glared at Milo. "They lied."

"We did not lie!" Milo protested. "But we just lost three people and I'm sorry, but getting a Thirty-nine out isn't our highest priority right now."

"You help the higher numbers escape?" I asked. I still

couldn't understand why.

"We make the higher numbers a priority because they're more useful to HARC. But we've gotten out lower numbers, too. It depends on who we can get to."

"Why?" I asked incredulously.

"Because we can't change anything with all of you working for HARC," Milo said. "If we're ever going to have a chance of getting rid of HARC, we need help. Like badass, trained-in-combat help. And we figured you all wouldn't turn down the chance to escape."

"But . . ." We weren't human. And I didn't want to break it to the guy, but if someone helped me escape I probably would just run away. I wasn't sticking around to help a bunch of humans. I found it hard to believe there was a Reboot reservation at all, much less one allied with these human rebels.

"Or at the very least, they need you gone so they have a shot," Leb said, like he could tell what I was thinking.

The shuttle began to descend, and Milo looked at Leb with wide eyes. "You can help me, right? You can get me out of this?"

"Maybe," Leb said, running a hand down his face. "I can try to set something up for when you're transferred to Austin. But they've got Suzanna Palm in Rosa tonight. You're just going to have to tough it out through questioning for now."

The color drained from Milo's face, but he nodded. "But you can get me out later, right? Because—"

"I said I'd try," Leb snapped. He turned to me. "They're

going to ask you what happened during the silence. You need to tell them the truth, sort of."

I blinked, confused. All the humans had lost their minds.

"A version of the truth. Tell them Milo started ranting about the Reboot reservation and people escaping. Tell them he said One-fifty-seven escaped. And that he wanted to help you. Then tell them that you think he's crazy. That even if he isn't, you wouldn't go. Do that thing where you look blank, like you have no feelings at all."

"I think that's just my face."

"Fine. You have to give them something. They're never going to believe he was just silent while your com malfunctioned." He looked at me pleadingly. "But please don't tell them about me or Adina. Can you just say I told you to remain silent? I have two other kids and my wife is gone. I can't get caught."

The shuttle jerked to a stop on the ground and I nodded. He didn't look entirely convinced I wouldn't rat him out.

"And you can't tell any of the other Reboots about this," Leb whispered, his words coming in a rush. "I can't get any more of them out right now. I came this close to getting caught last time. I'm not risking it again." He turned to glare at Milo. "Especially when certain people don't keep their word."

Milo glared right back as the door slid open to reveal Officer Mayer on the roof, his hands on his hips, anger radiating off his chubby body. Suzanna stood beside him, her anger controlled, if she felt any. She simply lifted her eyebrows at me. A corner of her mouth turned up as she regarded Milo.

I didn't blame the human for wincing.

"Take him down to interrogation for Suzanna," Officer Mayer barked to Leb, gesturing at Milo. "Then get down to the debriefing room and wait for me. You, come here!" He screamed the last sentence at me and I bolted out of the shuttle.

He grabbed me by the arm and hauled me down the stairs like I was a child who had run off. He didn't let go until we reached his ninth-floor office, dropping my arm to shove his key in the lock.

He slammed the door behind him and whirled around to face me, his face so close I could smell his sour breath.

He screamed something at me. I had no idea what it was.

Really. All the humans had lost it.

"I'm sorry, I don't understand, sir." I sounded calm.

He took a visible breath. "Why did you take your com out?" he asked through gritted teeth, gesturing to it, still clenched in my hand.

"It screeched in my ear. It's malfunctioning." I held it out to him. He batted my hand away and the little plastic device skidded across the tile floor and came to a stop underneath his long glass desk.

"And your camera?" Spit flew into my face as he talked and I resisted the urge to wipe my cheeks.

"I don't know; is it not working?" I asked innocently.

"What happened in that house?"

"The criminal started ranting about a Reboot reservation. Spouting nonsense about wanting to rescue us all. The officer came in since he'd lost communication, and together we took the assignment to the shuttle."

He wrapped a hand around his fist. I thought he might be preparing to punch me. "And?"

"He kept talking in the shuttle. He said One-fifty-seven didn't die; he escaped."

"And?" he growled.

"That's all. The officer told me not to speak. The human continued yelling about a Reboot reservation."

"Did he tell you where it was?"

"No." Not exactly, anyway. Northern Texas wasn't a thorough description. Everything north of us was a deserted wasteland, as far as I knew.

"Did he say they were going to help you escape?"

"Yes, he mentioned wanting to help me. But I think he was just crazy, sir."

Officer Mayer squinted at me, his wheezing and gasping the only sound in the room for several seconds.

"You think he was crazy," he said slowly.

"Reboots don't escape. I've seen them try. They're killed. Even if they did, there's nowhere to go."

"What about this Reboot reservation?"

"I find that hard to believe, sir." Not a lie. I couldn't picture it. How did they live? Where did they get food? Why would the humans just let them be?

He stared at me, searching my face for a lie.

"I didn't know it would get so hairy. But I sent you because I trusted you." He sucked in a ragged breath, taking a small step back. "These people . . . I know you can't understand this, but we saved them. We are the only state that survived, because we closed our borders early and stopped all civilian travel. And these people think they can go wherever they want and do whatever they want to do. We made these rules for a reason! We protected them and these rebels"—he spat out the word—"think they're on some sort of mission to save everyone. They're killing us faster. Traveling between cities, breaking the laws! This place"—he gestured wildly around the room—"is meant to protect humans. That's what you do. You know that, right?"

Protect was not the word I would use to describe what I did, but I could almost see his point. The humans chose to let the younger Reboots live so they could help clean up the cities. Weed out the criminals and the sick without the risk of becoming infected themselves and spreading the virus further.

"Yes," I replied.

He stepped forward, so close to me that I wanted to slam my hands against his chest and launch him across the room. "I will be watching every move you make. You breathe one word of this to anyone and you're dead. Understand?"

I nodded.

That sounded nothing like trust to me.

ELEVEN

WHEN I RETURNED TO MY QUARTERS THAT NIGHT, I CRAWLED into bed and faced the wall. I thought there was a good chance Officer Mayer was watching me at that very minute, and I wasn't sure my face didn't betray the thoughts racing through my head.

Escape?

It was ridiculous. HARC had planned the facilities to make that impossible. We were monitored constantly and surrounded by armed guards, our tracker locations were a secret, and every human in the cities was more than willing to turn us over to HARC if they spotted us.

Well, not every human, apparently.

I pulled my knees to my chest and frowned, trying to make sense of it. My initial gut reaction was that the rebels were setting us up. Helping Reboots escape with a story about a reservation, then killing them. But I couldn't see the point of that. If they really wanted to get rid of Reboots, wouldn't they just kill them while they were on assignments in the cities? Putting together an elaborate ruse to break them out of HARC first seemed dumb, even for a human.

But if they weren't setting us up, if they really were helping us with the hope that we'd help them, then that was smart. It was rather optimistic on the humans' part, to expect cooperation from Reboots, but it was a solid plan if they wanted to get rid of HARC.

I squished up my face. I didn't know how I felt about humans deciding to work with Reboots. It made it harder to hate them when they started introducing common sense into the equation.

I barely slept that night, and when I rolled over in the morning Ever was curled up in a ball, her fingers shaking as she clenched the covers to her chin. I sat up and swung my legs over the side of the bed, quickly averting my eyes when she noticed me staring.

I wanted to talk to her about what had happened the night before, but it seemed mean. If anyone needed to get out of here it was her, and Leb had made it clear he wasn't interested in helping any of us. What would I say, anyway? *Some Reboots get to escape, but looks like it won't be you or me?*

I slid out of bed and pulled on my running clothes, taking another glance at her before I left the room and headed down the hall. Twenty-two was waiting on the track, his eyes big and round and full of regret.

"Wren, I'm—"

"Let's just run," I interrupted, avoiding those eyes. They made me feel guilty again, and I didn't want to feel guilty when he was the one who thought I was a monster.

I took off running and he followed, both of us silent as we circled the track. He stayed quiet through the whole run, and through the training that afternoon. He continued to give me a look I took to mean he wanted to apologize, but I ignored it, speaking to him only about training.

"I'll meet you on the roof in an hour," I said when we'd finished training for the day. We had a sickie assignment that night, and I was grateful for the break. Extracting sick humans for delivery to the hospital was an easy assignment, one that was difficult to screw up. And it rarely involved violence.

Twenty-two nodded and I turned to leave, catching sight of Leb leaning against the gym wall, his eyes on me. I let Twenty-two walk in front of me, and as I approached the door I slowed, pausing with half my body out.

"Thanks," Leb whispered, his head lowered so he was speaking to the floor.

"Do you still have it?" I asked, my face turned toward the door. "The tracker locator?"

"No. I returned it so they wouldn't suspect someone inside had helped him."

I gripped the edge of the door, Ever's shaking body flashing in front of my eyes. "And you really can't—"

"No."

"But—"

"No." His eyes slid to the camera on the wall. "Go. Mayer's going to notice you talking to me."

He was right, and I sighed as I pushed through the door into the hallway. Maybe it wasn't even a good idea to try to help Ever escape. She wasn't in the best shape, and they would certainly send HARC officers out immediately to track down an escaped Reboot. It was hugely risky for any Reboot, but a Fifty-six who wasn't in top shape? Even if I found a way to go with her, the chances of her surviving were slim at best. Maybe she was better off here.

I stuck my helmet on top of my head and tightened the strap under my jaw, casting a nervous glance at Ever. She adjusted her com with trembling hands, much shakier than this morning.

"You need help?" I asked.

She shook her head, pushing the com into position in front of her mouth. "Is Callum doing better?"

"Fine," I muttered.

"He feels really bad, you know. Maybe go a little easy on him? The first few weeks here are hard."

I shrugged, even though I thought she could be right. Twenty-two's big, sad eyes floated through my head, and I let out a sigh.

Ever stood and her legs promptly gave out. She crumpled to the floor, gasping.

"Are you—" I stopped as her head shot up and her glazed eyes fixed on me.

She rocketed to her feet and flew at me. We hit the ground and she slammed my shoulders down, pinning me with her body.

I kicked my legs but she didn't budge, only bared her teeth and growled at me.

Two humans appeared outside our room, one holding a clipboard. Ever's head whirled around and she darted for them. The doctor with the clipboard quickly pushed the lock button.

I slowly got to my feet, keeping my glare on the floor instead of directing it at the humans.

Pound.

Pound.

Pound.

I closed my eyes, listening to Ever's rhythm. I didn't want to do this tonight. I wanted the real Ever back, the one who made me feel better and wanted to walk to the cafeteria with me.

I missed her.

I opened my eyes and sighed. Ever slowly turned, scowling at me as if that had offended her.

"Watch yourself, One-seventy-eight," the doctor outside called.

Oh, thank you, human. That is just so helpful.

She bounded to me like an animal, grabbing my shirt as I tried to duck away. I heard the tear as she ripped a chunk off the back. She seized what was left and tugged me to her, wrapping an arm around my stomach. I felt her teeth scratch my neck and I elbowed her in the side, wriggling out of her grasp.

I jumped onto my bed, but she was too fast. Her fingers circled around my wrist, jerking my arm from its socket as she pulled me to the floor. She leaped on top of me and clamped her fingers around my neck.

A tiny whimper escaped my mouth. I pressed my lips together, ashamed, and hoped the humans hadn't heard it.

But Ever had. Her eyes cleared and she snatched her hands off my neck, horror settling onto her pretty face.

"I'm sorry," she said, scrambling away from me. She looked from me to the humans outside, her eyes filling with tears.

"It's fine," I rasped, sitting up and leaning against my bed. My arm sagged strangely. "Will you put that back in?"

She grasped my arm and yanked it back into the socket, keeping her head down as tears began spilling over her cheeks.

"I'm sorry," she whispered again as the humans walked in.

"It's fine, Ever. Really." I smiled at her but she wasn't looking at me.

"Feeling a little weak?" the doctor asked in a kind voice,

like he wasn't the one who had done it to her.

She nodded mutely and he held out a syringe, gesturing for her arm.

"That'll help." He pushed the liquid in and patted her on the head.

She closed her eyes and took in a few breaths.

"Is that better?" he asked. "Do you think you can go out on assignment tonight?"

She nodded, wiping at her cheeks with her fingers.

The human chewed on his lip, considering for a moment. "It's just sick extraction tonight, isn't it?"

"Yes," Ever said.

"All right." He pointed at me. "Change your shirt. It's split down the back."

They left the room and I stood up, tugging off my black shirt and pulling out an identical one. I put it on over my undershirt, adjusting my helmet and camera.

"You ready?" I asked, offering Ever my hand.

She kept her head down as we walked to the roof, oblivious to the many glances I threw her way. We couldn't talk about it now, anyway, with our coms on and humans listening to every word.

Twenty-two and the other Reboots were already in the shuttle, strapped in. Hugo and his newbie were the only other training team going out tonight; the rest were veteran Reboots. Mostly Under-sixties, except for Marie One-thirty-five, who was on her second solo mission since our training. Sickie assignments didn't require much skill. I eyed the Under-sixties as I stepped inside the shuttle, looking for signs of the insanity I'd just seen from Ever. But their eyes were downcast, their expressions blank.

Two officers stood in the corner of the shuttle. A young guy named Paul, and one I didn't know. The stranger sneered at us and pointed his gun straight at me, showing off yellow teeth.

"Sit," he ordered.

Two officers wasn't a good sign.

I slid into the seat next to Twenty-two and ignored his efforts to catch my eye. Not in the mood.

We traveled to the heart of the slums in silence, filing out of the shuttle when Yellow Teeth barked the order. The slums were warmer tonight, the chilly breeze from the last few nights gone.

"Do you have your map?" I asked Twenty-two, handing the assignment slip to him as the shuttle door slammed shut behind us.

He nodded, holding it up to me.

"Sickie assignments are easier," I said as he studied it. "We're just extracting the sick who are contaminating the city."

"Why do they care?" he asked, gesturing to the shuttle.

"They're trying to rid the human population of disease. They can't if these humans walk around infecting everyone. They're preventing a second mass outbreak."

He frowned but said nothing. "That way?" He pointed.

"Yes."

We headed down a dirt street populated by little homes and tents. This area of town hadn't been completely built up yet, with some humans still living in makeshift houses until they constructed something sturdier. It was the worst of the slums, and the smell of death and sickness tickled my nose. The warmer weather made the stench worse, although not nearly as bad as the summer, when it got so strong I had to hold my breath.

I stopped in front of a tent made from some sort of plastic material. It wasn't particularly sturdy; in fact it was so full of holes I doubted it provided much shelter at all. The thin tree branches holding it up looked shaky at best.

"Bell Trevis," I called.

I heard a cough from inside; then the tent flaps parted and a young woman scooted out. Her greasy dark hair was matted to her head, her eyes sunken and black. Red flecks spotted her chin. Probably from when she coughed up blood.

She lifted her arms toward us. The sick rarely fought.

"I got her," Twenty-two said, scooping her up.

"You need to cuff her," I said.

"Why? What's she going to do? Run?" He looked down at the human. "KDH?"

She nodded, her head wobbling around like a newborn. He carefully placed it on his chest.

"Don't talk to her, Twenty-two."

He only frowned in response and turned away as he headed for the shuttle.

"Twenty-two!" I let out an exasperated sigh and spoke into my com. "Wren One-seventy-eight with Twenty-two. We have the assignment."

"Proceed to shuttle. Control your newbie, One-seventy-eight."

I jogged to catch up with Twenty-two, who had his head down, speaking to the human.

"You eventually won't feel anything at all," he said.

"Twenty-two!"

"Everything goes numb. You won't even realize it when you die—I promise."

"You don't speak to the humans," I said, grabbing his arm. He stopped and glared at me. He yanked his arm away but was silent as we continued. He set the human down gently in the shuttle with the other sickies, pretending not to notice my annoyed expression as we trudged to our own shuttle.

The other Reboots stood in line and we joined the end. I felt my stomach clench as the officers frowned at us. Something was off. I glanced at Ever but she stared blankly at the ground.

"We've got Reboots bringing in items from the field and threatening officers," Paul said. "We gotta search before boarding now."

I took off my top shirt and spread my arms, like usual.

"Everything," Paul said with a wave of his hand.

"Undershirts, too. Pull your pockets out and drop your pants. Leave the underwear. We don't need to be seeing that."

The other Reboots followed the order immediately, shirts coming off and pants hitting the ground with a soft swish.

I fingered the button on my pants, my eyes flicking to the bare chests down the line. None of them even seemed fazed by the order. They'd probably all seen one another in their underwear anyway. Out of the corner of my eye I could see that even Twenty-two had followed the order.

No one had ever seen me without my clothes on.

"Hey."

I looked up to see Yellow Teeth lift his gun at me. He jerked his head, indicating for me to follow the order.

My fingers trembled so badly I couldn't undo the button on my pants. It wouldn't go through the hole. This wasn't even the bad part. The pants, fine.

But the shirt. I couldn't take off the shirt.

"Who is that?" Yellow Teeth asked.

"One-seventy-eight," Paul said.

I shouldn't have to take them off anyway. I saved Leb. It wasn't me who pulled a knife on an officer.

"What's wrong with you?" Paul demanded, shoving his gun into my back.

Every Reboot head down the line turned to me. Marie One-thirty-five frowned deeply, almost concerned, as she nodded for me to follow their orders.

I saved him. I wanted to scream it at them.

"Hey," Twenty-two snapped, his hand shooting out and grabbing the barrel of the gun. I gasped. "Would you stop it? She shouldn't have to if she doesn't want."

Paul wrenched the gun back and slammed the barrel into Twenty-two's head. I winced as he stumbled, and I tugged at the button on my pants again. Paul stepped away from me, gun trained on Twenty-two instead.

Yellow Teeth let out an annoyed sigh and holstered his gun, striding over to me. He yanked me to him by the waist of my pants, tugging the button through the hole and pushing them down.

"Anyone else would have gotten a bullet in the brain," he muttered, grabbing the bottom of my shirt and jerking it over my head.

I pressed my arms against my thin white bra and tried to breathe, but my lungs wouldn't cooperate. My chest rose and fell too fast, my throat tightening up painfully.

"For the love of Texas," Yellow Teeth said in utter exasperation, pulling my arms out to the side. "You'd think you were a newbie."

Yellow Teeth grimaced at the sight of the ugly scars stretched across my chest and quickly averted his eyes. But the Reboots didn't. They all stared.

I turned my head away, trying not to let my arms shake. I failed.

Twenty-two didn't look at me. His face was turned firmly to the side so I couldn't see anything but the back of his head. He hadn't looked.

"All right, put 'em back on. Get in your seats," Paul ordered.

I grabbed both my shirts and pulled them over my head as fast as possible, my eyes on Twenty-two—on Callum—the whole time. He still hadn't looked at me.

I buttoned my pants and sat down in a chair next to him, quickly strapping myself in. My hands shook as I folded them in my lap, and I glanced over to see Callum staring at them. I pressed them together tightly to make the shaking stop, but it didn't work.

Ever caught my eye when I raised my head, and gave me a sympathetic look that made the pressure in my chest worse, not better. I focused my gaze on my lap.

When the shuttle landed I trailed out last. My trembling legs didn't work right anymore. I fell behind as the other Reboots marched across the roof and down the stairs.

Callum stood at the top of the stairs and waited, holding the door open for me. I gripped the rail as I wobbled down the stairs on my stupid little legs.

I felt something warm against my free hand and looked down to see Callum intertwining his fingers with mine. His skin felt pleasantly hot against my cold, dead flesh and I gripped the hand appreciatively and tried to smile at him. His big eyes flashed with worry and sympathy but he smiled back.

We slowly made our way down the stairs and through the eighth-floor door. I didn't want to let go of him but the boys' quarters were to the left, the girls' to the right. He squeezed my hand and I slipped it out of his, shoving it in my pocket to try and keep the warmth.

When I got to my quarters, I avoided Ever's eyes as I stripped off my field clothes and changed into sweats.

"Wren, it's really not—" she began.

I frowned at her as I climbed into bed, and she stopped talking. I pulled the covers all the way over my head and curled myself into a tight ball until the darkness engulfed me.

TWELVE

"YOU MISSED OUR RUN THIS MORNING. IT'S TOO BAD, BECAUSE I was pretty awesome."

Callum grinned at me as I walked across the gym and stopped in front of him. That big, sparkling smile had returned.

"I'm sorry," I said, my eyes darting around the gym. A couple Reboots stared at me. "I overslept." I focused on Callum again, my cheeks warming at the sight of that smile. "Thank you for going anyway. That's really good."

He shrugged. "Yeah, sure."

I caught Hugo staring at me from across the gym and I crossed my arms over my chest and glared at the shiny wooden floor. I wanted to crawl into the corner and hide my face and never look at any of these people again.

"You gonna hit me, or what?" Callum asked.

A surprised laugh escaped my mouth and I quickly cleared my throat to hide it. But it was too late; he'd heard it, and utter delight danced across his face. "Um, yes," I said, blushing when I looked into his eyes again.

Callum put his fists up in front of his face and I threw a light punch that he easily blocked. I threw a harder one, pulling back just before I made contact with his jaw.

"Faster," I said. "I almost hit you."

"You may have to accept that I'll never be good at this," he said, ducking as my fist flew toward him.

"No."

"No?" He jumped as I tried to kick his legs out from under him.

"Good."

"Thank you. No? You don't accept it?"

"No. All my newbies are good. I've never lost one during training. Only two after."

"Out of how many?" he asked, throwing a weak punch I easily dodged.

"Were you even trying there?" I asked, unable to keep a corner of my mouth from turning up.

"A little." He bounced on his feet.

"Try a lot."

He threw a harder punch but I still easily sidestepped it. At least it was better.

"How many?" he asked again.

"Twenty? Twenty-five? Something like that." We swung at each other harder now, my fist clipping his chin. I caught his arm as it came for me, yanking it so hard he fell on his butt. He immediately tried to take my legs out from under me, like I had taught him, and a smile spread across my face.

"Is this funny?" Callum asked, giving up after I jumped out of the way.

"No, it was good," I said, dipping my head so he couldn't see the bigger grin spreading across my face.

His fingers grasped my wrist suddenly and I stumbled, my knees smashing into his stomach as I landed on top of him. He let out a moan mixed with laughter.

"I win," he wheezed.

"You call that winning?"

He grabbed my hand as I started to climb off him, rising up on his elbows so his face was closer to mine. "Yes."

I looked at our intertwined hands instead of his dark, happy eyes, trying to fight the warmth spreading across my body. A full-body blush. Wonderful.

"I'm sorry about what I said," he said quietly, and I looked up at him. "I didn't mean it."

I slipped my hand out of his and slid off him onto the cold floor. He might be sorry, but he'd certainly meant it. "It's fine."

"It's not," he said, sitting up and leaning in close to me to talk privately. "I shouldn't have said you enjoy hunting people just because you're good at it—"

"I do enjoy it," I interrupted. "In a way. The chase, especially. But . . ." I didn't see how he could possibly understand—not at this point.

"But what?"

"But it's not like I have a choice," I said softly. "I barely remember my human life, and what I do remember is really bad. This is all I know. This is all I'm good at. So, yes, sometimes I enjoy it."

"That makes sense." He even sounded like he meant it.

"And I don't feel things. Not the same way. I'm a One-seventy-eight. It's true I don't really have any emotions."

"That's a lie," he said, amusement in his voice.

"No, it's not."

Callum leaned in closer, until I could smell the fresh scent of his skin. He smelled clean and alive and like a Twenty-two, and I wanted to wrap myself in something to hide my death stench. "Yes, it is. You beat the guts out of me the other day. That was anger. And that look in your eyes, when you talked about your human life, that's sadness." I could sense the heat of his breath against my face as he tilted his head closer to mine. A smile crossed his lips as I sucked in a tiny gasp of air in surprise. "You feel plenty."

"One-seventy-eight! Twenty-two! Back to work!" I snapped

my head up to see a guard glaring at us. I quickly stood, holding my hand out to Callum. He took it and hopped to his feet.

"Forgive me?" he asked as he put his fists in position. His eyes were big and round, like a puppy begging for a treat.

"Yes," I said with a laugh.

"Do it again," he said, bouncing up and down in happiness.

"Do what?"

"Laugh."

"Make you a deal. If you're able to punch me, I'll laugh."

"You're so weird."

I released Callum for dinner after the gym started to empty that evening. I was just starting to follow him to the gym doors when I saw Ever walk in and march across to the knife-practice area. She picked up one of the dull blades and took several steps back, her body stilling as she prepared to throw.

She tossed the knife. It bounced off the wall and hit the floor.

Callum looked at me expectantly as he held the gym door open, and I waved him away.

"Go ahead. I'll be there in a minute." I strode over and stopped next to Ever.

She glanced up at me as she reached for the knife with shaky fingers. "Hey. You doing all right?"

"I came to ask you the same thing."

She stepped back and threw the knife. It hit the wall a good six inches from the target. "Just fabulous."

I watched as she took several more tries, missing every shot. Most of them didn't even stick. She was pale and unsteady and whatever they had given her last night didn't seem like it had lasted long.

"Gee, I wonder why I'm no good today." Ever's voice dripped with sarcasm as she bent down to pick up the knife after another unsuccessful throw. "Isn't that strange?"

I crossed my arms over my chest as I tried my best to give her a sympathetic look. I wasn't sure how it came out. I wanted to say something, anything, but I couldn't think of words that wouldn't sound suspicious to a HARC officer listening in.

"I would think"—she grunted as she threw the knife again—"that this is the exact opposite of what they want." The knife lodged in the paper man's belly. She cocked her head. "Huh. Well I guess that'll slow him down."

"Ever—"

"One-seventy-eight!" I turned at the sound of the officer's voice. "Officer Mayer would like to see you in his office."

I nodded, keeping a straight face as my stomach twisted into knots. That didn't sound good.

I shot an apologetic look at Ever before walking out of the gym and up the stairwell. The cold, white hallway on the ninth floor was freezing, and I pulled my sleeves down my arm as I stopped in front of Officer Mayer's door.

The door slid open and the commanding officer peered up

at me from his massive glass desk. His fat fingers flicked across the screen, and he jerked his head toward a chair. "Sit."

I did, my back rigid. Did he know about my conversation with Ever? Or worse, did he know I'd lied about Leb and Milo?

"Interesting choice of newbie," he said, leaning back in his chair and folding his hands over his thighs.

I tried not to visibly sigh with relief.

"Care to explain?" he asked.

"I wanted to see if I could make a lower number better."

He nodded, swinging back and forth in his chair. "Not going well?"

"We've just started."

"He doesn't take orders well. He talked back to the officers in the shuttle yesterday."

"He's new."

"He ignores you." Officer Mayer squished up his red face. "Or jokes around like you're entertainment. I've seen you two in the gym."

I focused my eyes on his desk, nervously rubbing my palms together. I'd never been chastised for my newbie training.

"The lower numbers are often . . . difficult, but he's a whopper. I'm surprised you only pummeled him the once." He leaned forward, banging the chair on the floor. "And I hear you were trouble in the shuttle yesterday, too."

I cleared my throat. "I—"

"It's fine." He waved his hand. "I don't agree with you

disobeying orders, but I have told the officers not to make the girls remove their undershirts. We're not animals, for Tex's sake."

I nodded. "Thank you," I said softly. I even meant it, a little.

"I told them you were probably just frustrated with your newbie, which I understand. You should be frustrated. I'm frustrated."

I swallowed the lump in my throat and met his eyes. *Frustrated* was not a good word in Mayer language.

"We're not eliminating him yet. I already had to eliminate Forty-three for trying to kill an officer. Thank you for that, by the way. Leb was very complimentary."

I nodded again, twisting my fingers together. Not eliminating him *yet*.

"But he needs to shape up. You get him following orders or I'll have no choice. You feel free to tell him I said so."

My chest had tightened to the point where the edges of my vision were beginning to darken from lack of oxygen. They couldn't eliminate him. I couldn't let that happen. I had to make him better.

Officer Mayer focused his attention on his desk again, pressing his fingers to the glass. "That's all. You can go."

I stood up, ready to escape, but I paused when he said my number.

"I'm serious about the elimination. I don't like to see you wasting your time. Immediate improvement or he's out."

THIRTEEN

I NEED YOU TO BE BETTER.

I need you to be good.

The words ran through my head as I approached the red cafeteria doors. My newbies had never been threatened with elimination before. I didn't know how to have that conversation.

I need you not to die.

I pushed open the door and was met by a wall of noise. The guards rarely let us get rowdy, but it seemed they'd made an exception today. A few uninterested Reboots remained at their tables—all of the One-twenties, and a few of the Under-sixties—but everyone else was in the corner of the cafeteria in a giant clump. Some cheered, some punched one another, but everyone tried to push their way to the middle to see what was going on.

Callum. My eyes darted around the room, but I couldn't find him. I found Ever, pale and shaking at a table by herself, and she pointed a finger at the crowd.

I strode across the cafeteria, anger burning in my chest. I didn't have time for the Nineties' nonsense. I couldn't afford for Officer Mayer to see Callum getting his ass kicked by other Reboots.

"Move," I said, shoving aside a few Reboots to get to the center of the crowd. I heard them start to quiet as they noticed my presence, many of them running to their tables as they caught sight of me.

I pushed a Ninety out of the way and looked down at what they were all hollering about.

It was Callum, with a little Reboot. Thirteen years old or so. The boy was crazed, thrashing about and trying desperately to bite Callum. He'd already succeeded several times, from the looks of Twenty-two's bloodied arms.

I didn't know the kid's number, but I could guess. Under sixty. And recently given shots.

Callum desperately tried to run but the crowd had penned him in. The kid lunged and sunk his teeth into Callum's arm, tearing off a piece of flesh.

Callum snatched it away with a look of utter horror and

confusion. His eyes darted around the circle and rested on me, his relief obvious. I wasn't sure anyone had ever been happy to see me.

"Hey!" I yelled. The Reboots started scattering right away and I grasped the kid's shirt as he went for Callum again. I punched him across the face, hard, and tossed him along the floor, in the direction of the door. Weren't the guards going to come get him? They were just going to leave him in here like this?

A few of the Under-sixties headed for the kid so I turned back to Callum, kneeling down next to him. I opened my mouth to yell, to demand why he hadn't punched the smaller, weaker kid trying to devour him, when he wrapped his arms around my waist and hugged me.

"Thank you," he said, his breathing still heavy and panicked.

I stiffened at the warmth of the hug. It was too comfortable. And I couldn't remember why I wanted to yell at him.

"I'm sorry," he said, pulling away and bringing his arms in to his chest. "I'm getting blood on you."

The cafeteria was much too quiet. All eyes were on us so I lowered my voice.

"Are you okay?"

Wait. That wasn't what I meant to say. I was going to yell.

"That kid tried to eat me." He looked down at his arms. "Look at this! He did eat me!"

There were large chunks bitten out of his arms. I swallowed, trying to keep the disgust off my face. That kid actually bit into his flesh like some kind of animal.

What were they doing to them?

"Why didn't you fight back?" I asked. My voice came out steadier than I felt. I needed him to be calm, and better, not freaking out about HARC's current experiment.

"I . . . I don't know. He's just a kid. And I was sort of thrown off by the whole him-eating-me thing."

"You should have fought back."

"They had me cornered!" He glanced behind me before his voice dropped to nearly a whisper. "Besides, he's the same age as my little brother."

"He's not your brother."

"I know, but still—"

"I need you to be better," I said.

"You're really not concerned about him eating me?" he asked, holding his arm out again.

"It'll grow back in a minute."

"That's totally not the point. I'm traumatized."

"I need you to be better," I repeated.

"I—"

A scream echoed through the cafeteria and I spun my head around to see the crazed kid leaping through the air for a guard who had just come through the door. It wasn't natural, how high he could leap, even for a Reboot.

His teeth were in the human's neck before anyone could

react, and I grabbed Callum's head and pushed it down. I heard the other Reboots hit the floor. The guns were moving.

Callum's body jerked as several guns went off, firing ten or fifteen bullets before quieting. I stayed down a moment longer, until I was sure it was over, then slowly raised my head. The kid and the guard were both dead, although the guard had probably been gone the minute his throat was ripped out.

"What . . ." Callum's eyes were big and scared. "What was wrong with him?"

"He went crazy," I said. I didn't know how else to explain it. I certainly couldn't tell him the truth in the middle of the cafeteria, where HARC could hear every word.

He didn't say anything, but his eyes darted to the Under-sixties table. Clearly he had already heard something about that.

"Callum."

He turned to me. His expression was serious, but I liked how it softened slightly when he looked at me. Like the way he looked at me was different from how he looked at everyone else.

"I need you to be better. Really. I need you to follow orders and work harder. They don't tolerate stepping out of line here." I jerked my head toward the dead Reboot, and he swallowed. He understood. "Yes?"

"Yes."

Ever was perched on her bed when I returned to the room before lights-out, her whole body shaking. Her eyes were dead, hopeless, but she was herself. A shivering, sad version of herself.

I sat down on my own bed and she raised her head, her gaze sharp and angry.

"I'm dead."

"We all are," I said, attempting a smile.

A dry laugh escaped her throat, surprise crossing her face. "Did you just make a joke?"

"A little one. Not a very good one."

"I liked it." She pressed her lips together, bouncing her legs up and down, and I got the impression she was trying not to cry. "But I'm dead for real this time. They haven't killed me yet, but I'm already gone."

I opened my mouth and closed it again, glancing around. The humans probably recorded every word we said. They might be listening now. "You're not gone," I said very softly.

"Levi was dead," she continued. "Before he tried to eat Callum. He'd been dead for days. He was still walking around but there was nothing there anymore. It was just a crazy-ass shell." She grabbed the sleeves of her shirt, pulling on them so hard I thought they might rip. "And when he went for Callum, I understood. He smells so good. Like . . ." Her face twisted, and she whispered the next words. "Like meat."

My stomach turned and I focused on my feet, hoping she wouldn't see my discomfort. "It'll pass. It's probably just—"

"I'm sorry if I attack you tonight," she said. She shot to her feet, her fists balled at her sides, and screamed the next words to our glass wall. “BUT IT’S NOT MY FAULT!”

“Ever!” I looked out the glass nervously.

“What do they care?” she spat, throwing the comforter down the bed as she crawled in. “They’ve killed me.”

“You’re still here,” I whispered.

“Barely.”

FOURTEEN

EVER POKED A FINGER INTO HER MOUTH, SHOVING THE dangling beef in. Her cheeks bulged with food, her eyes drooping even though she had slept the whole night.

I'd ignored the One-twenties table and sat next to her as soon as I'd walked into the cafeteria at lunch and seen how high she'd piled her tray with meat.

"You all right?" Callum asked as he took a bite of his peanut-butter sandwich.

She swallowed some of her food. "I'm a crazy-ass shell."

Callum looked at me in confusion, but I avoided his eyes and stabbed at my own lunch with my fork.

I couldn't explain anything. Not with Officer Mayer

watching my every move.

Ever gripped the table as she swallowed her last mouthful of meat. She looked up from her empty tray with wild, unseeing eyes.

Her nostrils flared as she turned to Callum, baring her teeth as she let out a low growl. She grabbed his wrist and he dropped his sandwich, his eyes wide as he looked from me to her.

"Ever," I said, yanking her hand off his arm as she leaned down to take a bite. "Stop."

Callum jumped back as she lunged for him again, clutching his arms to his chest protectively. I got her by the waist as she tried to launch herself across the table. She thrashed against me and I held her tight with one arm, using the other to grab my beef and shove it in her mouth.

She snapped at my fingers but inhaled it with a little sigh of relief.

"Here," Callum said, sliding his meat across the table as well.

I shoved it past Ever's teeth and she chewed frantically, bits falling out of her open mouth. She began snapping at Callum again when she finished.

"Ever," I said, tightening my arm around her waist. "Please stop."

She stilled at the sound of my quiet words in her ear. I cautiously loosened my arm and she turned, her eyes shiny with tears and worry.

"Sorry," she whispered, scanning the mess of empty trays and bits of food on the table. She staggered to her feet and rushed out of the cafeteria, her walk wobbly and unbalanced.

Callum watched her go, and when he turned to me his eyes were big and questioning. I gave him the tiniest of shrugs, my eyes darting to the camera on the wall. He took the hint and returned his attention to his sandwich.

We headed to the gym after lunch and took our usual spot on the mat. I put my hands on my hips as I looked at him. It was time for him to be better.

"We're staying here today until you hit me," I announced.

"What?"

"You've never managed to make contact. You should be able to hit me by now. We'll stay here until you do."

"But I . . ." A sheepish smile spread across his face and he shrugged his shoulders. "I don't want to hit you."

"It's not a choice. I'm your trainer." I frowned up at him. "Have you not been giving it your all?"

"No, I have. Mostly, anyway."

"There's no more *mostly*. We will both stand here until you're able to hit me. And I'm not letting down my defenses."

He looked at me warily. He didn't believe it.

"Come on," I said, beckoning him over.

He took a cautious step forward, his smile slipping as he raised his hands in front of his face. But he made no move toward me.

"Go ahead," I said.

His fist swung at me, but I easily ducked it.

"What have I told you? Fast. Don't stop with one punch. I didn't try and hit you. What should you have done?"

"Tried to hit you again."

"Yes. Confuse me. Surprise me. Again."

He tossed punch after punch at me, none of them coming close to connecting. He was slow and clumsy, his feet moving one way as his arms went another. I could practically see his brain working, and I found myself avoiding punches almost as soon as he decided to throw them.

"Stop," I said with a sigh. He dropped his arms and gave me an apologetic look.

"I'm sorry, I'm trying—"

"I know you are."

I pushed a piece of hair behind my ear and frowned at the floor as a thought occurred to me.

"What?" Callum asked.

"Am I doing something wrong?" I asked it quietly, ashamed to let the other trainers hear. I was the best. I shouldn't be doing anything wrong.

"You're the only one doing it right. I'm the one who sucks."

"I must be explaining it wrong. Or not training you right. Do you want another trainer?"

"No," he said immediately.

"Are you sure? I don't want you to fail because of me."

"You know it's not because of you," Callum said, bringing

out his big eyes again. "Please don't give me to someone else."

"Then tell me what I'm doing wrong."

He hesitated. "I don't know. There's not something wrong, exactly. . . . It's more like I don't understand how I'm supposed to move so quickly. It's like I'm trying to remember all this stuff I'm supposed to be doing and I can't keep it all straight and my body won't keep up with my brain. It's sort of like when you first learn to dance and your feet are all over the place and nothing makes sense."

My eyebrows shot up. "You know how to dance?"

"Of course," he said, looking at me strangely. "It was required."

"Required by who?"

"The schools. It's a basic skill. Do they not do that in the slums?"

"No. Definitely not." I rolled my eyes. *Ricos.* "They were lucky if they were able to keep a history teacher for a few months."

"Oh."

I held out my arms, an idea occurring to me. "Teach me to dance."

His eyebrows lifted. "What?"

"Teach me to dance."

"We don't have any music."

"So? Pretend." I bounced my arms up and down impatiently. "Come on."

He stepped forward and wrapped an arm around my waist. I felt the blush on my cheeks right away, but the tingling his touch created on my back was unexpected. His hand was warm against my shirt and produced little flurries of excitement up and down my body.

"Your hand goes here," he said, putting it on his shoulder. His big hand covered mine completely as he took the other one, and I wanted to lace my fingers through his and pull him closer to me.

I blinked at that thought, lowering my gaze so it was even with his chest. I wanted to press my cheek there. Feel the warmth on my face and breathe in his fresh, alive smell.

"You're so short," he said.

I looked up to see a smile twitching at his lips. It was an obvious statement, but I smiled anyway. "I've noticed."

"Sorry. It's adorable."

Adorable seemed the wrong word to describe me. It suited him better.

"We're not dancing," I pointed out.

"All right. I'm going to take a step back. You take one with me." He looked down as I stepped on his foot. "You have to wait for me. I'm leading."

"Why are you leading?"

"Because you have no idea what you're doing."

"Fair enough."

He took a step back. "You're going to have to be faster than that," he said as I just stood there.

I laughed and his eyes fell to my lips as a huge grin spread across his face.

"We would have danced earlier if I knew I would get a laugh out of you."

I stepped to him, matching his smile with one of my own.

"Now step back," he said quietly, his eyes burning into mine.

I did as he said, almost tripping over my own feet when he tightened his arm around my waist. It would have been so easy to loop both my arms around his neck and press my whole body against his, to be lost inside those arms.

I glanced up at him and saw the amusement sparkling in his eyes. Maybe he knew exactly what I was thinking.

I accidentally stepped on his foot again and he chuckled. "At least you're not good at everything."

"What are you doing?" The gruff voice of a guard burst the spell and I jumped away from Callum.

"Training," I said, hoping my cheeks weren't too red.

The guard frowned. His mustache was so thick it covered his whole mouth, and I tried my best not to wrinkle my nose in distaste. "It doesn't look like it."

"We're trying something new. He needs different methods."

"I guess," the guard muttered. "Fine. But I don't want to see this going on for too long."

I nodded and he stomped away, taking his spot by the door again.

I gestured for Callum to come to me. "Come on, let's keep going."

He hopped over and pulled me into his arms so quickly I gasped.

"Where's that speed when we're fighting?" I asked as we began moving again.

"I like this better," he said softly.

I should have said it didn't matter what he liked. But I just shook my head. "I'm going to spin you," he said, stepping back and lifting his arm up.

I gave up trying not to smile as we danced. It was too easy to lose myself in his eyes and arms. I wanted to move like this with him forever, gliding across the gym floor to nonexistent music. I let it go on longer than I had planned, let myself forget that I was finding a way to make him a better hunter, a better killer.

Finally I took a step out of his arms and swung a fist in his direction, pulling up before I made contact with his face. He stopped and I shook my head, pointing to his feet.

"Keep moving them. And then swing."

He laughed. "Angry dancing."

I swung again and he blocked it, moving his feet like we were still dancing. I couldn't help beaming at him.

"Good," I said.

We continued our screwed-up dance for a long time, circling, swinging, moving in a way that made a funny little heat stir in my stomach. My eyes kept flicking over his body, watching the way his muscles appeared in his arms when he made a fist. The way I could see the outline of his thighs against his black pants. The intense look he got when he blocked a punch.

He made no sign he saw the other Reboots leave for dinner, no complaint that we had been at it for so many hours with few breaks. His eyes were trained on me, intense, focused, and I loved it. I felt like there was nothing else in the world, nothing but him, nothing other than his fists swinging at me.

I was overwhelmed by the urge to grab both fists, yank them behind his back, and kiss him. I had never kissed anyone, but I swear I could feel his lips against mine every time I looked at them.

When he broke the spell by dropping his hands and taking a step back I had to blink several times to clear the fog. It was all around him and for a brief moment I thought it might be real. But I blinked again and it was gone, and there was nothing but him and a silent, empty gym. My eyes found the clock. 11:16 p.m.

He was breathing heavily and I stared at the way his chest rose and fell, pressing against his white T-shirt like it wanted to burst through it.

"You have to keep going until you hit me," I said. My words sounded firmer than I had thought they would. I had expected my voice to waver and give away the fact that I didn't really care if he hit me anymore.

But I did. If he didn't hit me, if he didn't improve, he would be eliminated. The thought of him not breathing made my fists clench so tightly it hurt.

He said nothing. He put his hands on his hips and frowned at the ground, stared until I was worried it was some sort of silent rebellion.

But eventually he lifted his arms and motioned for me to come to him. His face was hard, determined, but I saw the twinge of defeat flicker across his eyes.

The difference wasn't noticeable right away. It took me a couple minutes to realize I was moving faster, ducking and blocking at the same time. The spell from earlier was broken and I was fighting, defending, moving in a way I only did when in the field.

When I saw his left arm coming at me I had only half raised my hand to block it before he grabbed my wrist and I felt his right hook smash across my cheek.

The punch was harder than I had expected. My knees hit the mat and I quickly wiped a hand across my nose, hoping he hadn't noticed the blood.

He had his back to me, his hands laced behind his head, his elbows folded forward across his face.

"Callum," I said. He didn't move. "That was really good."

He lowered his arms to cross them over his chest and turned to me. I had thought maybe he was crying, but his eyes looked clear. Clear, sad, angry.

"I'm sorry," he said quietly.

"Don't apologize," I said as I stood up. "I made you do it."

"Still feels wrong not to apologize," he mumbled, staring at his feet.

"Come on. I'll escort you back to your quarters so they don't give you any trouble."

He trudged behind me, ignoring every glance I shot back at him. I had a sudden wild impulse to ask if he was mad at me.

The answer was yes, no matter what came out of his mouth. I shouldn't care, anyway. My newbies were often mad at me. Hard not to be mad at someone who spent most of her time pummeling you. But it was strange to have one upset about hitting *me*.

"Training," I said as we passed the guard in front of the boys' quarters. He nodded slightly.

Callum stopped in front of a room and I took a quick glance inside. It looked exactly like mine, except for the boy sleeping in one of the beds.

"Good night," I said. My voice shook a little. Why did it do that? My chest felt heavy, like I was . . . sad. I didn't know what to think of that. Anger, fear, nervousness I could deal with. But sad?

I didn't think much of sad.

Callum's eyes were finally on mine. Then his arms were around me as well, tugging me closer than I'd ever been to him. His fingers lightly brushed the skin he'd just punched and the weight lifted from my chest. He left a trail of fireworks down my cheek and neck and into my hair and my eyes closed before I could stop them.

"Don't make me punch you anymore, okay?" he whispered.

I nodded, opening my eyes. "You have to punch other people, though."

When he laughed his chest moved against mine and I wanted nothing more than to kiss him.

I couldn't kiss him. What would the guard do? What would Callum do? Maybe he didn't even want a One-seventy-eight pressing her cold, dead lips to his.

"Deal," he said, leaning his head down so our foreheads almost touched.

Maybe he did.

But my toes wouldn't listen to me. They had to be first, those ten traitor toes. First to lift me from my sad little height to reach those lips.

They wouldn't move. He released me and I tucked a piece of hair behind my ear, not sure what else to do.

"See you in the morning," I mumbled, turning to go.

"Hey, I was better, right?" he asked.

You're fine the way you are.

I pushed the thought away, because he wasn't. He was dead if he wasn't better.

"Yes. You were better."

Although I still wasn't sure it was good enough.

FIFTEEN

I STOLE A GLANCE AT EVER AS I PULLED A SWEATER OVER MY undershirt. She looked more normal today. Balanced, calm, as she tied her shoes.

Too calm.

I didn't think she slept last night. She was awake when I returned to the room and perched on the edge of her bed when I woke up. She'd been in the same position, staring at the wall, when I returned from my run with Callum.

"Are you ready?" I asked, edging toward the door. She was scaring me. Her eyes were hard and icy and I half expected her to leap up and tear my throat out.

She stood slowly, letting out a little sigh as our eyes met.

Then she stepped forward and hugged me.

I stiffened, waiting for the catch, the real reason for the hug, but she just clung tighter.

I slowly wrapped my arms around her back, gently pressing my hands against the soft cotton of her shirt. She was warm—not Callum-warm, but certainly warmer than me, although her body shook with the intensity of someone who was freezing.

She pulled away and took a deep breath, attempting a smile through the tears that had formed in her eyes.

"I'm sorry," she whispered.

I heard the crack first. I hit the ground before I realized she'd slammed her foot into my knee, breaking the kneecap.

"Ever, wh—" I pressed my lips together to stop a scream as she grabbed my ankle and broke the other leg with one horrific twist.

I shoved the pain away, relegated it to a part of my brain I didn't acknowledge. It tickled at me, refusing to be completely ignored, but I was a master at numbing my body.

Ever sent an apologetic look my way as she ran out the door. She was herself. Why would she do that if she were herself?

I gripped the edge of the mattress and struggled to my feet. A grunt escaped my mouth as fresh agony ripped through my legs and I had to cling to the edge of the bed to stay upright.

Gunshot.

My head spun to the door to see the Reboots who'd been walking past freeze in mid-step at the sound.

Silence.

Silence was never good here.

I let go of the bed and promptly crashed to the floor, my broken legs not able to support my weight. I dug my fingers against the cold tile and crawled into the hallway, whipping my head one way and then the other.

The guard at the end of the hall was dead—sprawled out on the floor, a bullet through his head. His gun holster was empty.

"Who did that?" I gasped, even though I knew the answer.

The young Reboot standing a few feet away looked down at me sadly. "Ever."

I grasped her hand and she jumped, eyes wide with fear, as I used her as support to heave myself to my feet. My bones were beginning to heal, but I still wobbled.

I opened my mouth to ask if she would help me walk when another gunshot sounded. She jerked her hand from mine and sprinted in the opposite direction.

The wall didn't have much to hold on to so I leaned against it, dragging myself down the hallway. Reboots flew past me, everyone else headed away from the shots. More rang out as I threw open the door to the stairwell. I could walk faster with a solid grip on the railing, and I hobbled down the stairs as quickly as I could.

"Hey," I said, grabbing Hugo's arm as he ran up the stairs. "Where is she?"

"She was headed for the cafeteria," he said, eyebrows

lowered as he surveyed me. "What's wrong with you?"

I felt one of my kneecaps snap into place as it fully healed and I darted down the stairs, dragging the other leg.

"Where are you going?" Hugo yelled after me. "She's killing guards; you're gonna get shot!"

His warning faded as I raced through the seventh-floor door. Gunfire exploded in my ears and I looked from left to right frantically.

Two guards lay dead on the floor. Ever stood at the doorway of the cafeteria, a guard's helmet on her head. Several bullets had dinged it and her white shirt was covered in blood.

A guard flew around the corner and Ever whirled to face him, gun aimed. She fired off a round straight into his chest before he could react. Her face was hard, her lips pursed, her eyes scanning the area for another threat.

But she was still herself.

She reached up and unhooked the helmet, letting it fall to the ground as she pressed her hand to the cafeteria door.

What was she doing? They'd kill her the minute she walked in.

Both my legs had healed and I took off running as she opened the door, trying to yell her name. My voice didn't work.

"Wren!" I felt a tug on my arm and turned to see Callum's worried face. I yanked my arm away and bolted after Ever as she stepped into the cafeteria.

"Wren, stop!" Callum's footsteps followed me.

I burst through the door to see Ever climbing up on a table. She tossed aside the gun and made a gesture at the officers in the little room above the cafeteria like, *What are you waiting for?*

I ran for her, reaching out for her hand. "Ever, st—" My voice was lost in a barrage of gunshots.

I felt her blood splatter across my face.

Her head flew back.

And then I was on the ground, someone's arms tight around me, his body shielding mine. I think he was talking, but his words sounded garbled in my ear. His scent was familiar.

Callum.

"Clear the cafeteria." The sound over the intercom made me jump, the dull human voice piercing the fog.

His arms left, but I couldn't move.

Clear the cafeteria. I had to walk.

I couldn't walk. I couldn't move.

Callum grabbed me by the arms and pulled me to my feet. Cloth against my face, and I opened my eyes to see him using his shirt to wipe away Ever's blood.

"Walk," he said.

I blinked and attempted to put one foot in front of the other. I stumbled.

Callum wrapped an arm around my waist and held me against him, dragging me through the doors and out into the hallway.

He pulled me into the boys' restroom and propped me up

next to a sink, slowly slipping his arm from my waist. I leaned against the cool tile wall and closed my eyes, gripping the edge of the sink for support.

I felt something warm and wet on my face and neck and opened my eyes to see him cleaning me with a cloth.

"Are you wearing an undershirt?"

I couldn't comprehend the strange question. I touched my shirt and my hand came away wet, red. I took in a sharp breath.

He lifted up my shirt in back to check when I didn't respond. I was. Always.

He pulled off the black top shirt and threw it away, wiping my bloody fingers until they were clean. He tossed the cloth in the trash.

He reached for me and I pushed him away. I thought I might scream if he hugged me, held me close like Ever had a few minutes ago.

No screaming. That was my own rule.

He put his hands on my cheeks instead, making me look into his black eyes.

"I'm sorry," he whispered, close to tears.

I should have been close to tears. Ever would have been. A human would have been bawling.

Crying was the normal thing to do. She deserved tears.

I shook his hands off, pressing my palm to my mouth to stop the scream building in my chest. I couldn't break down in front of him.

I ran out of the bathroom, keeping my hand against my lips as I leaped up the stairs and headed for my quarters. I curled up on my mattress, pulling the covers over my face so I couldn't see her empty bed.

But still, no tears came.

SIXTEEN

CALLUM AND I WERE GIVEN AN ASSIGNMENT THAT NIGHT.

I almost didn't go. I wanted to crawl back into bed and wait to see if they'd take pity on me and assign a different Reboot to their stupid mission.

But I'd never seen any pity from HARC, and it didn't seem right to desert Callum. So I pulled on my clothes, plunked my helmet on my head, and trudged across the facility.

HARC had found an adult Reboot living in Rosa and needed him brought in immediately. They didn't give us specifics, but I suspected they'd use him for testing and then kill him. The hospitals made sure adults didn't Reboot, but if one died in the city and Rebooted we had to go get him before he started killing people.

Lissy and Ninety-three met us on the roof. Four teenage Reboots for one adult. It was necessary.

"How's he doing?" Lissy asked me, gesturing at Callum.

I blinked at her. I couldn't speak. Everything around me felt fake, far away, like if I reached out to touch it my hand would fall straight through.

Lissy peered at me like I was a moron as the shuttle approached. I felt Callum's hand on my arm and I turned to see a worried look on his face. He'd given me that look all day through training as I halfheartedly threw and dodged punches. He could have hit me multiple times, if he'd wanted to. I couldn't focus, couldn't stay in the moment.

The shuttle door slid open and we filed in, sitting when Leb gestured for us to do so. I buckled my strap and leaned back, letting my eyes close.

I'm sorry.

I took in a sharp breath and my eyes flew open at the sound of Ever's voice. I almost expected her to be in the shuttle with me, her voice was so clear, but only Leb stared back at me.

He was standing right in front of me and I frowned at his closeness. Why wasn't he in his seat?

"You all right there, One-seventy-eight?" he asked quietly.

Callum hovered next to me. The seats where Lissy and Ninety-three had been sitting were empty. We had landed.

Leb knelt down and unbuckled my strap for me. I slowly

got to my feet, confused where the minutes had gone. Nothing made sense.

I staggered out of the shuttle, turning my gaze to the ground when I saw the annoyance on Lissy's and Ninety-three's faces.

Callum pulled out his map and pointed west. Lissy and Ninety-three turned to me for confirmation.

I had no idea.

Lissy frowned at me and peeked over Callum's shoulder. She nodded and began walking west with Ninety-three. They'd dropped us on Main Street, and Lissy veered off the paved road and disappeared onto the dirt street behind a small house.

Callum laced his warm fingers through mine and I started to look down at them as we followed them. I caught myself just in time, snapping my head up before my camera recorded it. Officer Mayer would not approve.

"Is there anything I should know?" he asked, squeezing my hand. "About tonight?"

I didn't know what he meant.

"Fighting an adult Reboot," he prompted. He looked down at his assignment slip. "Gregor, adult Reboot."

I felt an emotion pressing against my chest, and this time I knew exactly what it was. Guilt. I should have prepared him. I shouldn't just stand there mutely listening to Ever's voice in my head.

"He won't run like a human; he will stay and fight if we

approach him," I said, my voice working for the first time all day. "In an adult, the Reboot causes insanity and extreme aggression. We're ordered to capture if we can, kill if we have to. His strength will depend on whatever his human strength was, because he probably hasn't been a Reboot long. But he will be quick. The Reboot reflexes kick in right away. Don't try talking to him. You can't reason with an adult Reboot. Whoever he was before is gone."

"Why are the adults different?" he asked.

"They say it's something to do with our brains not being fully formed. An adult brain can't handle the Reboot the way a kid's can." I shrugged. "I don't know. I think it's more about change."

"Change?"

"My parents always started screaming at each other when something changed. Like if we had to move or if HARC mandated another vaccine they couldn't afford. But I always just went with it. I think we adapt better."

A hint of a smile crossed his face. "That makes sense."

Lissy stopped in front of a house with a crooked roof and sheets covering the two windows in front. I quickly dropped Callum's hand as she turned. I missed the warmth right away, and I wanted her to point her camera in another direction so I could link my fingers through his again.

"You guys take the back," she said. "We've got the front."

I nodded and walked around, reaching for Callum's hand again as soon as we were out of sight. He kept his face pointed straight ahead but tugged me closer, until my shoulder touched his arm.

I closed my eyes briefly, letting the tingles of warmth dance over my skin. I could see Ever in the darkness, feel her hand as it pressed into my back.

I'm sorry.

My eyes popped open as a tiny gasp escaped my mouth. Callum's eyes were on mine now, full of concern, and I quickly looked away.

"Be prepared to fight," I said, clearing my throat and trying to push Ever's voice out of my head.

My hand was poised over the knob of the back door when I heard Lissy scream.

"One-seventy-eight!" Ninety-three yelled.

I took off with Callum close behind, rounding the corner to the front of the house in seconds.

Gregor was huge, so big that Lissy was a doll perched on his back, her arms around his thick neck. His eyes didn't focus right, like all of the adult Reboots I'd seen, and his mouth hung open, even when he wasn't growling. He brandished a large knife, wildly swinging it behind him at her.

Ninety-three lunged at him and Gregor whipped the knife in his direction.

I saw Ninety-three's head snap back as the blade slid in, but I slapped my hands over my eyes before I had to watch him slump to the ground.

"Lissy, get—" Callum's words cut off as I heard Lissy

scream, then another thump.

Take your hands off your eyes.

Move.

My brain wouldn't communicate with my body, wouldn't do anything I said. I dug my fingers into my skin, trying to wrench my hands away, but I was frozen.

A grunt from Callum broke the spell. I dropped my hands to see him tear the knife from Gregor's hand and hurl it as far as he could. Lissy and Ninety-three lay motionless on the ground, and Callum stumbled over the former as Gregor punched him across the jaw.

Callum's eyes darted to me as he sprung to his feet, his expression clear.

Help me.

My feet worked, even if the rest of me didn't. I raced across the dirt, launching my foot into Gregor's stomach. He barely stumbled, his dark Reboot eyes sparkling at the challenge of a fight.

I found I had that in common with adult Reboots. They seemed glad for a fight, eager to release the pent-up aggression and anger inside. I understood that. But tonight I couldn't find that energy.

Gregor threw a punch. I ducked, but another immediately followed. He'd been trained in combat as a human.

His fist slammed against my cheek and I hit the ground with a grunt.

I wanted to get up faster, to bounce up and revel in the fire of a fight burning in my belly, but my limbs were lead, moving like I was a human.

I was only up on my knees when he kicked me again.

He lifted his foot for another one, but Callum launched himself at the bigger Reboot, taking them both down. He tried to pin him to the ground but Gregor grasped his shirt and tossed him across the lawn.

I managed to stand before Gregor made his way over to me, lifting my fists to protect myself. I had to be faster than him. He was stronger, so I had to be faster.

I scrambled behind him as he swung, giving him a solid kick in the ass. He hit his knees and I reached for my cuffs, relief flooding me.

I yanked one arm behind his back but he spun around and grabbed my ankle, sending my butt to the ground. His foot connected with my helmet, smashing the camera.

"One-seventy-eight!" Officer Mayer yelled in my ear. "We've lost visual on your camera."

A pair of arms grabbed my waist, dragging me away as Gregor lunged for me. Callum darted around me and threw a punch directly into Gregor's face.

"One-seventy-eight!" Officer Mayer yelled in my ear.

"He . . . he broke it," I gasped, the world spinning a bit as I got up.

Callum turned at the sound of my voice and Gregor delivered a massive punch to his stomach, tugging viciously at

Callum's head. He succeeded in getting the helmet off, tossing it aside with a growl.

"One-seventy-eight! Get that helmet back on Twenty-two's head! All we see is the ground!"

I raced for them, fighting back the urge to rip my com from my ear. I threw myself in between the two Reboots, breaking Gregor's hold on Callum. I was messy, panicked, my eyes flying to my newbie to see if he was okay. I never saw the punches coming. Only felt the crack as he smashed my nose in.

My face was in the dirt again. I couldn't remember why I should get up.

"One-seventy-eight!"

Officer Mayer's voice was distant this time, and I squinted to see my com lying on the ground.

"One-seventy-eight, report—"

I slammed my fist down, the little plastic device making a pleasing crunch sound. I almost smiled, but a hand grabbed my shirt collar and I wiped at my eyes to see Gregor preparing for another hit.

I didn't care.

Callum grabbed the fist and Gregor let go of me. I collapsed back to the ground. Callum punched Gregor, the hardest hit I'd ever seen come out of him. The bigger Reboot stumbled and Callum struck him again.

"Would you shut up?" Callum yelled. Considering neither Gregor nor I had said a word, I could guess who he was talking to.

He went for a third punch, but Gregor snatched his arm and cracked it.

Callum didn't even wince. He slammed his palm against the bone, putting it back in place as he kicked Gregor in the stomach. He doubled over in pain and Callum kneed him in the face.

Gregor went down with a yell and Callum slapped the hand- and foot cuffs on him. His feet thrashed, but he wasn't going anywhere.

Callum knelt down next to me and I forced myself to sit up, wiping the back of my sleeve against my bloody face.

"I'm sorry," I whispered, unable to look at him.

"Twenty-two!" I could hear Officer Mayer yelling in his ear. "What is going on?"

I felt his hand on my cheek and I looked up at his bruised face. He gave me a little smile. He opened his mouth to say something, then frowned as Officer Mayer began yelling again.

I gently removed the com from his ear and set it on the ground.

"What a rebel," he said quietly. He scooted closer and gathered me into his arms. I felt like a little kid in his lap, but when I pressed my face to his chest and smelled his fresh skin through his clothes, I didn't mind.

"I'm sorry," I repeated. "I was useless—"

"No, you weren't," he said, running his fingers beneath my helmet and up into my hair. I liked his warm fingers there, liked the sensations they sent down my neck. "I'm sorry about Ever. She was your best friend?"

I'd never thought of her that way. "Yes," I said.

He wrapped both arms around my waist, holding me tightly. I could hear the muffled sounds of Officer Mayer yelling in the com from a few feet away, and I closed my eyes and blocked the sound. No one could see or hear us. I had been under the watch of a HARC guard every minute of the past five years.

I felt free.

It was a false freedom, of course, since my tracker gave away my exact location, but I sank into Callum for a moment and pretended.

When I pulled away he tried to bring me back, but I shook my head and gestured to his com.

"You should put it in," I said. "If you don't report they'll send in more Reboots. It'll be bad if they send more in and we're alive."

He sighed and reluctantly stuck the com in his ear. "Callum Twenty-two with Wren One-seventy-eight. Assignment secure. Lissy One-twenty-four and Raul Ninety-three are dead." He listened and looked around. "All right." He grabbed his helmet, plunking it on his head and adjusting the camera. "See? She's fine. Her com just got smashed." Callum winked at me. He knew exactly how that had happened.

He paused for a moment, then looked at me sadly.

"Can't you send—" He sighed. "All right." He jerked his head toward Ninety-three and Lissy. "They want us to bring them back."

I nodded, beating down the disgust. "Yeah, standard

procedure when Reboots die in the field. I've got them."

"I can do it, Wren—"

"It's fine," I said, attaching a leash to Ninety-three's wrists, then Lissy's. "You get him."

Callum secured Gregor, a frown crossing his face as he hauled the Reboot to his feet.

"No."

I frowned at him in confusion.

"No," he repeated into his com.

"What are they saying?" I asked.

"Nothing. You sure you got them? I can take one."

"It's fine. Are they telling you to do something?"

"Nope. Let's go." He nudged Gregor forward.

"Callum, you can't just ignore them."

He cast an amused smile back at me. "Come on. Everything's okay."

I doubted that, but I trudged after him, dragging the two dead Reboots behind me.

Leb ran around the corner, coming to a stop when he spotted us. He winced as his gaze fell on me, and I wiped at my face and found blood.

"Where's your gear?" he asked.

"Smashed," I replied.

He pulled his hand com out of his pocket and lifted it to his lips as he turned his back to us. "I have Twenty-two and One-seventy-eight. Smashed gear. Heading back now."

Callum and I piled the adult Reboot, Lissy, and Ninety-Three into the cargo shuttle and headed back to our own. We plopped down in our seats and Leb settled in across from us as the shuttle lifted off the ground.

Callum let out an annoyed sigh, giving his helmet a shove so the camera pointed up at the ceiling. He took his com out of his ear and sat on it.

"They won't shut up," he said, to our horrified looks.

"What are they—" I stopped, glancing at Leb as the shuttle lifted off.

"There aren't any other camera or audio feeds in here, if yours are gone. Just his," Leb said. He nodded to the com in his pocket. "They can't hear everything on mine. It mutes unless I'm using it."

Callum looked from him to me in surprise.

"What are they saying?" I asked, ignoring the look.

"They told me to kill Gregor."

I gasped, clapping my hand over my mouth to stop the wave of nausea that crashed over me.

"You shouldn't have done that, kid," Leb said. "They did not sound happy."

Leb's sympathetic tone made the pounding in my stomach worse, and I forced my hand away from my mouth and gripped my seat instead.

"You can't just disobey an order," I said, my voice shaking.

"I can, and I did. They can't make me do that."

"But you knew! I told you it was a capture-if-possible, kill-if-necessary mission."

"It wasn't necessary. He was contained. The only time it's necessary is in self-defense. They can't make me kill someone."

"But—"

But they'll kill you.

I couldn't say the words to him.

"I know what they might do to me," he said softly. "I'm not killing anyone for them."

I sprung out of my chair, not sure what I intended to do until I smacked his head. He lifted his arms to defend himself as I swung again, my rage at his stupidity burning a hole through my stomach.

I wanted to scream at him, to ask him how he could be so thoughtless when I had just lost her, but no words would come out of my mouth. My throat had tightened painfully.

"I'm sorry," he said, trying to catch my hands as I halfheartedly hit him.

"One-seventy-eight," Leb said. I felt his touch on my arms, pulling me backward, and I let him, my shoulders sagging.

"I'm sorry," Callum repeated, his eyes big and pleading. "Don't be mad. I just couldn't."

I turned away, watching as Leb sat down in his seat again with a sigh.

His gaze met mine and he took in a sharp breath, barely shaking his head.

He could tell what I was thinking.

I leaned down and put my hands on either side of Leb's chair. He pressed himself into the wall.

"Can you help us?" I whispered.

"No," he said automatically.

Out of the corner of my eye I could see Callum leaning in, trying to hear us, so I shot him a look. He sank back into his chair.

"Can you help just him?"

"No."

"Please. They're going to kill him."

A frown crossed his face. "I'm sorry about that, but even if I wanted to help, I'd need some time. Time he doesn't seem to have."

"I think I can convince Officer Mayer to let him continue training. I'll take the blame. Tell him I didn't prepare him properly."

"Then he'll be fine."

"No, he won't," I whispered. "How long do you think he has here, really? He'll disobey again and they'll eliminate him." Or a human would kill him. Or HARC would start giving him shots.

Leb's gaze turned to Callum for a moment. "I can't. It's too risky."

"Please. I'll do whatever you want. Name it."

The deep frown on his face slipped as something crossed his

eyes. I held my breath as he considered, but the frown returned and he dropped his eyes from mine.

"No." He said it firmly as the shuttle hit the ground. "Get in your seat."

Of course not. What did I have to trade, anyway? I could think of nothing a human would want from a Reboot.

I sat down as the shuttle door opened to reveal a furious Officer Mayer.

"Both of you, in my office. Now."

SEVENTEEN

OFFICER MAYER GLARED AT US FROM HIS DESK CHAIR, HIS face red.

"Sit," he ordered, and we did. "You." He looked at me. "That was the worst field assignment I've ever seen from you. I swear sometimes I thought you were just standing there watching."

I swallowed, not sure what to say, as that was entirely accurate.

"You." He turned to Callum. "You disobeyed a direct order and took your com out in the shuttle. Was there something you needed to say that you didn't want us to hear?"

"No, I was just tired of you yelling at me," Callum mumbled.

Officer Mayer slammed his fist on his desk. "You do not get to be tired! If I want to yell at you I will yell at you! Did your trainer not tell you to get in line? Did she not say that you were to follow all orders?"

"Yes," Callum replied.

"Then why shouldn't I eliminate you?"

"I don't want to kill anyone," Callum said quietly.

"I did not ask you to kill a person; I asked you to kill a Reboot. A crazy Reboot who killed two of your friends. I would think you would be glad to do it."

Callum shook his head.

"Then we should eliminate you." He nodded his head, like it was decided, and I felt like someone had just put their hand around my throat.

"No, that isn't—"

"I wasn't talking to you," Officer Mayer snapped at me before turning back to Callum. "You were warned and you chose not to follow a direct command. I don't see any improvement, and unfortunately there is no room here for Reboots who don't perform well."

"But he is better," I said, ignoring the glare Officer Mayer gave me as I spoke out of turn again. "He was the one who completed the assignment tonight. If it weren't for him I'd probably be dead and the assignment would have gotten away."

Officer Mayer pressed his lips together, looking from me to Callum, and I felt a tiny spark of hope amid my panic.

"And I didn't prepare him properly for a kill assignment," I said.

"Why not?"

"I'm not used to training such a low number. I didn't realize he'd be so emotional about it." The lie slid out of my mouth easily. Had I thought about it a little more, I would have known Callum wouldn't be okay with killing. "It's my fault."

"It's not—"

"You be quiet until you're spoken to," Officer Mayer snapped at Callum. He turned to me again. "Should I eliminate you instead?"

I swallowed, although that comment wasn't entirely unexpected, considering I'd just told him I'd screwed up. "I think if we continue training, he'll get better at following orders."

"So you don't think I should eliminate you, then." Officer Mayer had the tiniest smile on his face, and I was struck by the sudden urge to smack it away. He was enjoying watching me squirm.

"I would rather you didn't, sir."

He let out a long, exaggerated sigh as he sat back in his chair and crossed his arms over his chest. He looked from me to Callum for several agonizing seconds, the only noise in the room the hum of his computer.

Finally, he waved his hand. "Fine. Twenty-two, go to your quarters. One-seventy-eight, stay a minute."

I breathed a sigh of relief as Callum trudged out of the

room. Officer Mayer stood up, gathering a few papers and his computer into his hands.

"I'm sending you two on a kill assignment as soon as we locate the other adult Reboot," he said. "We've been tracking the other one for several days, so it shouldn't be long. If Twenty-two refuses to perform the assignment again, you'll eliminate him."

A flash of rage hit me so hard I almost gasped. It burned so strongly in my chest that I clenched my fists together and stared at my lap to keep myself from jumping up and snapping his neck.

I would eliminate him?

"You need to do it out in the field. This facility is . . . restless tonight after that crazy girl got herself killed."

That crazy girl. My best friend.

I could hear the snap it would make in my head. *Snap.*

He gestured for me to stand and I did, my legs shaking. He opened his office door.

"We'll say a human did it. Last thing we need is another elimination. We've had too many lately."

Snap.

Snap.

Snap.

Officer Mayer gestured for me to follow as he strolled into the hallway. "You gave it your best shot," he said, turning to walk away. "But he's bringing you down, too. We need to stop this nonsense."

I watched his back as he strode off. I could do it so quickly. He'd be dead before he hit the ground. Then I'd be dead a few minutes later. Perhaps only a few seconds later, depending on how far away the guards were.

I forced myself to move in the opposite direction. I certainly couldn't help Callum if I was dead.

I opened the door to the stairwell and stopped next to Callum, who stood in the dark alone.

Pound.

Pound.

Pound.

I turned toward the noise, coming from one floor down. The floor where the Reboots slept.

"What is that?" Callum asked.

I descended the stairs, gesturing for him to come with me. I pushed the door open and stepped onto the eighth floor.

Pound.

Pound.

Pound.

It came from my right, the girls' wing.

"Why are they doing that?" Callum whispered.

"Ever did that," I replied. "When she . . ."

When she went crazy.

Had they drugged them all? What good were Reboots if they were all totally insane?

"Get to your quarters," a guard barked.

I entered the girls' wing and stopped. In almost every room both girls were out of bed, methodically pounding on the wall.

Their eyes followed me as I walked to my room.

They weren't drugged.

They were rebelling.

EIGHTEEN

I SAT AT THE EDGE OF THE TRACK AND WATCHED CALLUM RUN the next morning. Even after the pounding stopped I barely slept, my eyes constantly drifting back to Ever's empty bed. I couldn't run today.

I wondered, if a human had helped her get out, would she have survived? Would she have improved once outside of HARC? Or would she have gotten worse?

Escape had never appealed to me, even when I heard about the rebels and the supposed Reboot reservation. The outside world was filled with humans who hated us, and a government set up to enslave or kill us. Outside, as a human, I had starved, caught several diseases, and ended up shot. Inside, I was fed regularly, clothed, and given a place to sleep.

But now, escape was all I could think of.

Rosa was surrounded by an electrified fence. Even if a Reboot could find and get rid of his tracker, he still had to find a way over or under the fence.

Going over it would be a little painful.

That was if we actually made it there. Armed guards patrolled the city line on every side, and sharpshooters were stationed in the towers strategically placed every half mile or so.

My plan so far was to run like hell, hope not to get shot in the head, and climb an electrified fence.

It was not the best plan.

I watched as Callum rounded the track in front of me, his breathing steady. He'd improved in almost every area. He was faster, stronger, more confident. His body was tighter, his movements sharp and controlled.

But I should have known he would never live up to the HARC standards. Even if he'd overcome his greatest obstacle—his sad little twenty-two minutes—he wasn't built to follow orders. He had too many questions. Too many opinions.

I had no idea how to save him without getting rid of our trackers. And there was no way to find a tracker without a HARC tracker locator. I'd never even seen one of those. I'd be surprised if they kept it in the same building with Reboots.

I needed someone who knew where those locators were. I needed Leb.

Relying on a human made my stomach clench. There was no reason he would want to help me and no reason I should trust him.

I pressed my hand to my forehead and forced my eyes away from Callum. I couldn't think straight when I looked at him. I was nothing but a pathetic knot of emotions and I couldn't think of what Leb needed, what he wanted, what a human couldn't—

His daughter.

He wanted his daughter.

They promised to help my daughter, he had said. *They lied.*

I slowly got to my feet, excitement swirling through my stomach and up to my chest. I had to find him. Now.

"Stop!" I called to Callum.

His chest heaved as he paused on the track and gave me a curious look.

"Come on," I said with a wave of my hand.

I rushed out the doors and down the hall, Callum's footsteps behind me. Leb was on duty today in the gym, and I had to get to him as quickly as possible. Officer Mayer would find us a kill assignment soon. I didn't have much time.

I rounded the corner and pushed open the door to the gym, scanning the room to find Leb. He was leaning against a wall, pretending he hadn't noticed me.

"Push-ups," I said to Callum, pointing to the floor.

He dropped down without comment, but his eyes followed

me as I took a few steps toward Leb. The officer shook his head slightly. He didn't want me talking to him.

Too bad.

I took a quick glance around the gym. Hugo and Ross were on the other side, engrossed in drilling their newbies. The rest of the Reboots were training or talking. I moved a little closer to Leb.

"Yeah, he is improving," I said loudly. I hoped whoever was watching the cameras didn't notice Leb hadn't actually asked me a question.

He stared stone-faced at me. He wasn't playing.

I turned to face Callum. "He's much faster now," I continued to Leb. I ducked my head and focused on the ground. "Your daughter," I whispered.

The silence stretched on for too long. There were about ten other Reboots in the gym, and for several seconds there was nothing but the sounds of fists smashing into bodies.

"What about her?" Leb finally mumbled.

"I can get her out."

He said nothing. He was so quiet that I finally peeked over my shoulder at him and found his face stricken, almost horrified. I might as well have just told him I was going to kill his daughter, not rescue her.

"They already tried," he stuttered.

"I'm better equipped than any human. I'm trained for this. If you want her, you need me."

He paused, looking at me with wide eyes. "How do I know you'll keep your word after you get out of here?"

"Trust?" One look at his face made it clear that wasn't an option.

We were silent again, and Leb stared at the floor with furrowed brows. Finally, he said, "You want to go to the reservation, right?"

"If it actually exists."

"It does."

"You've been there?"

"No, but the Reboots who meet with the rebels say it does." He looked almost excited as he spoke. "I could instruct the rebels in Austin not to give you a map to the reservation until you show up with Adina. Would you do that?"

The reservation was not my main concern—getting Callum out was—but Leb didn't need to know that. "Yes. You have to get me a tracker locator I can keep, though. I can't get her without it."

Leb nodded and my heart jumped with hope. This might actually work.

"Do it fast," I said, moving away from Leb. I jerked my head at Callum. "You can go shower."

Callum gave me another curious look that I ignored as we split off to our respective showers. My chest was pounding in anticipation but I couldn't decide if I wanted to say anything to him. What if I got his hopes up and everything fell through?

I grabbed a towel and stepped into a stall, snapping the curtain shut behind me. I tossed the towel over the side wall and gripped the bottom of my shirt.

"Wren?"

I whirled around to see the outline of someone standing on the other side of the curtain. "Callum?"

He pushed open the curtain and stepped inside the stall, amusement flickering across his face when he looked down at my fingers, still tightly clenched around the bottom of my shirt.

I quickly dropped it and smoothed the material over my stomach. He just stood there. Was I supposed to do something? Had he come thinking I'd want to have sex? My hands were shaking suddenly and I was relieved he hadn't immediately pounced on me.

And maybe a little disappointed.

"What have you been talking about with Leb?" he asked.

I crossed my arms over my chest and beat down the surge of disappointment that he hadn't come to kiss me.

"Plans," I said.

"What does that mean?"

I wanted to tell him that I was going to get him out of here. I wanted to tell him to hang in there, to be good for a little while longer until I could figure everything out. I knew he'd give me a look of happiness and hope and excitement. But I was worried he would be crushed if it all fell apart.

"Plans like he's going to help us escape?" he asked.

"I don't know."

His eyes were already hopeful. So much for not getting his hopes up.

"Will you please follow orders until I do know?" I asked.

He hesitated. It was brief, but it was there. "Yes."

I waited. He hadn't meant the *yes*.

The *yes* was a lie.

"Within reason," he finished.

There was the truth.

"They're sending us on a kill assignment any day now," I said quietly. "If it comes down to it, you need to do it."

"No."

"Callum . . ."

He smiled. "I like that you call me Callum now."

"You have to do it."

"No, I don't." He reached out, trying to pull one of my arms away from my chest.

I shook him off. "Leb can't help us if you're dead."

"They can't make me kill someone."

"It's an adult Reboot. It's not even a person anymore."

He looked down at me, a frown crossing his face. "Wouldn't humans say the same thing about us?"

"Yes, but it's true with an adult, they—"

"You don't know that. That's just what HARC says. I'm inclined to be suspicious."

"You saw Gregor last night," I said. "He was crazed. And

every person I've seen who Rebooted as an adult is like that. They can't even talk anymore, Callum."

"We were there to capture him so HARC could experiment on him. I'd fight back, too. And besides, I was hysterical after I rose. Weren't you?"

"Yes."

"So maybe—"

"It doesn't matter," I said in exasperation. "Either you kill the next one or HARC eliminates you."

"You've really killed lots of people?" he asked.

"Yes," I said, dropping my eyes. Without even thinking about it. Refusing had never even occurred to me.

"Humans, too?"

"Yes."

"They made you do that?"

"Sometimes I offered." I looked up as he took a sharp breath at that admission.

"Why would you do that?" he asked, his voice catching.

"When the assignment killed my fellow Reboots, I offered."

"So because you were mad."

I paused, hugging my arms tighter to my chest. "I guess." His face was full of confusion and horror and maybe even a little disgust. A rock had formed on top of my chest and I closed my eyes, trying to make it go away. "I was only twelve when I died; I've been here a long time and I thought I had to do everything I was—I mean, I do have to do everything I'm told. They were bad, the people I killed, and I didn't—"

"I'm not judging you," Callum interrupted, his face softening as he stepped closer to me. "Well, I was, but I shouldn't be. I'm sorry. I've been here only a few weeks and you . . . I can't imagine being here five years." A smile crossed his face. "Maybe I won't have to be. You and Leb looked pretty serious today."

"Or you won't be here five years because you disobey orders again and they kill you tomorrow."

"Or that," he said, patting my head with a little laugh. Apparently his own death bothered him very little.

"It's me, Callum. If you don't carry out the assignment I'm supposed to eliminate you."

"Oh." He looked at me questioningly.

"I won't do it," I said, my annoyance coming through in my voice.

"But then . . ."

"Then they'll probably eliminate me, too."

"Dammit, Wren . . ." He let out a whoosh of air, putting his hands behind his head. "That's not fair."

"It's the truth."

"No. They won't do it. You're their precious One-seventy-eight. Officer Mayer will just yell and have someone else kill me."

"I'm a Reboot like everyone else," I said. "They'll kill me if I start rebelling."

"So either I kill this person or I'm responsible for your death.

That's great. Wonderful choice you've set up for me there."

"I don't want you to die."

"Now you're sucking up." He tugged at my waist, trying to draw me closer. I let him, pressing my palm to his warm chest. "I just don't want to be . . ."

"Me?" I guessed.

"No. I don't want them to make me into that person. Into someone who kills."

I had nothing to say to that, as I was already that person. I pressed my lips together and looked at him pleadingly.

"That look," he moaned, putting his hands on my cheeks. "Don't give me that look."

"Will you do it? Please?"

He sighed and dropped his hands. "Do I have to decide now?"

"The assignment could come down any minute."

"I . . . could try, I guess." The defeat in his voice made my insides twist uncomfortably.

"Thank you." I took a step back, an indication that I was ready for him to go.

"Right, I'll let you shower." He grabbed the edge of the curtain but paused, the humor back in his eyes. "Or I could stay."

A little yelp escaped my mouth as I pulled my arms in and pressed them both against my chest. "I . . . um . . ." *Yes.* And *no.* I felt sick.

"I'm sorry," he said with a chuckle, holding up his hands. "You look horrified. I was mostly kidding."

"No, I'm not horrified," I said, forcing myself to relax. He gave me one last smile before pulling back the curtain and hopping out.

An Under-sixty leaned over and peeked around the curtain before I could shut it. A small crowd had formed, and the girls all had funny smiles on their faces.

"Aw, we knew you'd break down eventually," the Under-sixty said. "He's really cute."

I snapped the curtain closed and let out a long breath as I leaned my forehead against the cool tile.

I shouldn't have stuttered and mumbled like that. I shouldn't have looked horrified. I wanted to . . . well, I didn't know if I wanted to strip down and shower with him, but I liked his arms around me. I thought I would have liked to kiss him. Although I couldn't be sure, never having kissed anyone before.

Ever would have enjoyed this. She would have been thrilled if I had told her everything. Her eyes would have lit up with the hope I was a real person after all. She would have said something comforting and humanlike, although I had no idea what.

I missed her.

That evening, after dinner, I walked down the hallway, slowing as I spotted a human leaving my room. She caught my eye and pointed inside.

"Clothes drop-off," she said, and quickly scurried away.

I looked at the neatly folded clothes on my bed in confusion.

I'd had a clothes drop-off yesterday.

I grabbed a black sweatshirt off the top. It was way too big.

But there was a folded-up piece of paper beneath it.

I dropped the sweatshirt on the bed and held the paper close to my chest, turning away from my clear wall and unfolding it as discreetly as possible.

It was a map. A map of the five cities of Texas, with a route drawn in blue from Rosa to Austin. He'd drawn a circle around the intersection of Nelson and Holly in Rosa, a couple blocks from where the shuttle usually landed, and written the words *meet me here*. There was a star at the edge of the Rosa city line, directly in between two towers. Where we were supposed to exit the city, perhaps? The blue line stretched through the miles of trees between the two cities and stopped at the word *tunnel* scrawled near the edge of the *rico* side of Austin.

My breath caught in my chest and the map shook ever so slightly as I read the small words printed at the bottom.

I'm in.

NINETEEN

THE KILL ASSIGNMENT CAME THE NEXT DAY.

They gave me a gun and told me to either give it to Callum to kill the Reboot, or use it on Callum myself. I hadn't been given a gun to use in the field in a few months, and it felt cool and heavy against my hip.

I had the map in my pocket, even though I doubted Leb had managed to get his hands on a tracker locator in one day. I wouldn't run without removing our trackers first. There was no point.

If Leb didn't come through today, Callum had to perform the kill assignment.

Callum glanced down at the gun when I joined him on the

roof. A cool breeze blew across us, bringing with it the stench of the slums, and I saw his nose wrinkle. From the smell or the sight of the gun, I didn't know.

The shuttle hit the roof with a clunk and the door opened to reveal Paul inside. If Leb wasn't on this assignment, maybe he had the tracker locator and was waiting for us at the meeting spot.

I couldn't breathe. The air was gone and my chest hurt. This could be my last assignment. My last time in the shuttle. The last day at the place I'd called home for five years.

Paul gestured for us to sit and I stumbled on the way to my seat.

Callum was shaking as he strapped himself in. I wanted to tell him it was okay, that he wouldn't have to perform the assignment, but I didn't know that for sure.

The shuttle was silent as we rode to the slums. Paul dug into his pocket and produced four bullets as we landed, offering them to me.

"Take any unused ones out before boarding the shuttle," he warned as I closed my fist around the bullets.

I nodded and followed Callum into the cool night air. His eyes were glued to the gun as I loaded the bullets. I didn't want to tip off the HARC officers watching our video feed. They needed to believe we were following orders, for as long as possible.

I held the gun out to Callum, but his hands remained at his sides.

"Callum," I said quietly.

He wrapped his fingers around the gun, holding it away from him like it was contaminated. His eyes met mine.

"I have to?" he asked, his voice strained.

No. "Yes." I cleared my throat and jerked my head to the right. "Let's go this way. It's a shortcut."

Callum frowned down at his map and the assignment slip, then looked up at me, mouth open to most likely tell me we were headed in the wrong direction. He quickly snapped it shut as understanding crossed his face and I turned away so HARC wouldn't see the hope there.

I led him to the intersection of Holly and Nelson, whipping my head around to find Leb.

Nothing.

The night was quiet, nothing but the sound of wind in the trees and a few crickets as we stood in the middle of the dirt road surrounded by little tents.

Maybe he wasn't coming tonight.

"Can I see the map?" I asked, to stall.

Callum handed it over and I pretended to look at the straight lines representing the streets of Rosa. I didn't have long before the HARC officers watching me grew suspicious. I rarely needed to look at a map.

I stole another peek around but there was no one but me and Callum. I let out a long sigh.

"We should go that way," I said, trying my best to keep the

defeat out of my voice.

Callum's face fell and he looked down at the gun in his hand. "So I have to shoot her in the head, right? To kill my own kind?" He glanced down at the assignment slip. "Danielle. I murder Danielle?"

I winced at the word choice and the anger dripping from every syllable. HARC surely heard it.

"Yes," I replied. "Aim for the forehead, not the face. You want to destroy the brain. Two shots are best, to be safe."

"And then what? I drag her back to the shuttle?"

"Or I will." I turned away, unable to meet his accusing gaze. He might have been mostly mad at HARC, but there was plenty there for me as well. Would he ever be able to forgive me if I made him do this?

"I—" A high-pitched screeching in my ear interrupted me, and Callum and I both grimaced and pulled our coms out.

"What was that?" Callum asked, rubbing his ear. "Did our coms just go out?"

My eyes darted across the area, hope filling my chest so much it was difficult to breathe.

A man peeked around the edge of a tent, a broad figure in black. He rose from his knees and jogged to us, pushing the brim of his hat up as he stopped in front of me.

Leb. He held a knife with one hand and with the other pulled a black object out of his pocket, and Callum stepped forward, the gun half-raised to defend us. I shook my head at

Callum and he slowly lowered it, eyes still glued to Leb's knife.

"Stand still," Leb said, lifting the black object to my chest. It was a small device about the size of his palm, and it lit up with a red light when he scanned it over my upper right arm.

"Take off your jacket," he said.

"How'd you get it so fast?" I asked as I shook off my jacket.

"Getting it isn't the problem," he muttered. "It's the shit storm that will erupt when they realize it's gone that's the problem."

He lifted the knife and sliced a gash a few inches above my elbow, using the edge of the blade to knock a little metal device to the ground. I wrapped my fingers around the bloody wound. It wasn't deep enough to be painful, but my fingers still shook as I clutched them to my skin.

I stared at the bloody silver tracker. Freedom. I could run now, and no one would know where I was. What I was doing. What I was saying.

Leb waved for Callum to come closer, but he just stood there, staring at the blood seeping out of my arm. He looked shocked, on the edge of happiness, like he couldn't believe it was real.

"Would you hurry up?" Leb snapped, grabbing him by the arm and waving the locator over his body. "The shuttle officer is probably already on his way."

Leb spun Callum around and ran the locator down his back until it turned red. He lifted his shirt and cut a short line across his back just under his shoulder blade. He grabbed the tracker and carefully set it on the ground.

Leb took off down the street, motioning for us to follow him. We ran two blocks, coming to a stop behind a dark house with an assortment of trash and broken toys in the backyard.

Leb shoved something into my hand and I looked down to see some papers, the locator, and a map of the Austin slums. I didn't think I needed a map—I remembered it well enough—but he'd marked a particular spot in the middle of a residential area.

"Her name is Adina," he said, tapping an envelope and a picture of a dark-haired Reboot below the map. "She's on assignment Tuesday and Wednesday night. The shuttle usually lands at the end of Guadalupe Street. Give her that letter. I marked the rebels' address on the map. If you get Adina, go there and they will tell you how to get to the reservation."

"Fine," I said, shoving everything into my back pocket. "Do you have any bullets? We only have four."

He pulled his gun out and emptied about ten into my hand. "They're militant about keeping this location secret from HARC. Go at night. Don't call attention to yourselves." He dropped the knife in my other hand. "Take that, too. Go."

"Thank you," I said as Leb turned to run. He gave me a slight nod over his shoulder before disappearing down an alley.

I was frozen. Leb had said *go*. Which way? Where? To some mythical Reboot reservation that probably didn't even exist?

Panic gripped my chest as I realized what I'd done. I was in the slums, surrounded by humans, and I wasn't going back to HARC.

I wasn't going home.

"Wren." I looked up to see Callum's excited face peering at me. He broke the camera off my helmet, took my com from my clenched hand, and tossed them both on the ground. "I think wc should run."

TWENTY

I GRABBED CALLUM'S HAND AND WE WOVE THROUGH A DARK alleyway, breaking into a full sprint as we headed for an abandoned shelter. In the years after the war it was meant to help the humans get back on their feet. When the drug dealers and gangs took over Rosa, HARC boarded it up.

We were at the edge of Rosa, near the city line and in the heart of the slums. HARC was on the other side of town, past the fields, but it wouldn't take them long to dispatch officers. In terms of hiding, this was not the best place. The houses were tiny and the tents on the next road over would provide even less cover.

An alarm pierced the silence and a spotlight swooped across

the area. I scrambled to the back of a shack, pressing myself against the rickety wood. Callum did the same, his eyes on the sky as a shuttle spotlight surveyed the area. It moved down the street and he looked over at me.

"Should we keep going?" he whispered.

Yes. Maybe? I wasn't sure. Almost every decision I'd made over the last five years wasn't really mine. I knew the rules of HARC and I followed them.

The spotlight swung to us and Callum gripped my hand as we took off across the patchy grass surrounding the shack. I heard the bullets before several pierced my shoulders and bounced off my helmet.

"This way," I called, dropping Callum's hand as we crossed the dirt road. The spotlight lost us as I wove in between houses and darted over lawns, but I could see officers in the distance, a huge group of them dispersing on the streets.

I came to a stop at the back of the old shelter and yanked so hard on the door that the building actually swayed like it was going to fall over. I stumbled as the door swung open easily and stepped inside only to reel back, hitting Callum's chest.

People. Humans, everywhere. They smelled like grime and filth and infection. I knew that smell.

I recognized the humans huddled in their own little corners, some using only clothes or sticks to mark their territory. Saw the track marks on their arms, the shaky hands, the desperation etched on their faces.

As a child, I lived in a similar place for months while my parents floated on an intense high, a drug that lasted so long they often didn't have time to come down before finding an opportunity to shoot up again. The squatters in the abandoned buildings were the worst off of the slum dwellers, the ones who gave every cent they had to the drug dealers and criminals who had stalled Rosa's progress.

I'd forgotten most of my time squatting with my parents, but I remembered the smell and how I used to hold the blanket to my nose at night to block it while I slept.

Callum gagged, which drew a few interested looks. Some of the humans blinked and stared, too high to recognize the two Reboots standing in front of them. But others weren't that far gone.

I raised my fingers to my lips, begging for silence, but it was useless. A regular human was bad, but these people were worse.

They screamed and I was struck by the sudden impulse to pull out my gun and start shooting. There were about thirty of them. How long would it take to kill them all?

"We can go out that way."

Callum's voice sliced through my thoughts and I looked over at him in surprise. I had almost forgotten he was there.

It occurred to me that he would be horrified if I started killing people. He'd give me that look, like I was a monster. He had been willing to die because he refused to take a life.

But me, I contemplated shooting everyone.

"Wren," he said, pulling urgently on my arm.

I let him drag me to the front door and out into the darkness. We took off in the opposite direction of the spotlight.

I forgot that I hated humans. I had been clinical about the assignments; that's how we were trained. But I hated them, even when I was one.

Dirty, disgusting, violent, selfish, impulsive, and now I had to spend days—weeks—wading through them to find Adina and this mythical Reboot reservation.

I wanted to hate Callum for it, but my brain immediately screamed at only me. Me, the one who could never get Callum to follow the rules. Me, who couldn't train him well enough to survive inside HARC. Me, who brought him into this madness, where he was most likely going to be killed anyway.

Bullets peppered the ground as we ran, biting at Callum's ankles and spewing blood across the dirt. It slowed him down, so I pulled ahead and grabbed his arm to tug him along.

The houses were closer together, the night quieter as we crossed into the nicer area of the slums. The bullets from above stopped and I thought maybe they had lost us.

But the ground crew had found us. The officers, six, seven—no, nine of them, came barreling around a corner, their guns poised.

"Duck," I said, pushing his head down as they fired.

I left him on the ground and flew at the soldiers. I recognized a couple familiar faces through their plastic masks, although the terror splashed across them was new.

I slammed my foot into an officer's chest as he fired at my head, dodging the shot and knocking the gun out of his hand. The others tried to grab me but I darted away, faster than their little human eyes could keep track of.

I lifted the gun. One, two, three. I shot each one in the chest, ignoring the bullets that tore through my jacket and bounced off my helmet.

One of the soldiers unhooked a grenade from his belt and tossed it frantically in my direction, missing by several feet.

Callum.

The grenade sailed past him and hit the house just behind him. He dove for the ground as the blast blew out the back of the little wooden shack, engulfing the lawn, and him, in flames.

The barrel of a gun pressed against my forehead. The panic hit, for only a moment, and I kicked his legs as the bullet grazed my ear. My fingers tightened around my gun and I fired a shot into his chest.

Another blast rocked the ground, and I snatched a grenade off the dead officer's belt and launched it at the men running for me.

One remained, and I turned to see him taking aim at Callum, who was on the ground, trying to extinguish the flames lapping up his legs.

I fired three times, my aim messy as fear took over. The final soldier fell after the third shot and I dove for Callum, jumping on top of him and rolling us through the dirt. I smothered the lingering flames with my hands and hopped off him, pulling him to his feet.

He swayed, his hands shaking as he lifted them to examine the damage. His skin was red, charred in places. His shirt was almost totally gone, his pants nothing but scorched threads.

"Are you all right?" I asked, swiftly taking a glance around.

"Yes," he stammered. "I'm—I'm sorry, I tried to get away, but as soon as I got the first fire out they threw another one and—"

"It's fine," I said, taking his hand as gently as I could. "Can you run?"

He nodded, wincing as we took off. We only had to go a block; I was headed to the closest hiding place I could think of.

The large square trash receptacle was piled too high, as usual, and sat not far from the brick wall of the schoolhouse. I pushed the large gray container closer to the wall, gesturing for Callum to get behind it. My first instinct was to jump inside and bury ourselves beneath the trash, but if I were an officer, I would immediately look in every place with a lid or door that shut. We weren't entirely covered behind the trash bin—they'd be able to see us from the side, at the right angle—but it was such an open place to hide I hoped they wouldn't even think to look for us there.

I edged around and leaned against the wall next to Callum, casting a worried glance in his direction. I'd never been burned to the extent he was—his arms were black in places—but I remembered the pain of lesser burns well. The stinging had been impossible to totally shut out, mixing with the uncomfortable sensation of new skin stretching over the dead.

He held his arms away from his body and scrunched his face up in a way that made me want to gather him into my arms. That would only make it worse, though.

I couldn't look at him anymore, so I pressed my palms against my eyes and wished I'd paid closer attention to Callum's healing time. Ten minutes? Twenty?

I squeezed my eyes shut, but when I pushed the image of Callum's pain-filled face out of my head all I saw was the drug den.

"Stay really still."

I took in a sharp breath as the memory came crashing down, as clear as if it had just happened.

"Don't look at her."

It was my mom speaking, her putrid breath caressing my face as she whispered in my ear and locked her arm around my tummy so tight it hurt.

I didn't listen to her. I had looked up, past the other humans huddled in fear around the den, to the face of the Reboot in the center of the room.

She saw me staring, her light green eyes shining in the darkness.

"One-thirteen." She spoke to the other Reboot and he

turned. She pointed at me.

"What?" he asked.

"It's a kid."

"So?"

"So she shouldn't be here, should she? Look at this place."

"That's none of our concern. We're just here to get the assignment."

"But—"

"Seventy-one," he interrupted sharply.

She closed her mouth, turning to look at me sadly as she left. I'd stared even after she was gone, wishing I could follow her.

My mom must have noticed, because she pushed me off her lap, her face angry and disgusted.

My heart beat strangely from the memory, the faces of my parents flooding my mind. My mom had been blond, like me, although her hair was darker from the dirt and grease. My dad had big bushy eyebrows that were constantly knitted together in sadness or deep thought.

I clenched my hands against my helmet, willing the images out. I hated it here. I didn't want to remember these things. I didn't want to go to Austin. The pain that hit my chest was so intense that for a moment I thought someone had shot me.

"Wren."

Callum's voice jolted me out of my thoughts and I looked up to see his adorable worried face.

"Are you okay?" he asked.

His skin hadn't healed everywhere yet; I could see wounds closing and turning pink in front of my eyes. But he looked so much better that I was struck by a wild urge to throw my arms around his neck.

"Yes. Are you?"

Callum turned and pressed his body against mine, placing his palms flat against the wall behind me. I mashed myself into the brick, taken aback by his sudden closeness.

"How did you do it?" he asked, eyes twinkling as he smiled at me. "How did you get Leb to help?"

"I went on a solo mission with Leb, and I captured this human who said they were helping Reboots escape. Sending them to some Reboot reservation. I made a deal."

"Something about his daughter?"

"I had to promise to go rescue her. She's a Reboot in Austin." My words came out strained, breathless. I couldn't speak right with his body so close to mine.

"What is this Reboot reservation? Reboots are really just living there? Free?"

"I don't know. I doubt it, to be honest."

"So we get Adina, meet these humans, and then go to this reservation?"

"Yes."

"Where are we going to go if it's not there?"

"I don't know," I said, the panic gripping my chest again. "I didn't think about it. I was just . . ." I stopped, hoping I wouldn't have to finish the sentence. But he only raised his eyebrows in question. "I didn't want you to die."

He slipped his hands over my cheeks and tilted my face up so I had no choice but to stare into his dark eyes. I'd thought he couldn't get any closer, but he leaned in and my body folded into his. His chest rose and fell against mine and I let my hands rest on it.

"Thank you."

I blinked, not expecting gratitude. Not sure if I deserved it. I didn't know what to say in response, but he wasn't looking at me like he expected one.

He had to give his helmet a little shove and dip his head down to kiss me, but I didn't believe he was actually going to do it until I felt his lips gently press against mine. My body jolted in surprise and I felt him smile against my lips.

And I was totally gone.

My toes needed no urging this time. I rose up on them as far as I could go and wrapped my arms around his neck. He dropped his hands to my waist and hugged me against his body.

It wasn't how I had thought it would be. Kissing had sort of puzzled me. As a human I had thought it seemed dangerous—an easy way to spread germs. As a Reboot it had confused me. I wasn't entirely sure why people liked doing it.

Now I was only confused as to why a person would want to kiss anyone but Callum.

When he lifted his head from mine I almost pulled it back

down again, but he smiled and I didn't want to miss that.

"I told you you liked me."

I laughed and utter delight danced across his face, like he hadn't been sure that statement was true.

He stepped away and pulled what was left of his shirt over his head. He unhooked his helmet, carefully placed it on the ground, and studied his pants, which were more like shorts with a few strands of fabric. I could see his black underwear poking through. He plopped onto the ground and I slid down the wall next to him. My brain wanted to continue running but my legs were limp and wobbly suddenly.

"That really hurts, by the way," he said, holding his arm out to look at his new skin. "Have you ever been burned?"

"Not like that," I said quietly, my voice shaking.

"What's wrong?" he asked, scooting closer to me. "Were you worried about me?"

I crossed my arms over my chest and mock frowned at him in response, which made him smile wider. He reached for me and I felt a blush cross my face.

"Callum, you're in your underwear."

"I have pants on. Sort of." He reached for me again, his eyebrows furrowing when he took one of my hands in his. "You're cold. Come here."

"Aren't you cold?" I asked as he pulled me into his lap and I wrapped my arms around his bare shoulders.

"No. It's not cold."

I thought he was going to kiss me, but instead he leaned forward and buried his head in my neck, his lips gently pressing against a spot that made my stomach do a happy dance.

"You smell so good," he mumbled, kissing my neck again.

"No, I don't," I said, trying to move away in embarrassment. "I smell like death."

"You're crazy," he said with a chuckle, holding me tighter. "You're not dead. You don't smell like death."

"I was dead a long time."

"And now you're not. Hence the alive smell." He lifted his head and pressed his lips to mine.

I meant to push him away with more force, but my body didn't actually want him to go anywhere. His lips left mine only by about an inch.

"We shouldn't stay here too long," I said.

"Why not? It's so cozy. The fresh night air, mixed with the perfume of rotting trash. It's beautiful."

"They'll be—" I stopped as I heard the sounds of footsteps approaching.

"No visual," I heard an officer say. "Nine dead, couldn't have been long ago."

Callum looked at me in surprise at the number and I focused on the ground, afraid of seeing disgust in his eyes.

"Get ready to run," I whispered in his ear.

"Check in there," an officer yelled.

Footsteps crunched on gravel in our direction and I held

my breath, afraid to move even an inch. The lid to the trash bin banged open, hitting the side of the schoolhouse above our heads. Trash rustled as the officer dug around inside.

"All clear," he yelled. The footsteps faded, the yells from the other officers disappearing in the distance.

Callum grinned, bouncing me in his arms until I cracked a smile. "Why am I not surprised you picked a good hiding spot?"

"We got lucky," I said, unhooking my helmet and setting it on the ground.

"I wouldn't look too hard for us, if I were them. Not if they know it's you they're up against."

"I . . . um . . . those nine guards . . ." I cleared my throat. I wanted to ask if he was horrified that I'd killed all those humans, but he didn't look horrified. I didn't want to bring it to his attention that perhaps I was a monster, and not someone he should be kissing.

"I know," he said quietly. "You had to save us."

I gave him a relieved smile, letting out a slow breath. Maybe, if I'd tried harder, I could have just injured a few. I decided not to point that out to him.

"I want to do something while we're in Austin," he said, giving me his big eyes. "I want to go see my family."

I immediately shook my head. "No. That's not a good idea."

"But we have to go anyway, right? To get Adina?"

"Yes, but—"

"I just want to see them. Tell them I'm okay."

"They won't . . ." I couldn't say it. I couldn't tell him they wouldn't want to see him. That they would consider their son dead, and this boy only an illusion who looked similar.

"They'll want to see me," he said in response to my unspoken words. "I know HARC says we can't have contact with our families, but they don't know my parents. And my brother, David . . ." He rubbed his hand over his short, dark hair. "We were actually sort of close. I think he'd want to see me."

I didn't know his parents, either, but I could guess their reaction if a monster who looked like their son showed up on their doorstep.

"How old is your brother?" I asked.

"Thirteen."

"He didn't get sick when you did?"

He shook his head. "No, he was fine when I died."

A thirteen-year-old would probably be more accepting of a Reboot than an adult, given that it could still happen to him at any time. Still, with his parents there I didn't see that going well. "I don't think you should go."

"I have to," he said, pushing an escaped strand of hair behind my ear. "And I'd prefer it if you came with me."

I sighed. He'd go whether I came or not.

"You know I'd probably get killed in under an hour without you," he said.

"With the way things are going, I'd be shocked if we even make it out of Rosa."

"You just took down nine officers by yourself. I think we'll be fine." He inched back against the wall, wrapping his arm tightly around my waist when I started to scoot away. "Are we going to try to leave Rosa tonight?"

"I think tomorrow night will be better, don't you? They're all on high alert and they'll be expecting us to try to break out now."

He nodded in agreement. "We should stay here awhile. They probably won't check this area again."

"Hopefully," I said, sliding off his lap and settling next to him. He slid his hand into mine and leaned over to press a soft kiss onto my cheek. I shifted a little closer, until his warm arm rubbed against mine, and lowered my gaze to hide the goofy smile spreading across my face.

TWENTY-ONE

"WREN."

The soft voice made me stir, and I winced at the pain that shot through my neck. I was leaning against something, my cheek pressed against a lovely warm and solid object, and I forced my eyelids open.

My head was on Callum's shoulder. I'd fallen asleep. I took in a surprised breath and jerked into a sitting position, swinging around to see if we were safe. The streets were deserted, bright with early morning light.

"I thought you might want to move before everyone starts getting up," Callum said, a smile tugging at the edge of his mouth.

"I fell asleep?" I asked stupidly.

"Yes."

"I'm sorry." I couldn't believe I'd passed out. For hours. Anyone could have snuck up on us.

"It's okay," Callum said, stretching. "I stayed awake and kept watch. Plus you look all cute and nonlethal when you sleep."

A blush crept up my cheeks and he leaned forward to kiss me, making me blush more deeply.

"Um, yes," I said when he pulled away. "We should probably move before the streets get too crowded." I wasn't sure of the best place to hide, but we did need to get to the other side of town, closer to the fence at the city line.

"Should we try to get me some clothes?" Callum asked as he reached for his helmet and strapped it on. "I don't really mind being in my underwear and shorty shorts, but this might attract unwanted attention."

"Maybe," I said, holding back a grin. I glanced around and stood up to slowly peek into the open waste bin.

"Are you really looking for clothes in the trash?"

I held up a dirty paper bag. "We could make holes in this."

"I think my wearing a paper-bag dress will actually attract more stares," he said dryly.

I tossed it back and reached for my helmet, glancing around. I couldn't see any humans, but I could hear the shuffle of a few of them nearby. We would need food eventually—my stomach was feeling a little empty—but my first concern was getting across the city before it got too crowded.

"No one has come over here recently?" I asked.

"No. I've heard officers occasionally, but not for a couple hours."

"Thanks," I said, leaning back against the wall and smiling at him. "For keeping watch."

He brushed his fingers against my hair, running them down the ponytail. "Of course. You can sleep on me any time you want."

His eyes were soft, different than I'd ever seen them, and I wanted to crawl into his lap immediately and take him up on that offer. When he leaned forward to kiss me I let him, just for a moment.

I pulled away and took a quick glance around, strapping my helmet on as I jumped up.

"Time for our morning run," I said. "Maybe we can get to the other side of town without being spotted."

He nodded as he got to his feet, and I wrapped my fingers around his wrist as we sprinted out from behind the trash bin and took off down the alleyway. We hit the dirt road and I let go of Callum to pump my arms as we cut away from the center of town, to the tents and the worst of the slums. My feet pounded the dirt, and I glanced over at Callum to see if he was okay.

He was gone.

I skidded to a stop, my breath coming in big gasps as I

frantically whipped my head around. I took off back in the direction of the school, flying around the corner again.

There was nothing. Not even a human. Clothes flapped on the line in the backyard of a house next to me and I jogged away from the noise, straining to listen for a sign of him.

Panic surged up my chest with such force that I clapped my hand over my mouth to keep from screaming his name. Giving away my location was not the smart thing to do.

I closed my eyes and listened. I could hear people running, a few shouts, but nothing that sounded like Callum.

But humans shouting and running couldn't be good, especially with a Reboot on the loose. I sprinted in the direction of the shouts, coming to a quick stop at the corner of a building when I realized it was HARC officers yelling orders at one another. I couldn't see them but they were close, no more than a block or two away.

What if they'd already found him?

What would I do if I couldn't find him? Just head to Austin without him and hope he made it by himself?

The idea was so ridiculous I almost laughed. I turned down a random street and broke into a run. I never would have escaped without him. I would have stayed in my little white cell, happily, numbly, until I died.

I wasn't going anywhere without Callum.

I stopped in my tracks, all thoughts of staying hidden and safe flying from my brain.

I screamed his name so loudly my throat ached in protest. But I yelled again, listening desperately for a response.

"Wren!"

The distant yell came from back toward the schoolhouse, and I took off at top speed, ignoring the gawking humans wandering out of their houses.

I recognized the sounds as I passed the schoolhouse and headed for the center of town. The hysteria, the angry shouts. I'd heard it before, when humans had caught themselves a Reboot.

I rounded a corner and spotted Callum running toward me as fast as he could. His battered pants flapped as he sprinted, his knees and thighs exposed and bloodied.

Behind him was a horde of angry townspeople. There were about fifteen of them, most of them without weapons, but they were being joined on all sides as humans ran out of their houses to see what the fuss was about. It wasn't often they got to face a Reboot without HARC's protection, and clearly they wanted to take advantage of it. They kicked up dirt as they ran, and the air was full of it, obscuring their faces and making some of them cough.

Callum had already taken a beating. His face was bruised, one of his arms bent at a funny angle, and I barreled toward him.

A boy about our age caught his uninjured arm and yanked him to the ground, but Callum kicked him in the chest so hard he flew to the other side of the road. If I hadn't been focused on getting him to safety I might have smiled in pride at how quickly he reacted.

He scrambled to his feet, fending off a woman trying to bash his head with a baseball bat. Relief flooded his eyes as I surged forward and caught the bat, snatching it out of her grasp and tossing it as far as I could. A hand clamped down on my shoulder and I heard gasps from several humans as I landed flat on my back.

They all grabbed for me, yelling things that I couldn't understand. A hand went for my neck and I snapped it, my eyes burning into the man's. I kicked and grabbed the gun from my pants, their greedy little hands all trying to get to it so they could put a bullet in our brains.

Callum shoved aside a man directly in front of me and pulled me to my feet, dragging me out of their grasp. I whirled around, pointing the gun in their direction. A few backed off, hands raised in surrender, but most kept right on coming.

I only had a few bullets left, so I fired one shot into the leg of the human who looked the fastest and took off in the opposite direction with Callum.

"You're monsters!" I heard a woman scream. "You're soulless monsters!"

The humans were tiring, falling farther and farther behind as their inferior lungs and legs gave out. We flew down the streets, over the dirt roads, into the ugliest part of town. As we approached the old medical building I glanced behind us again and realized we had lost them for good.

I came to a stop next to the one-story building and pressed my hands against my thighs as I gasped for air.

"I'm sorry," Callum said, leaning against the building as his chest heaved up and down. "I should have . . ." He shook his head with a little shrug.

I looked up at him, the anxiety from earlier setting in even though he was standing in front of me. I tried to hide my fear, to push back the sick feeling that kept resurfacing as it hit me that I'd come very close to losing him, but I must have failed, because he gave me a questioning, confused look. I dropped my eyes from his. I didn't know how to put the sentence together, to tell him that I had been terrified of something happening to him. It sounded pathetic in my head. It would sound worse out loud.

I cleared my throat. "What happened?"

"A couple guys grabbed me. I tried to yell, but they had me by the head. They dragged me to an alley so . . ." He frowned at me. "So they could all get a hit in, I guess? They really hate us, huh?"

I hesitated, then nodded, because it was the truth. He lowered his eyes in disappointment.

"I'm sorry," I said quietly. "It's my fault. I've worked this area a long time. They despise me. They probably wanted me."

He shrugged. "It's not your fault." He reached up, rubbing

his hand against his head. "But they took my helmet."

I hadn't even realized it; I was so distracted by my ridiculous feelings. There was no point in disguising my horror.

"Yeah, it's not good," he said with a sigh.

It was definitely not good. The officers would aim for his head and there would be nothing to block their bullets.

"Do you know where they took it off?" I asked.

"When we got to the center of town, I think."

I glanced back, like I might actually be able to see it from here.

"You can't go back," he protested.

The alarm sounded, proving him right. The roaring of shuttles approaching filled the air and I shoved the gun in my pocket, and pressed myself against the side of the building with Callum.

"What should we do?" he asked, looking up at the sky.

"Shhh."

The shushing noise came from inside the building, followed by a sniffle, and Callum and I spun around. The wood was old, the white paint peeling everywhere, and I caught movement inside through the cracks. I leaned closer and someone gasped.

The door next to me swung open and I jumped away from the little girl who appeared. She blinked at me with tired eyes, squinting in the sunlight.

"Grace!" a terrified voice called, but the little girl just stood there, looking up at me.

A messy-haired teenager ran to the door and scooped Grace up in her arms. "We didn't do anything," she said, backing away as she hugged the girl to her chest.

"We're not here for you," Callum said, his voice edging on annoyed.

Her eyes lifted to the shuttles in the sky, then dropped back to us. "You can't stay here."

I looked out at the open space in front of us. The patchy grass led to a small clump of trees several yards away, but they were skinny and missing half their leaves. They wouldn't provide any cover, and we were sure to be spotted if we spent too much time out in the open.

"Did you escape?" she asked.

Neither of us responded and I felt a twinge of pride that Callum didn't trust this human.

"You can't stay here," she repeated. "I'm sorry. I know you . . . can't help it"—she gestured to us—"but you have to go." She pointed to the left. "There's a ditch over there. It's kind of covered by some trees. You could try hiding there."

I looked at her in surprise as Callum tugged on my arm. "Come on," he said, studying the sky. "We have an opening."

I let him pull me, glancing back at the teenager. "Thank you."

"Yeah. Good luck."

I took off in a slow run behind Callum, one eye on the shuttles. They were scattered in other areas, but one was facing partly in our direction.

I sprinted across the grass to the patch of trees, praying they hadn't spotted us. The small hole looked like someone had started digging a grave and changed their mind about halfway through. It wasn't very deep, but it might do.

Callum jumped in and I followed, sliding down the dirt. The ditch wasn't big enough to stretch out so I pulled my legs to my chest.

I pressed my face into my knees as a shuttle whirred closer, willing them to keep going. If they saw us we were dead. One helmet, wide-open space, and a gun with only a few bullets left.

The shuttle landed with a thunk and I tried to fight back the rising sense of dread.

"Did I say thank you?" Callum whispered. "For getting me out? If we die I just want to say thank you."

I pressed my lips together and stared at the ground. *You're welcome* seemed a stupid thing to say since we might be seconds from death. *I'm sorry* might be more appropriate.

Boots crunched on the grass, saving me from having to speak at all.

"That building's deserted," a HARC officer said. "Check it out in case they're hiding inside."

I let out a long sigh as I realized they hadn't seen us run to the ditch.

"There's just some kids in there," another voice answered. "They said they hadn't seen anything."

"What are they doing in there?"

"Living there, from the looks of it."

"All right, pack 'em up. We'll drop them at the orphanage on the way back."

I closed my eyes, a weight settling on my chest. There were few places worse in the slums than the orphanage. I had made elaborate plans as a kid to avoid it at all costs in the event of my parents' death.

"No!" I heard the shrill scream. "We're fine! You can't!"

I clenched my hand around a fistful of dirt, pushing back the odd urge to jump out of the hole and help them.

The yelling continued for a long time, while the officers combed the area. I wanted to press my hands against my ears like I did when I was little, but I was afraid it would look weird and pathetic to Callum.

When they piled into the shuttle and took off I breathed a sigh of relief more for the end of the screaming than for my own safety.

Callum leaned his head back against the dirt, giving me a tentative smile. "You all right? You looked really intense there for a while."

"I'm fine." I stood up and peeked out of the hole. It was quiet and deserted, the door to the medical building swinging open in the wind. Only one shuttle remained in the air, about half a mile away. The others must have landed around Rosa.

"I need to get you a helmet," I said.

"What? No. We should stay here. We're probably safe here until tonight."

"And then we have to get over the fence at the city line, where there will be armed guards. The chances of us making it across are pretty slim with helmets. Without . . ."

"What are you going to do? Go back into town and look for it?" he asked.

"I think I have a better shot at taking one of the officers'."

He moaned. "That plan sounds worse."

"You should stay here," I said. I didn't want to take the chance of losing him again, and he was right. We'd found a pretty safe spot.

"I don't think you're actually listening to me," he said with a hint of amusement.

"I'm listening; I'm just not responding."

He shook his head, a smile twitching at his lips. "Fine. I'll stay here. Try not to die."

"If you have to move for any reason, come back as soon as you can. I'll wait here for you."

"And if you don't come back?"

I paused, not sure. "I'll come back."

"Excellent Plan B." He laughed, running a shaky hand over his face. I frowned and he looked at me curiously. "What?"

"Why are you shaking?"

"Oh." He glanced down at himself. "I don't know. Maybe I'm hungry."

I dropped my eyes to his other hand, shaking in his lap. Panic swelled in my chest so suddenly I turned away so he couldn't see my face.

Shaking.

Like Ever.

I took a deep breath, determined not to freak him out. It could just be hunger. He'd been at HARC only a few weeks. They probably wouldn't have started him on the shots yet.

They couldn't have.

"I'll try to get some food," I said, digging my fingers into the dirt to hoist myself out of the hole.

"Don't worry about it; I'm fine."

I swung my legs over and got to my feet, turning to face him. He looked small, his bare chest dirty and bloodied, the skin of his long legs peeking through his torn pants in weird places.

"Maybe I can get you some clothes as well."

"Sure. Grab me a book, too, while you're out. Something funny."

I thought he was serious, until a grin spread across his face. "Just come back, okay? I don't need anything else."

I smiled and nodded, letting out a whoosh of air as I turned my gaze back the way we'd come.

All the humans would be on the lookout for Reboots now. I looked down at my clothes. Even the ones who hadn't seen me would immediately recognize the all-black clothing as Reboot attire.

I pulled my shirt over my head, turning away from Callum as I made sure my white undershirt covered my chest. It did. I passed the shirt down to him, took my helmet off, and removed my hair band, shaking my hair out in front of my eyes.

"Are you doing a striptease first? I'm on board with that." Callum smiled up at me.

"I'm trying to blend in. Do I look human at all?"

"Just keep your eyes covered. That's really the only difference between us and them."

It wasn't, but I nodded anyway and pulled my gun out of my pants, leaning down to hand it to him. "Only use that if you have to. There aren't many bullets left."

"Maybe you should keep it."

I shook my head, stepping back from him as he tried to hand it to me. "At least fire it if you're in trouble, okay?"

"Okay."

"And put my helmet on," I said, tossing it to him.

"No, you should take it. It's too small anyway."

"It's fine. I can't wear it without drawing attention." I nodded as he strapped it on. It sat too high on his head, but it would work well enough.

I took a few steps, making an effort to slow down and add a bounce to my step. Humans were more clumsy, disjointed, and haphazard, but I had to make an effort to conceal my stride. I glanced back at Callum and tried to return his smile. Sucking in a deep breath, I faced forward, head down.

I turned onto the paved street that separated the slums, ducking my head farther even though I didn't see any humans. The houses grew sturdier and bigger as I headed back to the center of town.

I'd grabbed assignments out of several houses on this street. It was slightly less depressing during the day. I'd always thought of all the houses in Rosa as ugly crap piles, but they looked almost cute in the sunlight. They were mostly identical, little two-bedrooms with a tiny window in front, but a few of them had flowers in the yard or a garden off to the side.

I'd never noticed the gardens before.

Footsteps sounded on the pavement behind me, and I took a swift look back. It was just an old guy, swinging a bag as he walked.

I quickened my pace, my feet barely skimming the sidewalk until I remembered that would attract more attention. I slowed and shoved my hands in my pockets, letting my shoulders rise up to my ears.

"You look like a monkey when you do that." My mother's laughing voice filled my head.

"Stand up straight, Wren. Lift that pretty face. I don't know where you got that face from, darlin', but you don't need to be hidin' it."

I closed my eyes as the old man passed me, my mother's face filling the darkness. She'd been right; she wasn't pretty. She was gaunt even before she slipped fully into her addiction, never possessing the full cheeks or round hips that earned other women appreciative looks.

I hit a cross street and glanced to my left. Humans scurried past, probably headed for their homes. Two officers appeared from behind a building, guns ready.

I darted to the other side of the brick building, peeking around to see the officers slowly surveying the street.

My hand instinctively went to my head to make sure my helmet was straight, but touched only my hair. *Right. I left it with Callum.*

One good shot from the officers and he'd be waiting forever.

I should have told him to go without me if I didn't come back. Maybe he would anyway.

An odd nervous flutter crept into my chest, and I tried to push it down with a deep breath. So I didn't have a helmet. I was still stronger and faster than these humans. I could take them down before they got a shot off.

I heard someone approaching and I took a deep breath before turning to look straight into the woman's eyes. Her mouth formed an *o* as she backed away, and for a moment I was worried she wouldn't scream.

But of course she did.

I raced to the other side of the building, pausing long enough to let the officers see where I was going. The woman took off as they pursued me.

I leaped out just as they rounded the corner, aiming my foot for the shorter officer's neck. The other one lifted his gun and I slammed two punches into his face before he could pull the trigger. He hit the ground next to the other human with a grunt.

I leaned down, my fingers poised to snap his neck, when he held his hands up in surrender and frantically shook his head.

I paused, glancing at the other officer wheezing on his knees. I should kill them anyway. Surrender shouldn't mean anything. I reached for his neck again, but stopped when he squeezed his eyes shut and looked away. It didn't feel right with him just lying there like that.

I grabbed his chinstrap instead and unsnapped his helmet, yanking it off his head. I tucked it under my arm and grabbed their guns off the ground.

"Please," he said quietly.

I frowned and straightened, shoving the guns into the back of my pants. "Give me your shirt."

He looked at me strangely but unbuttoned his black shirt and held it out to me. I backed away slowly, my eyes fixed on them, but neither made a move to follow me.

I regretted my decision as soon as I disappeared behind the building and broke into a run. I should have killed them. They were probably on their coms now, telling the other officers my exact location.

I ran another block and crouched down against the side of a house, listening for the sounds of officers coming.

Nothing. If anything, it was quieter, as if the humans had

all locked themselves away in their houses.

I straightened my legs and lifted my nose, searching for one more thing before I went back to Callum.

Food.

I didn't want to risk returning to the shops at the center of town. Stealing from one of the houses was probably the best bet.

I pressed my ear to the house right next to me, but I could hear voices inside. I scurried across the lawn to the next one, and the next one, listening for silence.

The fourth house was quiet. I walked around back and leaned in to listen again, but still nothing. I yanked on the back door until the lock broke and it swung open. The tiny kitchen was deserted, but a loaf of bread sat on the wooden counter. I snatched it and checked the refrigerator, but there was no meat. I should have expected that. Most people in Rosa considered it a frivolous expense.

"Looking for somethin'?"

I jumped, pushing the door closed and aiming my gun at the young woman in front of me. Her eyes met mine calmly as I backed toward the door.

"Don't scream," I said. "I'm just going to take this and go." I hugged the bread to my chest.

She held her hands up. "I'm not screamin'. But—"

I gestured for her to be quiet as the sounds of yelling and running drifted in from outside. Officers shouted orders at one another and I gripped the gun tighter, my eyes searching her face for a sign I should wrap my hands around her neck to stifle a scream.

She just stared at me.

The voices faded and I peeked out the door to see them scattering in all directions. I turned back to the woman.

"Will you keep quiet for a few minutes?" I asked.

"Will you leave me half that loaf? My kid will be hungry when he gets home from school. There's not much else. You may have noticed."

I lowered my gun, uncomfortable under her gaze. I wasn't used to humans looking into my eyes, and her light eyes were locked on mine.

The guilt that pressed down on my chest was the worst I had ever felt, and I let out a sigh and put the loaf on the counter. I would have been thrilled to come home from school to find a loaf of bread on the counter. Although I think I was thrilled by any food at all as a kid.

The woman took a knife out of the drawer and held it over the bread, until I shook my head.

"It's fine," I said, pushing the door open. "Get your lock fixed; I broke it."

She stared at me again, her face impossible to read. There wasn't a trace of fear, or hostility, or anything, really. She just stared.

I turned to leave, tucking the gun in my pants.

"Kid, wait," she said. She sliced off a generous piece of bread, wrapped it in a cloth, and handed it to me.

I slowly took it, holding it out for a moment to give her the opportunity to change her mind, but she didn't.

"Thank you," I said.

"You're welcome."

TWENTY-TWO

CALLUM LOOKED UP AT ME FROM THE HOLE, RELIEF AND JOY spreading across his face. He had one arm wrapped around his knees, my helmet sitting in the dirt beside him. I was so happy to see him I didn't even bother to point out he should have been wearing it.

"You got it," he said, looking at the helmet tucked under my arm with genuine surprise.

"Yes." I jumped into the hole and handed it to him. "I took his shirt, too. Hopefully it doesn't stink."

He brought it up to his nose. "Nah, it's fine."

I held the bread out to him. "This is for you, too."

He unwrapped it and looked at me in amazement.

"Seriously? You're scary good sometimes."

"You can have it all; I'm not hungry," I lied.

He frowned at me as he set it on the ground. "Don't be ridiculous. We haven't eaten since last night." He put his arms through the shirt, leaving it unbuttoned as he split the bread in half and offered part to me.

"You take it; I'm fine for now," I said as I slid down to the ground.

"Wren. Eat it. I am actually a little tough, you know. You don't have to take care of me."

The edge in his voice made me pause. "I didn't mean—"

He cut me off with a kiss, which I returned, relieved I didn't have to finish that sentence. He pressed the bread into my palm and I took it, smiling at him as he pulled away.

"Where'd you get it?" he asked as he took a bite.

"Just some house," I mumbled. "Do you want to sleep for a while? I'll keep watch."

"Nah, I'm not tired," he said, finishing his bread.

"But you didn't sleep at all last night."

"I don't sleep all the time. I just can't."

"Ever didn't sleep much," I said, running my fingers through the dirt. "Is that common with the Under-sixties?"

"Yeah, that's what I heard. I was sleeping more the last week or so, but I feel all awake again."

"Do you feel okay?" I asked.

"I feel fine. They gave Ever the shots, didn't they? The ones that make us crazy."

I nodded, keeping my gaze on the dirt.

"What if . . ."

I looked up to see his face worried, anxious. "What if they gave them to you?" I guessed.

"Yeah."

"They didn't, that you know of?"

"No. But my roommate and I didn't talk much. I don't think he would have told me."

"You feel all right, though?"

"Yes, except . . ." He looked down at his shaking hands.

"You're probably just hungry. You never ate enough. And tired. You should try to sleep."

"I guess. But if it's not just that? Then what?"

"You're out now," I said with a confidence I didn't feel. "They couldn't have even given you that many shots. They'll probably just wear off."

He nodded, leaning back against the dirt. "Yeah. I'm sure it's fine. I wasn't there that long."

He was trying to convince himself more than me, but I smiled and nodded. "Exactly."

"I'll try and sleep," he said, closing his eyes. He cracked one open and held his arm out to me. "Want to come closer?"

"I can't. One of us has to stay up and keep watch."

"One cuddle. Maybe two. Fifteen, max."

"Callum," I said with a laugh. "Go to sleep."

"All right," he said with an exaggerated sigh, a smile twitching his lips.

When I poked my head out of the hole hours later, the night looked deceptively calm. A soft breeze blew across the field, rustling the few leaves left on the trees. It felt so nice I had a brief, wild thought of just lying back down beneath the trees with Callum.

He popped up next to me, glancing around. He had tried to sleep, or pretended to try, for quite a while, until he finally gave up and stared at the side of the ditch. It reminded me of Ever so much it became difficult to breathe. It felt like someone was standing on my chest.

I held the map out in front of us, pointing to the area where Leb had indicated we should make our escape.

"We'll run through here," I said, tracing the route with my finger. "I'm hoping we can get pretty close to the fence before the guards spot us. From there we'll head into the trees and go north until we lose the humans. Then we'll turn and go south."

Callum nodded. "Got it."

I pulled myself out of the hole and Callum did the same. The lights of the slums were ablaze as HARC officers continued to scour for us, but it was dark in the field.

I started in the direction of the city line and Callum followed. He took my hand as we walked, lacing his fingers through mine. We were a little slower than usual. My feet felt heavy and my stomach was growling for food. I was almost tempted to stop and find something, but I didn't want to risk drawing HARC officers out this way again. We needed to get as close to the city line as possible without being noticed.

Callum seemed in better shape. He hadn't mentioned being hungry, and when he glanced down at me he looked steady and calm.

"Do you know who shot you and your parents?" he asked.

"No. It doesn't matter anyway."

He paused, glancing over at me. "Do you miss your mom and dad?"

"I don't know." It was the only way to truthfully answer the question.

"You don't know?"

"No. I don't. I don't remember much of them, and what I do isn't great. But sometimes I feel . . . weird."

"Weird like sad?"

"I guess."

"You wouldn't want to see them again if you could?"

"Callum, you'll never get me to say that's a good idea. And no. I wouldn't want to see them again."

He was quiet for a few minutes as we made our way through the neighborhood, staying close to the backs of houses as we got closer to the city line.

"What did you do?" he asked. "As a human?"

"I was twelve. I went to school and worked."

"Where did you work?"

"A pub. Washing dishes. A lot of kids wanted the job but they liked how small I was. I didn't take up much space."

"There weren't age rules for working in the slums?" he asked.

"No. If you could do the job you could apply. They have age rules in the *rico*?"

"Sixteen. After graduation. The wealthy ones go on to trade school; the rest of us start working."

I looked at him in surprise. "I thought you all went to trade school."

"Nope. Too expensive."

"What did you do, then?" I asked.

"I worked the fields." He laughed at the stunned expression on my face. "What? Someone has to do it."

"Well, yeah, but . . . I didn't think it was the *rico* folks."

"Who else?" he said with a shrug. "They won't bring in workers from the slums for the food crops because of the risk of disease. They don't want Reboots touching their food. HARC tried to bring them in a while back and people protested. They're terrified of us."

"They should be."

The lights at the edge of town appeared and I stopped and checked the map. The houses had thinned out and then disappeared completely. There wasn't much on the south side of Rosa. HARC was to the west, the worst part of the slums to the east.

The trees were scarcer as well, leaving nothing but flat dirt dotted with grass in front of us. HARC had no doubt cleared it out so there would be no way to sneak out of the city. The whole area was lit up brighter than daylight.

"Leb didn't give us an area with much cover," I said, ducking behind a tree and gesturing for Callum to follow.

"I doubt any section has cover," Callum said. He moved closer to me until both our bodies were hidden behind the tree trunk.

He was probably right, unfortunately. Leb had drawn the star directly in between two of the tall metal watchtowers, which he must have thought was the safest route. The watchtowers were spaced several hundred yards apart. I peeked out from behind our hiding spot to see an officer strolling up and down in front of the fence, a massive gun at his waist.

"Let's just run," he said. "What do we have to lose?" He took a step forward, like he was going to take off right away.

"Our heads," I said in annoyance, tugging him back to me by the arm. "They're going to have sharpshooters up there."

"What else are we going to do?" He knocked on his helmet. "Besides, we have these."

He was right, but I still felt a burst of irritation at his disregard for his own life. Again.

"Those helmets don't hold up forever," I said. "I didn't save you from getting shot on the inside so you could die one day later out here. At least pretend that you care about dying." I looked down at the map again. "This can't be the best place. It seems so stupid."

He looked at me in surprise. "I care if I die."

"You don't act like it."

"I already died once. Turned out all right." He smiled at me.

"That's not funny. You'll be dead for real this time. And then what? I'm supposed to go to this stupid Reboot reservation by myself? I never would have left if it weren't for you."

"I didn't ask you to do that," he said. "And what do you mean, you never would have left? You were fine with it? Being a prisoner?"

"Yes. It was better than my human life."

"But they made you kill people."

"I don't—" I wrapped my arms around my waist and stopped myself. I couldn't tell him that.

"You don't care?" he guessed. "You don't feel guilt? Sadness?"

"No," I said, looking at the ground. "I did at first. But now . . . no."

I stole a glance up at him to see a heartbreakingly crestfallen look on his face.

"I don't know why you keep saying that," he said.

"Because it's true."

"No, it's not. I saw your face when they took those kids away. You feel everything, just like the rest of us." He paused, considering me before a mischievous glint sparkled in his eyes.

"And you totally have the hots for me."

A surprised laugh escaped my mouth.

"What? You do."

I couldn't argue with that, so I just smiled. He grabbed my hand and tugged me to him, planting a soft kiss on my lips.

"Leb wanted us to get out," he said. "We can't rescue his daughter if we're dead. He must have thought this was the best way."

"Yeah," I admitted, tucking the map into my pocket. "I'd just prefer it if our heads didn't explode."

"Let's run fast, then." He lifted his eyebrows, looking at me for approval.

I nodded. "Start going in a zigzag pattern when they spot us. Should make it harder for them to hit us."

"Got it."

I took one more glance around before ducking out from behind the tree and heading for the open field.

We had taken only a few steps when the siren sounded. It was louder here, screeching from one of the towers. I felt the bullets before I heard them.

They pelted my shoulders and knocked against my helmet. My feet flew over the dirt, Callum at my side even as I picked up speed and began running in a crooked line.

The world was white suddenly, the ground rumbling as I fell against it. A second blast, closer, threw me across the dirt and sent a searing pain up my leg.

I couldn't hear. I couldn't see. I scrambled to my feet only to have the world shake again, the blast so intense I landed several feet away.

A bullet clipped my ear as I jumped up. They whizzed by, hitting the dirt like heavy drops.

Callum. I couldn't see him.

"Callum!" I ran into the smoke and directly into a hard chest.

I couldn't make out a face, but he lifted a gun to my head. I ducked, smashing my fist into his gut and knocking his knees out from under him. I snatched the gun from his hand and smashed the barrel against his head.

"Wren." I heard Callum's voice, quiet, but when I looked up he was right next to me, yelling. His helmet was half-gone, the left side of his head totally exposed. I took his hand and we sprinted for the fence.

His eyes were wide with fear as he turned to look behind us. I whipped my head around to see a massive group of HARC officers hot on our trail.

I lowered my chin into my chest as they fired, dropping Callum's hand so I could run faster.

The fence was so close I could see it clearly now. It wasn't terribly high—fifteen feet or so.

But it was electrified.

I could hear the buzz as we approached. We were going to have to hold on to it for several seconds to be able to get up and over it, but the force of the shock might knock us off right away.

Callum hit the fence a second before I did. I saw the jolt go through his body as his fingers wrapped around the wire, but he held on, his face determined.

I grabbed the wire and gasped as my insides lit on fire. The shock was so intense I almost screamed, almost broke my own rule.

I hauled ass up the fence as fast as I could, my hands black by the time I reached the top and hurled myself over.

The twitching was so intense it was hard to stand, let alone run. But I heard the buzz stop as they turned the fence off for the HARC officers. They'd catch us if we didn't move. Callum's body jerked as badly as mine so I grabbed him around the waist and turned him in the direction of the trees.

We needed to go north, and panic flashed through my brain as I struggled to remember which direction that was. Austin was south, but I didn't want HARC to see us headed there. If they knew where we were going, they'd be waiting for us.

A shuttle roared through the sky, bringing a fresh round of bullets with it. I heard the crack, then felt the blast against my head.

The remains of my helmet toppled to the ground.

Right. North was right.

My brain didn't want to run but my legs carried me anyway, floating over the dirt and grass faster than a human could keep up with.

We were in the trees, the beautiful trees, slapping against branches as our feet pounded the dirt. My insides jiggled around, unsettled, but I pressed on until the officers' voices grew distant.

I came to a sudden stop, looking up as the shuttle zoomed by. I gestured for Callum to follow me as I darted farther into the trees and hid behind a thick one. I couldn't see them anymore, but I could hear officers running and yelling from several directions.

I looked over at Callum to see the twitching gone, his fingers wrapped around the trunk of the tree as his eyes scanned the area. The rest of his helmet was gone, too, probably lost and shattered somewhere like mine.

"You all right?" I asked, breathing heavily.

"Yes. I can keep going."

I glanced up at the sky as another shuttle flew overhead, and hesitantly took a step out from behind the tree. Nearby, boots crunched against leaves and I squinted in the darkness. They weren't using flashlights, which was smart. Easier to sneak up on us that way.

I nodded at Callum, putting a finger to my lips as I took a careful step to the west. He followed my lead, and I wanted to hug him for his quiet footsteps. I eased past a fallen tree branch and glanced over my shoulder.

We crept through the trees until I couldn't hear our pursuers anymore. It was quiet, the only sounds the breeze rustling the leaves and the distant hum of a shuttle engine.

"Run?" I whispered to Callum, turning to face south.

He nodded in agreement, his eyes serious when they met mine, but a hint of a smile starting to form on his lips.

I let myself smile, too, just for a moment. And then we ran.

TWENTY-THREE

THE QUIET SWIRLED AROUND ME. I'D NEVER EXPERIENCED such quiet before. I knew the sounds of the city, or the sounds of the shuttles, or the sounds of Ever's breathing as she tried to sleep, but this type of quiet was entirely foreign. I felt like an intruder in this world. We were still just outside Rosa, but I was on a new planet, one where there was nothing but Callum and a breeze blowing softly against my skin.

The trees provided solid cover, but the ground was uneven, littered with leaves and holes and fallen branches. I hopped and dodged and stumbled but my breathing steadied as I healed, matching Callum's as our feet hit the ground.

The healing provided only momentary relief, and I slowed

as my stomach turned over in protest. We'd only run about four miles, but my face was hot and my legs were unsteady. Callum glanced in my direction, his eyebrows knitting together. He slowed, pulling on my hand to stop me.

"Are you all right?" he asked.

I nodded. "Yeah. I'm just hungry, I think." I hadn't eaten a real meal in more than twenty-four hours, and my body did not appreciate the long run on so little fuel. My body didn't appreciate so little fuel at all, actually. It was used to being fed well, and regularly, for the past five years.

I felt worse standing still, and I winced as I reached for my left shoulder. I could feel the hard lump just behind my shoulder, from a bullet lodged there. My skin had closed up over it.

I tried to push the pain away, but it was harder when I was weak. It throbbed, refusing to be ignored, and I frowned. How annoying.

"What?" Callum asked, reaching for my shoulder.

I shrugged him off, turning my face away. It was embarrassing for someone to be able to read the emotions on my face. I didn't think anyone had ever been able to do that, even when I was a human.

"It's nothing," I mumbled. "There's a bullet in there."

He reached for me again, and I let him press his hand to my jacket, his fingers finding the spot. "Want me to get it out for you?"

I hesitated, glancing around. It was dark, deserted. We

were still quite a ways from Austin and far enough outside of Rosa to have lost any shuttles or officers. A breeze tugged a few escaped strands of hair from my ponytail into my face, and I batted them away. "Maybe we should just keep going."

Callum smirked as he held his hand out. "Just give me the knife."

I pulled it from my pants and handed it over. I felt a little burst of relief that he hadn't agreed to keep running. It was the last thing I wanted to do.

"Probably easiest if you sit," he said as I shrugged off my jacket.

I glanced around one last time before slowly sliding down onto the dirt and crossing my legs. I closed my eyes briefly as everything in me collapsed in a heap of exhaustion. Callum's fingers brushed my arms as he sat down behind me and I shivered at his touch. His fingers found the hole the bullet had made in my shirt and when he spoke I could feel his breath on my neck.

"You need to take this one off," he said.

I pulled my arms through the shirtsleeves and let it hang around my neck over my undershirt.

"Um, do I just dig in there with the knife?" he asked, holding my shoulder steady with one hand.

"Yes. You don't have to be careful. Quick would be best."

"Okay." He exhaled slowly and I felt the tip of the knife poke my skin. I shut my eyes as he pressed harder. It was easier to block out the pain with his breath on my neck and the warmth of him behind me.

The bullet hit the ground with a thud, and Callum set the knife to the side, his hands sliding down my arms. He leaned forward until his cheek brushed my face, the slight stubble tickling my skin. He laced his fingers through mine, turning his head so his lips brushed against my temple.

"That's the grossest thing I've ever done," he whispered, a trace of amusement in his voice.

I laughed and he squeezed my hand, his lips forming into a smile against my skin. I turned and our eyes met, then our lips for the briefest moment. He was the one who pulled away, the concerned look back on his face.

"Do you want to try to find food?" he asked. "You look exhausted."

I scooted away from him, sticking my arms back into my shirt. "I'm fine. Let's just keep going."

He looked like he might argue, but when I pulled my jacket on and started walking he followed without a word. I briefly considered trying to catch an animal, but I saw none, and we couldn't build a fire to cook it anyway. HARC might see the smoke.

It was different going without food as a Reboot. As a human, it had been uncomfortable, painful, consuming. The hunger took over until I could think of nothing else.

My mind was clearer as a Reboot. I could focus on other

things, but the gnawing in my stomach was worse. It felt like a monster was eating me from the inside.

Food hadn't occurred to me when I was planning our escape. I hadn't considered so many things, like where we would sleep or find water and fresh clothes. In my panic to get Callum out I hadn't stopped to think that maybe we would be worse off outside. Maybe HARC had been right, and they were doing us a kindness by sheltering us and feeding us. Yes, we were technically their slaves, but maybe that was better than what we would face out here.

I'm sorry. Ever's voice rang through my ears, as clear as the day she'd died. She wouldn't have been worse off on the outside. In fact, if I'd paid closer attention, if I'd worked harder to escape when I first discovered it was possible, she might still be alive.

I closed my eyes against the guilt pushing at my chest. She would have liked it out here, hungry or not.

"The reservation is that way, right?" Callum asked, pulling me from my thoughts. He was looking up at the black sky and pointing north.

"Yes."

"So all the HARC shuttles went in that direction. Do you think they know where it is?"

"Yes. That seems logical."

"You really don't think it's there, do you?" he asked.

"No, I never did. If anything it's probably just some Reboots running from place to place, hiding from HARC." I sighed as his face dropped in disappointment. "I'm sorry. Is that the sort of thing I should lie about to make you feel better?"

He laughed. "No. I like that you always tell the truth."

"I don't really see the point in lying."

"That's very cool."

"Thank you," I said, a warmth spreading through my chest and all the way up to my cheeks. At least he didn't seem alarmed by the fact that we had no idea what we were doing. His optimism was comforting, and I reached for his hand as we walked.

As the sun began to rise the thick trees gave way to open land, the green and brown grass spreading out in front of us. We were still a good ten miles or so from Austin, and we'd be easily visible to any passing HARC shuttle.

I ran a hand over my face as I stopped. We should have run. If we'd run we'd already be there, and we could have found food more easily in Austin.

"Should we rest for a while?" Callum asked.

"I think we have to until the sun sets," I said, turning to trudge back to a thicker area of the trees. I plopped down against one, stretching my legs out in front of me. Callum stayed where he was, turning his head as he surveyed the area.

"How far from Austin are we?" he asked.

"We're about halfway. Ten miles or so."

"I'm going to go look for food," he said, facing me. "You want to wait here? I won't go too far."

"Look for food where?" I asked, casting a baffled glance at the trees around us.

"I'm going to go that way," he said, pointing. "Uh . . ." He turned around a few times. "East. Right? That way is east?"

I nodded. "What do you expect to find out there?"

He quirked an eyebrow at me. "They do have food outside a cafeteria, Wren."

I tried to hold back a smile, but it tugged at the corners of my mouth anyway. "I have heard that. You really think you're just going to find food?"

"I worked the fields. I know what to look for. And me and some of the others used to scrounge on the walk back to the city when the HARC farmers weren't looking."

I started to get to my feet, but he shook his head.

"You can rest," he said. "I won't go far. There's no one around here anyway."

I looked up at the sky. He was right: It was blue and clear and there wasn't a shuttle in sight. If I was being honest, my body had no interest in walking anyway.

"Just don't get lost," I said, leaning my head back against the tree. "Yell if you run into trouble."

He nodded and turned to walk away, tossing a smile in my direction even though his pace was slow and heavy. He must have been tired as well, and just as hungry, but he was hiding it better. I had to admire his ability to keep that smile on his face, even when things sucked.

I squinted my eyes as the sun peeked out from behind the leaves, my head beginning to droop to one side. I wanted to keep my eyes open, but they kept falling shut, and eventually I let them stay that way.

I woke with a start, my legs jerking against the dirt as my eyes flew open. A leaf was tickling my arm, and I pushed it away, quickly turning to look at the sun. It was higher, up above the trees now.

"Callum?" I called softly, getting to my feet. I turned in a circle, but I was alone, the only sound the flapping of wings as a bird took off from somewhere nearby.

I pulled my jacket tighter around me, glancing at the sun again. Where had it been before? I couldn't have slept that long. Maybe an hour. Less, probably. It had been dumb to let him go by himself. Getting separated was the worst thing that could happen to us right now, and I had let him wander off in the middle of the wilderness by himself.

The bird overheard screeched and I jumped, stuffing my cold hands into my pockets. Escaping from HARC in the summer would have been a much smarter plan. Actually, any plan except for this one would have been a much smarter plan.

I swallowed, trying not to panic as the minutes stretched out with no sign of Callum. I shifted from foot to foot as I pushed back the urge to run into the trees and find him. He was fine. If I kept repeating it to myself it had to be true.

A rustling noise made me turn, and I tensed, my hand flying to my gun. Callum's triumphant face appeared a moment later and I exhaled, returning his grin.

"Sorry it took so long," he said. "I went a little farther than I thought I would."

He was holding his shirt out in front of him, and I frowned as he dropped to his knees and emptied the contents before me. I knelt down and picked up a small, black, round object.

"A squishy black thing?" I asked, eyebrows raised. I looked down at the hard brown balls mixed in with them. "Are those ones nuts?"

"Wren," he said with a laugh, scooting over and taking the nut. "It's a pecan. You've never seen a pecan?"

"Oh. Never in the shell, I guess."

He glanced around and selected a rock, placing the pecan on the ground. "We're going to have to get a little creative, since we don't have a nutcracker." He smashed the rock down and the shell shattered. He picked out the pieces of the nut and plunked them into my free hand.

"Thank you," I said, blinking at them in surprise.

"And that's a persimmon," he said, pointing to the black fruit. "You just kind of squeeze it into your mouth. Not my favorite, but it'll do."

I ate a couple pieces of pecan as Callum continued cracking them on the ground, then I squished the persimmon with my fingers and held it over my mouth. It was sweet and messy, and my hands were black with juices as I tossed the skin aside.

We ate in silence and I wiped my hands on my pants when we'd polished everything off. Callum scooted back against a tree, opened his arm up, and I gladly crawled over next to him.

"Thank you," I said, resting my head on his chest.

"You're welcome." He rested his chin on top of my head as he trailed his fingers down my arm. He was quiet for a long time, and I closed my eyes as my head moved up and down with his breath.

"Did you always intend to go to Austin?"

"What do you mean?" I blinked my eyes open, startled at the sound of his voice.

"When you promised Leb you would go get his daughter. Did you really mean it? Or were you thinking about just running away?"

"I didn't know where I'd go," I said. "If the reservation is real I'd like to know where it is. Clearly I'm not exactly equipped to survive in the wild."

He chuckled. "I think you'd do fine."

"And I don't want to prove him right," I said softly. "I know Leb is expecting us to run off. They don't trust us, and I don't want to prove them right."

He reached up and pressed his hand to my cheek, and I felt him plant a soft kiss on top of my head. "Good point," he whispered.

TWENTY-FOUR

WE LEFT OUR HIDING SPOT AFTER THE SUN SET. TWO HARC shuttles had passed during the day, but I hadn't seen any in hours.

I'd fallen asleep again for a little while but Callum was awake and alert. He still hadn't slept at all since we left the facility and I could see his hands shaking again. Although he saw me notice, we both said nothing. He hadn't displayed any of the other signs of insanity and I refused to talk about something that very likely wouldn't happen.

That *couldn't* happen.

We headed to the edge of the trees and I took in a deep breath as I glanced at the sky. All clear.

We took off, boots pounding the ground as we sprinted across the grass. The wind whipped through the bullet holes in my jacket and I scrunched up my face against the cold. My chest was tight and my throat burned as we sprinted, but we kept up a quick pace, casting nervous glances into the sky.

It was about five miles before a patch of trees appeared again, and we slowed to a walk as we disappeared into them. I took in a deep breath, crossing my arms over my chest to trap some of the warmth.

"How long is it going to take us to get through this tunnel thing?" Callum asked after we'd caught our breath.

"No idea. It just says *tunnel* on the map. We can always hop the fence again if it's not there."

"Awesome. That wasn't at all hard last time." He swung an arm around my shoulder and pulled me close.

The trees were thinner here, scattered and providing less cover than the ones closer to Rosa, but we walked anyway, both too tired to run anymore.

The skyline of Austin came into view as we got closer, and a trace of a smile crossed Callum's lips. "It's nicer than Rosa."

"We're coming in from the *rico* side." The tops of the buildings looked vaguely familiar. There were three tall glass structures, surrounded by a few shorter ones I could barely see over the trees. The tallest building was on the west side of town, and the very top was bright white, like it was guiding people home. It was amusing, considering the rico side of Austin had no interest in letting anyone in.

"Have you seen this side of the city before?" Callum asked.

"No. We passed through on the way to the holding facility after I died, but I think I was still in shock. I don't really remember it."

"Do you remember dying?" he asked. "Or waking up?"

"I remember waking up."

"Did you know you were dead? I didn't know."

"Sort of," I replied. "I was hysterical, so everything is jumbled. I only remember waking up in the Dead Room and screaming."

"They took you out of the Rising Room? That's terrible."

"Yes. They thought I was permanently dead." The hospital moved all young people who might Reboot to the Rising Room, where they were strapped down to beds. If they Rebooted they moved on to the holding facility; if they didn't, they went to the Dead Room.

No one should have to wake up in the Dead Room, surrounded by the day's deceased humans, waiting for cremation. It had been a full room the day I was there.

I glanced at Callum, pushing the memory away. "You didn't realize you were dead?"

"No. I thought I'd gone to sleep. I kept asking for my parents. I thought I'd feel different as a Reboot. But I feel the same. It never felt real until I got to Rosa."

"Yeah," I agreed.

The trees grew thicker as we neared the city, and as I pushed a low branch away from my face, the gray wire fence and flashing red lights came into view. I stopped and pulled out the map. The fence was making a soft buzzing sound, indicating that this one was electrified, too.

We retreated back farther into the trees, until the fence was no longer visible. If Leb's map was correct, the tunnel should be right in this area.

"It's here?" Callum asked, peering over my shoulder at the map.

"Supposedly," I said, squinting at the ground. It was too dark to see much at all. I tilted the map in his direction. "Are we in the right area? It looks like the tunnel should come out not far from downtown."

Callum glanced at the map, then at darkness around us. "Let's try a little farther west," he said, pointing. "I don't think we're close enough to downtown."

I nodded and followed him, kicking at the dirt and every suspicious rock. I wasn't sure what I was looking for. I probably should have asked Leb what the tunnel looked like. Or what they used it for. Or if Leb was sure it was still there.

I stuffed the map in my pocket and let out a sigh. Callum and I walked west, then back east, then west again, combing the area and searching through fallen leaves and branches.

"We're going to have to get electrocuted again, aren't we?" Callum asked, squinting up at the sky. The first hints of morning light were creeping through.

"Maybe."

"Wonderful. I think my insides liquefied last time. It was all jiggly in there."

I shot an amused smile his way. "Let's try a little closer to the fence."

He followed me as I headed toward it, stopping when I could hear the hum of electricity. I turned when Callum dropped to his knees and pushed aside a pile of branches. He pointed at a small hole and grinned, bracing his hands against the sides as he peered inside.

"It looks tiny."

"I'll go first," I said.

I knelt down next to him and looked into what seemed like nothing more than a poorly constructed hole in the ground. I paused, glancing back at Callum. Crawling through a tiny, dark hole in the ground actually made me a little nervous. I had no idea what was in there, but I had to believe that Leb wouldn't lead us into danger with his daughter at stake.

"We can still get electrocuted if you want," Callum said, pointing back at the fence.

"I think we should go with the quieter approach." I ignored my nerves and crawled into the hole. I heard Callum follow a moment later.

The tunnel was barely big enough for us to fit through on our hands and knees. I had a bit of breathing room, but when I twisted around to look at Callum, I could just make out the outline of his back brushing up against the top of the tunnel.

The ceiling was supported by some sort of white wooden beams that looked less than sturdy. Other than that it was nothing but dirt underneath my fingers.

"What happens if this caves in?" Callum asked. "Are we just stuck in here buried alive forever?"

"Yes, probably."

"Oh, good. Thanks for making me feel better about that."

I wanted to turn around and smile at him, but the idea of the tunnel caving in and trapping us wasn't that far-fetched. Perhaps as little movement as possible was the way to go. Besides, it was too dark for him to see it anyway.

I shuffled forward on my hands and knees, taking a deep breath in an effort to slow the rapid bursts of air coming from my lungs. Despite his words, Callum's breathing was slow and steady, and when I closed my eyes and listened, it calmed me as well.

I crawled until my head bumped against something solid. I stopped, reaching out to touch it.

Was the tunnel sealed?

Callum ran into my feet and I felt him come to a stop as well. "What?"

"It's blocked," I said, pushing against the solid object. It was rough against my skin. "Maybe we should—"

The blockage moved before I could get out my cowardly

words that we should forget this plan and Leb and Adina. I shoved it again and a streak of light appeared. It was two logs, most likely put there to hide the entrance.

I threw my shoulder against them until the top one fell to the ground with a thunk, and I was able to push the other one away. I squeezed out of the tunnel and sank onto the grass with a sigh. The air was chilly, the grass damp with dew beneath my fingers, but for once I didn't mind the cold. I sucked a generous amount of the fresh air into my lungs.

There were no gunshots, no bombs, no yelling, just the cool morning air and the sounds of leaves rustling and crickets chirping. Escaping from Rosa was a faraway nightmare compared to the ease of our break-in to Austin.

Callum brushed off his clothes, then reached over and playfully mussed my hair, sending dirt flying. He smiled briefly at me, but his eyes were focused on something in the distance.

I turned. The tunnel had let us out on a hill, and it gave me a clear view of the *rico* part of Austin. I didn't remember ever seeing it so clearly during my time in the slums.

It was small, probably somewhere between ten and fifteen square miles. It was the second Austin. The original was several miles south and, from what I'd been told, nothing but a pile of rubble. The Reboots had destroyed most human cities in the war.

I'd heard Austin called the best city in Texas. Judging by the other cities I'd seen, it seemed an accurate statement. It was nestled next to a lake, sparkling in the morning light. The buildings in the center of town were taller than those in Rosa, some ten or fifteen stories high.

A wide street ran up the center of town, beginning not far from the trees surrounding the lake and ending at a cute little round building. It was designed to replicate the original Austin's capitol. Texas had no capitol, so I didn't know what they did in the building now. Perhaps it was empty.

"Which way is your parents' house?" I asked as I piled the logs back up in front of the hole.

"Past the capitol, down Lake Travis Boulevard," he said, pointing to the wide street. His eyebrows lowered as he crossed his arms over his stomach.

"What?" I asked, getting to my feet and wiping my hands on my pants.

"I'm really . . ." He took in a deep breath as he pressed his hand into his stomach. "I'm really hungry, I think."

He'd gone pale, and his hands were shaking worse than before. I swallowed, reaching for his hand.

"Your parents will have food, right?" My voice was steady, even though I was beginning to tremble myself. Ever had been famished in the cafeteria, shoving meat in her mouth as fast as possible.

Callum nodded. "They'll have a little, probably."

"Come on, maybe we can find something else on the way, too," I said. The sun was getting higher in the sky, and we didn't have long until the humans were everywhere.

He let me pull him down the hill and across the grass, the buzz of crickets fading as we neared the buildings. The only way to get to the other side of the capitol was through the city, since the HARC fence wasn't far from the edge of town and I didn't want to risk getting too close to it.

We crept along an alleyway behind the brick and wooden buildings. I glimpsed a few humans walking on the next street over and I quickened my pace, tugging on Callum's hand. His eyes were downcast, his other fist pressed against his mouth.

"What is that?" His voice was muffled behind his fingers.

"What?"

"That smell." He stopped, leaning forward and pressing his hands into his thighs. He took in a deep breath and I stepped closer to him, placing a hand on his shoulder. "It smells like meat or something?"

I lifted my nose but all I could smell was fresh morning air and maybe a hint of grass or weeds.

He smells so good. Like . . . meat.

Ever's words raced through my brain and I turned to the humans, dread trickling down my stomach.

He smelled the humans.

I grabbed his arm and he stood with a start, blinking at me.

"Let's get you meat, then," I said. "Where's the nearest restaurant?"

He didn't answer. Instead, he turned to stare at the humans, his expression unreadable. "Remember when that kid tried to eat me?" he said softly.

"Or a butcher," I said, ignoring him. "Or a grocery store. Are there any around here?"

"And then Ever acted like she was going to eat me, too. Remember? She was all weird and crazy." He looked down at his hands.

My heart was beating too fast. I refused to answer these questions because then I'd have to admit that we should be scared of what HARC had done to him, and he already looked terrified.

"You won't let me, right?" His words were quiet, his eyes bouncing between me and the humans.

I shook my head, too vigorously. "No. I won't let you."

He nodded, shoving his hands in his pockets. "There's a restaurant up about a block. They have meat, I think."

I looped my arm through his and we rushed along the block. Callum tucked his chin down, and he kept taking in deep gulps of air, trying to hold his breath as much as possible.

"That one," he said, pointing to a slightly cracked wooden door behind a smelly Dumpster. The sound of dishes clanging and food sizzling drifted out through the opening, and I slipped the gun from my pants and flung the door open.

Two humans were working in the kitchen. A man and a woman, probably in their thirties, and pleasantly plump in that well-fed, *rico* way. The man saw us first, and he let out a yell and clutched the woman.

Perhaps we looked worse than usual, or maybe *rico* folks weren't used to seeing Reboots, but their terror was the sharpest I had ever encountered. The woman immediately began crying as she tried to drag the man toward the other door.

"Stop," I said, pointing the gun directly at the man. "We won't hurt you; we just want food."

They both froze, clutching each other and sobbing.

"Would you stop with the crying and just get us food?" I snapped in annoyance. *Why must people cry?*

The woman let out a gasp and untangled herself from the man, rushing to the refrigerator. Callum pressed his face into the top of my head, a whimper escaping his mouth.

"Meat," I clarified.

She turned around with two large packages of raw meat in her hands, holding them out to us with shaky terror.

"Cooked meat, you . . ." I took a deep breath. "We're not animals." I gestured to the steak on the grill and the man started piling it into a container. "The bread, too."

He put the whole loaf into a bag, placing the container of meat in with it. He moved to hand it to me and the woman snatched it away, pushing him behind her. She let the bag hang from one finger as she took a cautious step in our direction.

I didn't realize the flash at the corner of my eye was Callum until he was on top of her.

Teeth bared.

Growling.

The humans screamed.

I wasn't annoyed by it this time. My eyes flew to Callum's. Glazed eyes.

My feet refused to budge as he shoved away her frantic hands and tried to get his face to her neck.

You won't let me, right?

His words jolted me out of my frozen state. I launched myself at him, pushing the man out of the way. I grasped Callum's collar and hauled him off the sobbing human so hard he hit the wall. He blinked and shook his head, but he still wasn't Callum.

He wasn't Callum.

The humans huddled on the ground as I snatched up the bag and ran to him.

"Callum," I said, my voice shaking slightly.

He blinked once more and confusion colored his face as he looked down at me. I quickly shoved him to the door before he noticed the state of the humans.

"What—"

"Go," I interrupted, taking his hand and breaking into a run.

I pulled hard when he slowed, yanking him down the alleyway. We sprinted through the city and onto a wide paved road leading to houses in the distance. It split off in two directions and I whipped my head around to look at Callum.

"Which way?" I glanced behind me for a sign of HARC, but

there was nothing yet. The sky was clear, the morning air quiet.

He pointed right and we took off. Callum pulled me to a stop as we neared the houses, gesturing to a row of bushes.

"I have to eat something before we get near them again," he said, nodding at the meat. "I can't see my family like this."

I looked behind us again. Still nothing. "Maybe we should keep going. Those humans will alert HARC any minute and—"

Callum snorted. "No, they won't. You think they want everyone knowing there were two Reboots in that restaurant? No one would ever go in again." He pointed up to the empty sky. "They didn't tell anyone."

I scanned the area. He was right. There wasn't a shuttle or a guard to be seen.

I followed Callum over and plopped down beside him in the grass behind the bushes. I opened the container of meat and offered it to him. He took a piece and immediately bit into it, eating with fervor I'd never seen from him. I took a small piece for myself and pushed the rest to him, which he ate without protest. I nibbled at the bread as I watched him.

When he finished he ran a hand over his mouth, turning his gaze to the grass. He picked at it, his fingers almost steady again. "I just attacked that woman, didn't I? I sort of blacked out, but I remember. . . ." His voice was strained, quiet.

I didn't answer, but he didn't need me to. He knew what happened. We sat there in silence for long seconds before it occurred to me that maybe this was a moment when I should say something comforting.

"Maybe it will wear off," I said. "Or we can ask for help when we get to the reservation. They must have seen this before."

He nodded. "That's true."

I hopped to my feet, holding out my hand to him. The sun was rising higher in the sky, and we didn't have time to waste. There was a chance the couple would change their minds. "Until then, we'll just keep you well fed. I'm sure it will be fine."

He took my hand as he stood up, a hint of relief on his face. He believed me.

I tried to smile like I believed it, too.

TWENTY-FIVE

WE HEADED DOWN THE PAVED ROAD AND TURNED ONTO A narrower street. The houses were smaller than I would have thought, but clean and well kept, without any of the trash that littered the lawns in Rosa's slums.

"Are we close?" I asked. I pointed to the thick trees near the edge of the city line. "I could go wait there. Maybe I'll go check the security around the slum wall."

"No, you have to come with me," Callum said, looking at me in surprise.

"I don't think that's a good idea," I said. "But I'll stay close by."

"No, you have to come. They'll want to meet you."

"They will absolutely not want to meet me."

"Yes, they will. You saved me."

I sighed. "I'll go but I'll stay back. I'll terrify them."

"You will not. You're not scary until you start attacking people."

"I will. And so will you."

"I am certainly not terrifying. I'm not even close."

I let out a sigh of defeat and he smiled.

I really hoped he was right.

I glanced behind us, where I could see the tops of bigger houses peeking out from the trees. I couldn't see much beyond the roofs, but the size alone suggested wealth.

"What's over there?" I asked.

"The rich people," he said.

"I thought you were all rich people here."

He gave me an amused look. His color had returned after eating the meat and he almost looked like his old self again. "Mostly we're just here because property is passed down through families. My parents never had any money. Neither did my grandparents."

"What do they do?" I asked. I hadn't thought rich people did anything, but if Callum worked the fields, his parents must have had jobs.

"My mom's a teacher and my dad works in the food-processing plant. But they fired my mom when I got sick, so I don't know if she still teaches."

"Why?" I asked.

"Risk of infection," Callum said. "She got one of the lighter strains of KDH when I got sick. They don't risk infecting children with anything here."

"Maybe they gave her the job back after she got well." The little homes had backyards with wooden fences, and I caught glimpses of gardens and flowers. Everything seemed cheerier here.

We rounded the corner and Callum came to a sudden stop, his face scrunching up with unhappiness.

I followed his gaze to a small white house with blue shutters. A stone path led up to the front door and the little windows facing the street gave it a cute, quaint look.

But in front, on a wooden sign in big, black letters, were the words: *Quarantined until November 24. Auction on December 1.*

I looked at him quickly. "Auction? Does that mean . . ."

"They lost it," he said, his voice catching.

"Lost it? How?"

"They had a lot of debts. They spent everything they had trying to save me and they must . . ." He swallowed and I took his hand.

"Did they have friends?"

"Yes, but no one would have room. And they wouldn't be willing to take on three extra mouths when everyone is already in bad shape."

"So where would they go?" I asked.

"I don't know. Over there, I guess." His gaze went east, to the slums. "HARC shuttles the homeless over there. They don't want that sort of thing here."

A man a few doors down wandered out of his house, banging the screen door behind him as he headed for his flowers.

"We shouldn't stay in the open like this," I said. Callum still stared in the direction of the slums, and panic rose up in my chest at the prospect of going there now. I thought I had more time.

"Let's go in," I said, tugging on his hand. "At least until the sun sets. No one's going to set foot in a quarantined house."

"We could just go to the slums now."

"It'll be safer at night." I tugged on his hand again, and he finally looked down at me. His expression softened. Perhaps the panic I felt was splashed across my face.

"Yeah, okay."

We walked up the stone steps to the little white front door. It was locked, but a hard kick from Callum knocked it open.

At first glance, the house looked bigger than it was. The rooms were sparsely furnished and open, the floors a shiny wood I had never seen before. There was no table in the kitchen, nothing but a dingy couch and a television in the living room. It was as if the place had been cleared out by thieves.

Sunlight poured in from a side window, bouncing off the floor and dancing across the bare cream walls. Whatever had been there before was gone, the small nail holes all that remained.

"I guess they let them take the pictures," Callum said, walking toward the back hallway.

"And some of the furniture?"

"No, this is all we had."

I dropped my eyes from his, embarrassed, even though his parents had far more than mine ever did.

"Come on," he said.

I followed him down the dim hallway, the gray carpeting plushy under my feet. He took a quick glance into the first door on our left, which was a small room, empty except for a few posters of comic-book characters on the wall. He walked through the second door on the left.

It was his room. It looked like it hadn't been touched since the day he died: the bed unmade, papers and books scattered across his desk, pictures and electronic equipment I couldn't identify littering his bookshelf.

The wooden furniture was old and chipped but the room was fairly neat. Cozy, even. The thick blue comforter at the end of the bed looked nicer than the thin blanket I'd had at HARC, and the sun streaming in through the sheer white curtains made the room warm and open.

"They should have sold this or given it to David," he said, running his fingers over what I thought was his school reader. We often used old paper books at the slum school, but I'd seen a few readers.

"They couldn't. When you die and Reboot all your previous possessions become property of HARC." The cost of safety, they said.

"Oh."

He sat down on his bed, flipping on the radio on his nightstand. The sounds of a fiddle and a man's voice filled the room.

"I miss music," he said, his eyes on his lap.

"I did, too, at first."

"I shouldn't have let them pay for treatments," he said, rubbing his hands over his face. "I knew the survival rate. I knew deep down it was pointless. I was just so scared I would Reboot. I was so terrified I made myself sick at the holding facility." He looked up and smiled at me. "Until I saw you. I remember lying on the ground staring up at you thinking, *If girls that cute are here, it can't be all bad*."

I turned away, trying to hide my smile as heat spread across my face. The bed creaked as he rose and planted a light kiss on top of my head.

"I'm going to check and see if the water still works. Maybe we can shower." He turned to grin at me as he left the room. "Separately, of course."

My full-body blush hadn't faded in the least by the time he returned. He went to his closet and pulled down a towel, black cotton pants, and a green T-shirt.

"It works," he said, holding the clothes out to me. "These

are going to be way too big, but I figure you'll want to change."

"Thanks."

"It's the next door over."

The white-tiled bathroom was clean and private. I'd forgotten what a private bathroom felt like. I stripped off my clothes and carefully stepped underneath the stream of water. The shower was warm and glorious, the water red as it circled the drain. I was covered in blood, evidence of the numerous gunshot wounds I had suffered.

I emerged from the shower clean and smooth, my mangled chest the only blemish on my skin. I pulled on Callum's clothes and eased a comb through my hair. I gathered up my own clothes in my arms and dropped them in the corner of Callum's room.

He was putting new sheets on the bed, gray and so soft looking that I immediately wanted to crawl in.

"I thought you might want to sleep," he said, putting on the last pillowcase. "Feel free to get in; I'm going to take a shower."

I nodded, but I sat down at his desk as he left the room. I reached for a photo screen, pressing the button on the edge to bring up the first image.

It was Callum.

Sort of.

Human Callum had shaggy hair and light brown eyes, an easy smile on his face. His arm was around another human boy, but I could only look at him. At his imperfect skin, at the goofy grin on his face, at the innocence that radiated from him.

His skin had been darker as a human. Reboots were paler, evidence that death had touched them, but I rarely noticed anymore. Humans had a brightness to them, a glow that only death extinguished.

I pushed the button and flipped through dozens of photos of Callum with his friends. I barely recognized him.

I raised my head as Callum came up behind me and was almost relieved to see he was how I remembered. His face was hard and strong, nothing like the boy's in the picture. His dark eyes circled the room in a way that was probably instinctual now—he was looking for threats. He gazed over my shoulder at the picture, reaching down to take it out of my hands. A frown crossed his face.

"I don't look like this anymore," he said.

"No."

"I didn't think I had changed. It's only been a few weeks."

"You have," I said, touching his fingers. "I like you better this way."

He raised his eyes from the picture to me, then to the wall just behind me. I turned to see what he was looking at and saw our reflections in a mirror.

"I don't look human anymore," he said.

"No. You're not."

He looked down at the picture sadly. "When I woke up, after I died, I thought I looked mostly the same."

"Well, you do, in a way," I admitted, nodding at the picture in his hand. "Your human memories start to get blurry right away. Especially the things you don't want to remember."

He lifted an eyebrow at me. "You know a little bit about that."

I shrugged and he put the photo screen on the desk, taking my hand and tugging me out of the chair.

"Want to dance?" He scooped me into his arms before I could reply. "We have music this time. And I don't have to punch you when we finish."

"You don't have to. But if I step on your feet too many times you can feel free."

"I will pass on that offer, but thank you."

He twirled me once, twice, three times, until I collapsed against his chest in laughter. I rose up on my toes for a kiss and he grabbed me under the arms and lifted me up in the air until I wrapped my legs around his waist.

"That's better," he said, brushing his lips against mine.

I closed my eyes and let myself fade away inside the kiss. I liked that I didn't have to worry about sneak attacks or humans walking past. I liked yielding completely to the kiss, to his arms and the warmth of his body.

"There's no dancing going on here," I finally said with a smile.

"Sure there is," he said, moving in a slow circle. "And this is my favorite dance, by the way."

"Mine, too." I leaned my forehead against his, letting the tickling happiness creep up my body.

When the song ended he sat down on the bed with me in his lap, running his hands into my damp hair and kissing from my jawline to my neck.

I wanted to reach under his shirt and touch the warm skin of his back with my fingertips, but I hesitated, my mind immediately trying to sort out how many people or cameras might be watching us.

But there was no one. It was just us.

So I trailed my fingers down his back and closed my eyes and focused on only him.

His breath against my mouth.

His arms as they circled tightly around my waist.

My lips against his cheek.

My eyes finding his, my smile at the desire in his gaze.

His fingers against my back, the cool air tickling my skin as he pushed my shirt up just slightly.

I stiffened, jumping away from him so quickly I almost fell off the bed. I missed the warmth of him immediately, but my stomach had twisted into nervous knots and I couldn't bring myself to even look at him.

When I suggested we stay in his house I hadn't considered there would be a bed. I hadn't considered that we'd be alone.

I hadn't considered what those two things might mean.

"I'm sorry," Callum said. His voice was soft, slightly

confused. "Not okay?"

"Um." It was the only word I could come up with.

Was it okay? I'd never considered whether I wanted to have sex, with anyone.

I'd certainly never considered that someone would want to have sex with me.

"I've, um, never . . ." I finally looked up at him to see genuine surprise flash across his features.

"You're kidding," he said. "You were there five years and you never did it with anyone?"

"Of course not. No one wanted to touch me. You were the first person to even kiss me."

He cocked his head to the side, studying me curiously. "That's ridiculous, Wren."

"It's the truth."

He scooted closer until his leg brushed against mine. "No one touched you because you didn't want them to."

Maybe he was right about that. I pressed my palms against my thighs but my hands were shaking, so I quickly clasped them together.

"I never did, either," he said.

Unexpected relief flooded my chest. "Really? Sex is usually the first thing newbies do."

"I think people immediately assumed I was yours so they stayed far away." He met my eyes and smiled. "I was. I am." He leaned forward and brushed his lips to mine. "Yours."

I swallowed, a strange weight dropping in my stomach. I felt funny, hot, and nervous, and I wanted to pull him to me and never let go. I laced my fingers through his. I was the shaky one this time. He was steady.

"We—we can," I stuttered. "But we have to leave my shirt on."

His eyes dropped to my shirt briefly. "Why?"

"It's gross. It's better to leave it on."

"Gross?" he repeated in confusion.

I said nothing and understanding crossed his face. "Oh. Is that where you were shot?"

"Yes."

"I don't care if you have a scar, Wren."

"It's ugly. And it's more than one."

"Someone shot you more than once?"

"Yes. Three times."

"Who would do that to a twelve-year-old?"

"I don't know," I said, my voice strained and quiet. "I don't really remember."

"Any of it?"

The screaming—my screaming—echoed in my brain, making me a liar if I answered that question with a no.

"I remember some of it," I admitted. "It was a man, I think. We were living in an apartment and he came in yelling at my parents. I don't remember what about, but it was probably drugs. They were both really high, like always." I frowned as the images flashed through my brain. "My mom took me back to the bedroom and I think we were trying to climb out the window. I remember looking down at the grass thinking it was really far down. I heard gunshots and I screamed and my mom put my hand over my mouth and—"

"Are you trying to kill us?"

I swallowed at the sound of my mom's voice in my ear. "That's really all I remember."

Callum took a deep, shaky breath. "I'm sorry." The horror was spread across his every feature.

"Sorry you asked?" I said with a little laugh.

"Of course not."

"So we can do it if you want, but this should stay on," I said, crossing my arms over my chest.

He laughed. He saw my confusion and tried to stop, but another one escaped and he shook his head.

"No," he said, tucking my hair behind my ear and softly kissing my cheek. "I think I will wait for you to have a bit more enthusiasm than 'we can do it if you want.'" He chuckled again.

My cheeks flushed as I focused on the floor. "Oh. I didn't, that wasn't—"

"It's fine." He pressed his lips to my forehead and slid off the bed. "I wasn't expecting that, for the record."

I wanted to melt into the floor. To become a big pile of bright red, mushy Reboot.

"I can go sleep in my parents' room," he said.

I quickly grabbed his hand. "No, will you stay?" I still wanted him close, even if I didn't want him *that* close.

"Of course." He was pleased I'd asked; I could see it in his eyes as he crawled into bed.

I slid in next to him and scooted closer until he wrapped his arms around me. I pressed my face into his chest and he leaned in until his lips brushed my ear.

"When we do have sex, there will be none of this keeping-your-shirt-on nonsense."

"But—"

"Nope, sorry. I don't care about the scars and neither should you. All or nothing."

"Then you may get nothing."

"Please. You're not going to be able to resist me for much longer."

I laughed and tilted my head up to kiss him. He held me tighter against his chest as our lips met, and for a moment, I thought he might be right.

TWENTY-SIX

"WREN." CALLUM'S BREATH TICKLED MY EAR AND I STIRRED, my forehead brushing against his chest. "The sun is setting."

I peeked through my eyelids to see the room bathed in orange light. Callum's skin was bright and almost human-looking in its glow.

I stretched my legs against the softness of the sheets. I had the plushy material of the comforter clenched in a hand under my chin. I was inside a cloud—a luxurious, bubbly cloud where my body sank into a bed softer than anything I'd ever felt. The cloud smelled like Callum. Like soap and spice and warmth and the unmistakable hint of Reboot.

He pushed the hair off my forehead and pressed his lips

against the skin, sparking a trail of fire all the way down to my neck.

"We should go soon." His dark eyes met mine and I saw no point in trying to pretend I wasn't scared. He could already see it. His thumb rubbed warmth onto my cheek and his steady gaze suggested he didn't mind my fear.

I nodded but didn't move. I would have rather stayed in this bed with him all night, all day, all week. Forget Leb's daughter, forget the nonexistent reservation, forget everything but his arms and smile.

But he was shaking. His fingers jerked against my skin and he rolled away, swinging his legs over the side of the bed. He stole a quick glance at his trembling hands before reaching for his clothes.

The panic that tore through my chest took my breath away, made me press my face into the bed for fear I would scream.

"Maybe I have a smaller shirt you can wear," Callum said, hopping off the bed and striding across the room to his closet. "Something from when I was four or so."

I laughed against the mattress, sitting up and pushing the panic off my features. It sat on my chest, insistent, mocking.

"At least seven," I countered. "I'm not that small."

"Here," he said, throwing me a light blue shirt. "That's still going to be too big, but maybe you can tie the bottom."

He left the room to change and I pulled on my own pants and his shirt, which came down to the middle of my thighs. I tried to tie a knot with the extra material, eventually giving up and shoving it inside my pants. I took the black sweatshirt he'd thrown over the desk chair for me and smiled as I pulled the soft material over my head.

Callum returned and put the photo screen and a small camera in a pack, along with a couple pieces of clothing.

"We can go check if my parents left any food, but I really doubt it," he said, zipping the bag up and tossing it over his back.

The kitchen was bare except for a few abandoned, chipped plates. Callum shrugged and held his hand out to me.

"Ready?"

Never.

"Ready," I said, taking his hand.

I glanced around one last time as we headed down the hallway and into the living room. Callum seemed to be making an effort not to look, his gaze on the floor as he opened the front door for me. The temperature had dropped several degrees from the previous night, and the evening air was chilly. Even Callum shivered.

"One stop before we cross over," he said, pointing to the house next door. "I need to find out where my family went."

"What are we going to do? Pop in and ask?"

"Yep," he said, pulling me around to the back of the house. He rapped on a back window before I could protest.

The curtains parted and a human boy not much younger than us peeked through, letting out a yell and snapping them shut when he spotted us.

"Eduardo!" Callum yelled. "I just need to know where my parents and David went!"

Eduardo peeked out again, his eyes wide as he pressed his forehead against the glass to stare at us. "Callum?"

"Yes."

"Is it bad?"

The question could have meant several things, but Callum nodded.

"Yes. It's bad."

Eduardo's breath fogged up the window as he blinked in horror. "Did you escape?"

"Yes. Do you know where my family went?"

"My mom said Tower Apartments."

"Thank you," Callum said, taking a step back.

"Wait," Eduardo said, pushing the window up. Callum took another step backward. "What's your number?"

"Twenty-two," he said, holding his wrist up.

Eduardo snickered. "Aww, that's precious."

I laughed and Callum smiled at me.

"Who's that?" Eduardo asked.

"Wren. One-seventy-eight. Don't call her precious."

"One-seventy-eight!" Eduardo exclaimed too loudly. "For the love of Texas!"

"Thank you," Callum said as he pulled me to his side and we started to turn away.

"Wait, wait," Eduardo called. We faced him again and he chewed at his lip nervously. "After you died my mom asked me what I would want if I got sick."

"What you would want?" Callum repeated.

"Yeah, you know. If she should make sure." He made a gun with his fingers and held it to his temple.

I'd heard of it. No one had ever asked my opinion on the matter, and I found I wasn't sure what to say. I looked up at Callum to see a similar expression on his face. He lifted his eyebrows at me in question.

"No," I said.

Eduardo looked at Callum for confirmation, and for a long beat I thought he might disagree.

"No," he finally said. "Take your chances Rebooting."

"Are you just saying that because your brain is all messed up now?" Eduardo asked.

"Maybe." Callum shook his head in amusement and Eduardo grinned.

I gave Callum a baffled look as he laughed and turned away. I'd never witnessed such a friendly exchange between a human and a Reboot.

"Do you know where Tower Apartments are?" he asked, swinging an arm over my shoulders.

"I could probably get us to the general area." I twisted around to look at Eduardo's closed window. "He was your friend?"

"Yes."

"He wasn't too scared of us."

"Most kids are more terrified of Rebooting than the actual Reboots themselves."

"That makes sense, I guess."

We walked along the back of the neighborhood in silence. With every step my dread increased, the slum I had known beginning to take shape in my head.

As we approached the wall I stopped and stared. Someone had painted it, a beautiful mural of children playing and people running in the sunshine. I wanted to strangle the artist.

There were zero officers on this side of the wall. Who would want to sneak into the slums?

"Wren," Callum said, gesturing for me to follow him.

"I'm scared." The admission came out of my mouth before I could stop it.

He looked up at the wall. "Of going back?"

"Yes."

"Maybe it's better than you remember."

I drew myself up to my pathetic little height and took a deep breath. It wasn't like I had a choice. I had to go.

"Let me check it out first," I said. I hoisted myself up and peeked over. I saw nothing but grass until I looked to the left, and spotted an officer stationed several feet away. "Quietly," I whispered to Callum.

I jumped down, my feet making a soft thud. The officer

turned as Callum landed next to me. We took off, but only silence followed us. The officer was either a rebel or couldn't be bothered to care about a couple of crazy kids sneaking into the slums from the *rico*.

It looked familiar. The center of the slums in the distance, the medical center looming to my right, the rows of shacks to my left.

It smelled like death. The pure air of the *rico* was gone, the scent of flowers and grass just a memory.

It felt like home. We were in the worst area of the slums, the part I had once lived in, and I squeezed my eyes shut when I recognized a large building full of little apartments.

"Are you trying to kill us?"

My foot caught on something and my face smacked into the dirt. I gasped, pushing the images of my parents out of my head.

"Wren," Callum said, kneeling down next to me.

My breath escaped in short gasps, like I was a human. I struggled to my knees and pressed my hands into my thighs.

Why had I agreed to come here? Why had I done this to myself?

Callum scooped me up off the ground and carried me in his arms. I put my face in his chest and tried to slow my breathing, but it still came in gasps that rocked my body.

He ducked behind the medical building and gently set me down. I clutched my legs to my chest and he crouched in front of me, running his fingers into my hair.

"I don't want to be here," I whispered, burying my head in my knees in shame.

"I know." He kept stroking my hair and it calmed me, my breathing slowing until my body stopped shaking.

"Tell me a good memory," he said.

"There aren't any."

"There has to be at least one."

"If there is I don't remember it," I said.

"Think harder."

That seemed useless, but I shut my eyes and did it anyway. Nothing came except yelling and gunshots.

"My mom told me I looked like a monkey," I finally said.

He looked at me in confusion. "Sorry?"

"She said when I slumped I looked like a monkey and I had a pretty face and I shouldn't hide it."

"You do have a pretty face," he said with a little smile.

"So that's sort of happy, I guess. It doesn't make me feel bad, anyway."

"What was she like?" Callum asked.

"I don't know. I remember only bits and pieces of her."

"More now?" he guessed.

"Yes."

"Maybe that means you miss her."

"Maybe it means my subconscious is mean."

He laughed, leaning forward to gently kiss my forehead.

"You miss your parents," I said. It wasn't a question.

"Yes." He looked almost ashamed.

"Let's go find them, then," I said with a sigh, slowly getting to my feet. "I need to get to Guadalupe Street to watch for shuttles soon. Adina's supposed to be on assignment tonight."

"Are you okay? We can rest for longer if you want."

"We rested all day."

"Well, it wasn't all resting," he said with a teasing smile that made me blush. He grabbed me around the waist and kissed me. It was true that we'd spent a very good portion of the day doing more kissing than sleeping.

"Thank you," he said when he released me. "For coming with me. For not giving me shit about wanting to see my parents."

"I have most definitely given you shit."

"Then thank you for giving me minimal shit."

"You're welcome."

"That way?" he asked, pointing.

I nodded and laced my fingers through his as we started down the road. There were no humans out tonight. Not a single one, which confirmed that I remembered right—there was a strict curfew in the Austin slums.

I kicked at the dirt with my boot, the wind blowing it back onto my pants. The chilly breeze slapped at me, and I wrapped an arm around my stomach and scrunched my face up against it.

My feet dragged, the sound of my boots scraping against the ground comforting and familiar.

"Do you want to stop?" Callum asked, casting an amused glance down at my feet.

"No. It reminds me—" I looked up to see the schoolhouse on my right. The three white buildings looked the same. It was bigger than the schoolhouse in Rosa, and definitely cheerier. They painted it with whatever materials they had. Someone had drawn big dripping flowers in some sort of thick black liquid.

The side of the biggest building was covered in something, and I took in a sharp breath as I remembered what it was.

"Can we pause for a minute?" I asked, slipping my hand out of Callum's.

"Sure. What is it?" he asked, following me.

"They do a photo collage. Of all the kids who died."

His face lit up. "You're up there? The human you?" He bounded ahead of me.

"Probably not. I think the parents give them the photos. But I thought maybe . . ."

I stopped in front of the wall. Hundreds of photos were stuck to the building, protected behind thick plastic. Every month or so the teachers would remove the plastic and put the new ones up and we would gather around and tell stories about the kids we'd lost.

"What about this one?" Callum asked.

I looked at the lanky blond girl. "No."

My eyes scanned the pictures, but I didn't see my human self in any of them. I doubted my parents had that many pictures of me, and I found it hard to believe anyone went looking for them after we died.

Then I saw her.

The little girl didn't frown at the camera, but she was obviously displeased. Her blond hair was dirty and her clothes were too big, but she looked tough. As tough as an eleven-year-old human could look. Her eyes were blue, the only part of her face that was pretty.

It was me.

I put my finger to the plastic, touching the ugly human's little face.

"Is it you?" Callum asked, appearing next to me. "Oh, it's not."

"Yes, it is," I said softly.

He squinted at the picture in the darkness. Maybe he was looking at the sunken cheeks or the pointy chin or the way she stared past the camera.

"Are you sure?" he asked.

"Yes. A teacher took it, I remember."

"You look different now."

"She was so ugly."

"You weren't ugly," he said. "Look at you. You were cute. Not particularly happy, but cute."

"She was never happy."

"It's freaking me out how you keep referring to yourself in the third person."

A smile crossed my lips. "Sorry. I don't feel like that person anymore."

"You're not." He glanced at it again. "I never thought about it before, but I'm glad you're not a human. Is that a weird thing to say?"

"No. I'm glad you're not a human, too." I held my hand out to him. "Let's go."

"Wait," he said, taking a camera from his bag. He held it up close to the picture and snapped a shot. "You need at least one picture of her."

He stowed the camera away and took my hand as we headed into town. The road widened as we walked past the market and shops. The center of town was a long, straight road, one I had replaced in my head with the one from Rosa.

It wasn't the same. The wooden buildings were all painted, like they belonged to rich people with money to spare. But they weren't painted normal colors like white or gray. They were done up with elaborate designs—huge pink flowers, orange-and-red flames spewing across doors, funky colorful skeletons dancing on the sides of buildings.

"It's nicer here than in Rosa," Callum said in surprise.

"Those are Tower Apartments," I said, pointing to the three-story complex at the end of the street.

He gave my hand a squeeze. We had reached Tower Apartments faster than I had expected. I was surprised I had taken us in the right direction, much less directly there.

"They . . . could be worse," Callum said as he looked up at them.

They could be worse. Someone had painted a sun at the top edge of the building, and little trees and sky between the apartment windows. I remembered none of that, only that at three stories, it was the tallest building in the Austin slums.

We approached the door and Callum studied the Human Occupancy Register affixed to the wall.

"Apartment 203," he said, pointing to the name Reyes.

He pulled on the main door, but it was locked. He yanked harder, until the lock gave in and we slipped through the door.

I trudged up the stairwell behind him and onto the second floor. The walls were a plain, dingy white, the concrete floors dirty. I could hear the muffled sounds of humans talking and Callum pressed his ear to the door marked *203*.

He gestured for me to come closer but I moved forward only a few feet, dread setting itself squarely in my tummy. I should have fought him harder on this.

He knocked, softly, and I heard the voices on the other side of the door go silent.

"Mom? Dad?" he whispered.

A bang erupted from the apartment and Callum jumped. I wanted to cover my eyes with my hands, hide until it was all over, but I stood firm.

The door opened a crack. I couldn't see anyone, but Callum smiled. The door inched open wider.

The man holding it ajar looked very much like Callum. He was tall and lanky with dark hair that was shaggy like the old pictures of his son.

His mouth opened in shock, his body trembling. His eyes traveled up and down Callum frantically, as if looking for something.

A woman appeared behind him, her dark hair pulled back in a messy bun. She had the same olive complexion as Callum, although her human skin was a bit darker, and while she had similar dark eyes, hers were wide and crazy. She pressed her hand to her mouth, weird animal sounds coming from behind it.

"It's okay, it's me," Callum said, his smile fading.

I sucked in a breath and for a moment, hoped for the best.

The tears could be because they were so happy to see him.

The shock could be because they never expected to see him again.

They were going to wrap their arms around him and tell him they missed him.

His father let out a choked sob and squeezed his eyes shut.

He couldn't look.

"It's still me," Callum said desperately.

His mom wailed and I took a quick glance around. The human in the apartment across the hall was peering out his cracked door.

I stepped forward and touched Callum's arm, his parents slipping into further hysterics when they saw me.

"Let's go," I said gently.

"Mom!" Callum exclaimed. He was on the edge of tears. "Don't you . . ." He grabbed her hand in both of his. "It's still me, see?"

She put her hand over her face to cry harder, trying to yank the other one from his grasp. He would have felt cold to her. Dead.

"Dad, look at me," he said, giving up on his mom and desperately trying to get his dad to meet his eyes. "Just look!"

They didn't look, either of them. His dad began making a desperate waving motion with his hands. His eyes darted down the hallway as he tried to shoo his son away.

"Go." His voice was low, strangled, as he pushed his wife behind him. "If they see you here . . ."

HARC would arrest both his parents if they found Callum here.

"But—" Callum took in a shaky breath as his eyes found something behind them.

I stood on my toes to see past his mom. A dark-haired boy stood next to the couch. David, I assumed. His eyes were fixed on Callum, but he made no move toward his brother.

"Go," his father repeated, taking a step backward into the apartment.

He slammed the door shut.

TWENTY-SEVEN

DISAPPOINTMENT PUSHED AT MY CHEST AS CALLUM BLINKED at the spot where his parents had been. Maybe I had thought he was right about them.

I held my hand out to him, but he was alone in another world and had forgotten I existed. I slipped my hand into his and he jumped.

"Let's go," I said, gently tugging on his arm.

He let me lead him through the hallway and down the stairs, but he kept looking behind him, even after the door was no longer visible. I was worried he'd dart away from me and try again, so I gripped his fingers tighter as we made our way out into the cool night air.

Callum stopped in front of the building, his jacket blowing open in the wind as he turned to look at me. He was so still, so calm, that I was scared to move for fear of breaking him.

But we were out in the open, surrounded by apartment buildings with curious humans pressing their faces to the windows. I could see David two floors up, his hands against the dingy glass, his mouth open wide.

So I gently pulled on Callum's hand and he followed me when I broke into a run. We headed back down the long road and past the brightly painted houses again. I didn't know where I was going, but when we approached the market Callum veered off the road. He pressed his hand to the back of his neck as he walked around the side of the wooden building and I silently followed him.

He reached out and touched the tips of his fingers to the wall, letting out a heavy sigh. "I need a minute."

He'd closed his eyes but I nodded anyway, because I didn't know what else to do. I should have already considered ways to comfort him. I expected this. Why hadn't I thought about it?

Standing there staring at him was undoubtedly not the right thing to do. I wrapped an arm around his waist and pressed my cheek against his shoulder.

"I'm sorry," I whispered.

A few tears fell as he opened his eyes and planted a soft kiss on my forehead. He cleared his throat as he pulled away from me and wiped his fingers across his eyes, his expression tinged with embarrassment as he tried to remove the evidence of his crying.

I thought it was more embarrassing to not be able to cry at all.

"We need to go get Adina, right?" he asked.

I took that to mean he didn't want to talk about it. I couldn't blame him.

His hand was shaking violently when I slipped my fingers through his. I took in a deep breath. It could be because he was devastated about his parents.

Or it could be because he was about to go insane.

Either way, I refused to let him see my fear. I held his hand tighter as we ducked out of the alley and hurried down the street. The tiny houses were lined up right next to one another in this part of town, an occasional apartment complex stuck at the end of a street. They were painted as well, some with colorful drawings, others with words. Fighting words. Words that would result in immediate arrest in Rosa.

Take Back Texas.

Texans for Freedom.

Callum squinted at them as we passed. "It's weird here," he mumbled.

He was right. I remembered nothing clean or colorful or rebellious about the Austin I grew up in. Something had changed.

The roar of the shuttle made me turn. It touched down at

the end of Guadalupe Street, and we hid against the side of a house as five Reboots stepped out. They all looked the same in their black clothes and helmets, but I could see a long, dark ponytail sticking out of the back of one helmet.

"I think that might be her," I said, peering around the corner of the house as the Reboots split up. The dark-haired girl headed down First Street and disappeared from view.

We took off after her at a slow pace, running behind the houses to stay out of sight of the other Reboots. We crossed onto First Street and I spotted Adina standing in front of a house, looking down at her assignment slip.

Callum slumped against a wire fence, breathing heavily as he clutched his arms against his stomach. "I don't think I should go in there with a human."

I hesitated, glancing from him to her. He was probably right. "All right. Don't move, okay? Yell if you start feeling . . . weird. And be ready to run when we come back."

He nodded, waving me off. Adina was at the front door of the house, knocking as I silently hurried across the lawn. She lifted her foot and smashed in the front door.

There were no human screams as I crept up the stairs behind her. She stood in the middle of the small living room, her hands on her hips as she scanned from left to right. The house appeared to be empty.

I grabbed her around the waist and a gasp escaped her mouth. My other hand found her camera, ripping it off her helmet and tossing it against the wall.

She tore my arm off her stomach and swung at me, just barely missing my cheek. I tried to catch her eye but she came at me again, hard and fast. I ducked and swiped at her legs with my foot. She jumped over them and smashed her right fist into my cheek.

I blinked, surprised. She was good for a Thirty-nine.

I dodged the next punch, grabbing her arm and twisting it behind her back. I pulled her closer to me, until her face was inches from mine. I didn't want to speak while her com was still in her ear, so I stared straight into her eyes.

Her face crumpled in confusion and she shoved me away, lifting her arms like she was going to keep fighting me. I raised my hands in surrender, pointing with one finger to my bar code.

She hesitantly took a step forward, nudging her helmet farther up to reveal wisps of long brown hair. Her wide brown-gold eyes flew up to mine, full of suspicion and curiosity.

I reached into my pocket and she grabbed my wrist, her fingers digging into my skin. I gave her an annoyed look and shook her off, pulling Leb's note out. I held it toward her and she frowned at it for several seconds before plucking it from my fingers.

Her eyes skimmed over the words quickly, her expression unreadable. When she looked up at me again I reached for the com in her ear. She let me take it out and I clenched it in my fist.

"Do you want to come with me?" I whispered.

"To this reservation thing?" she asked, glancing down at the note.

"Yes." I took a quick glance behind me, through the front door. Callum was still slumped against the fence, his face lifted to the sky.

She didn't answer for several seconds. She pressed her lips together, her eyebrows lowered in thought. When she looked up at me again I was almost certain she would say no. A few weeks ago, before Callum, I would have said no.

She barely nodded.

"Yes?" I asked.

"Yes," she said, carefully folding the note and slipping it into her pocket.

I crushed the com in my hand and dropped the pieces on the ground. I pulled the tracker locator from my pocket and waved it over her body until it lit up, above her left collarbone.

"Your tracker," I whispered as I took my knife and sliced just under her neck. She didn't flinch as I pulled the tracker out and carefully placed it on the ground.

"Wren," I said.

"Addie," she said. "You know my father?"

"Yes, but we need to run. They—"

A scream pierced the night, strangled and terrified. I whirled around to the front of the house, my eyes searching for Callum.

He was gone.

I bolted out the door, Addie's footsteps following behind me as I flew down the steps and onto the grass.

The fence next door was open.

The front door broken down.

I raced through the yard and what remained of the front door. The kitchen was in total disarray, chairs scattered around the room, the table overturned.

"Callum?" I yelled.

A grunt came from the back room and I ran down the hallway. I came to a sudden stop at the bedroom door.

The human was sprawled out on the floor, Callum's hands around his neck. The man's eyes stared blankly past me.

He was dead.

Callum loosened his grip and opened his mouth wide, poised to take a big chunk out of the human's neck.

I dove across the room, pushing Callum off before he could sink his teeth in. We hit the floor together and his teeth scraped against my arm as he growled and flailed. I pushed his arms into the wood as I hauled myself on top of him.

"Callum," I said through gritted teeth, slamming his arms down as he struggled against me.

I looked from the dead man to Callum. I couldn't let him see that. If I got him out of the room I wouldn't have to tell him at all. He didn't need to know.

"Get his feet," I said to Addie, grabbing Callum underneath the arms.

She did as I said, yanking Callum's feet together when he tried to kick her.

"He's an Under-sixty?" she asked as we lifted him off the ground.

"Yes. Twenty-two."

"She's gone! Thirty-nine is gone!"

The man's yell from next door made both our heads snap up. We had to hurry. Addie ran backward through the room and for the door at the rear of the house, whipping her head around every few seconds to see where she was going as we lugged Callum with us.

The front door banged open as we flew out the back and I looked desperately for a hiding place. There was no way to run far with Callum like this, not with them right behind us.

The backyard was fenced in by some rotting wood and I sprinted across the grass, Callum bouncing in my grasp. He wasn't struggling much anymore. Instead he was blinking and shaking his head, as if trying to clear his thoughts.

Addie unhooked the gate and we scrambled into the alley, yells and footsteps not far behind us. I dug my fingers into Callum's shoulders as we ran. I couldn't come this far and get caught.

Addie made a sharp turn as we approached a poorly paved road dotted with run-down homes and a few shops. I let her lead since she knew the town better than I did, and I didn't have any other bright ideas.

The shouts were louder as she tore through a yard and around to the back of a house. A dim light flickered inside and I tried to run as quietly as possible.

We were headed for a shed, a tiny rectangle-shaped one that looked like it was barely big enough to fit all three of us. Addie dropped Callum's legs and they skidded against the dirt until he found his footing. He gently shrugged me off and I let him go as Addie threw open the shed door.

We raced inside and I stumbled over a rake and a toolbox before finding a spot against the wall. Callum slid down next to me and I wanted to tell him not to sit, to be prepared to run, but he looked so utterly freaked out that I couldn't find the words.

Addie tried to close the door but it looked like she'd broken the lock, so she gave up and held on to the handle, keeping it closed as she leaned forward to listen. There was yelling nearby and I closed my fingers over the gun on my hip.

"Is that Adina? What happened?" Callum whispered, turning his face up to mine. His eyes were huge and worried, like he already suspected something.

"You lost it for a minute there," I whispered as the voices outside began to fade.

"And yes, I'm Addie," she said.

Callum looked at her, but she stayed focused on the outside. His head swung back to me and I had to drop my eyes because I didn't want him to see the fear there.

"Wren." His voice was firm, controlled. "What just happened?"

I should have come up with a lie. A story to tell him to fill in the holes. Maybe I could just tell him he attacked someone and I pulled him off in time.

But that lie made me feel sick. He'd thank me and his gratitude would likely make me hurl.

I'd waited too long to answer and he was staring at me like he already knew something terrible had happened. I was shaking a little as I crossed my arms over my chest.

"I'm sorry," I whispered. "I shouldn't have left you."

"I hurt someone?"

I nodded. My throat burned again and I tried to swallow. It didn't help.

"I killed someone?"

"Yes," I choked out. He was silent and I looked up. He was perfectly still, the horror creeping over his features.

"It's not your fault," Addie said. "I've seen what the shots do and been there myself and—"

Callum held his hand up and she closed her mouth, shrugging her shoulders at me like she didn't know what else to say.

I didn't, either. The footsteps outside were gone so I slid down the wall beside him. His eyes were closed, his hands clasped together at the back of his neck.

"I'm sorry," I whispered. "It's my fault. I said I wouldn't let you hurt anyone and I did."

What was one more body to add to my tally? I wanted to point that out to him, to remind him that I'd killed more people than he ever would. But I doubted that would be comforting.

He shook his head, dropping his hands from his neck and looking me straight in the eye. I thought he would be sad, but his eyes were hard, angry. I braced myself, thinking he was going to yell at me, but he slipped his hand into mine and squeezed it.

"It's not your fault," he said. "It's HARC's fault."

Addie muttered something that sounded like agreement. My head snapped up as it occurred to me that she might be in the same situation as Callum.

"Are you okay?" I asked. "Did they give you shots?"

"Yes. I'm fine for now, though. I'm between rounds."

"What do you mean?" Callum asked.

"They do multiple rounds," Addie said. "You must be on the first."

"I guess. I was only there a few weeks."

"Yeah, probably on the first, then. You start going off the deep end, then they'll give you something that makes you feel normal again. Some sort of cure or antidote or something. Then they start it up again."

Callum's eyes widened with hope at the same time mine did.

"I don't know that for sure," Addie said quickly. "But my friends said I was a mess last week and now I'm fine. Good timing, by the way. Thanks for that."

"Your dad might have known," I said. It could be why he was so quick to get us the tracker locator. I made a fist and dug my fingers into my palm. Leb hadn't bothered to check on Callum's status.

"If there is an antidote, maybe the rebels will have it," Callum said hopefully. "Or they'll get it for us."

I gave him a doubtful look. I'd barely persuaded Leb to help us, and only in exchange for something.

"I can't stay like this." He swallowed, turning to Addie. "I'll just get worse, right?"

"Probably," she said quietly. "The ones who didn't get multiple rounds, the ones they let run the course . . . yeah, they never got better."

The lump in my throat was unexpected, and I had to swallow several times before I could speak.

"We have to at least ask the rebels," he said.

I nodded. "We will. And when they say no we'll go get it ourselves."

Addie raised her eyebrows. "Seriously? You know you'll have to go inside HARC to get it."

"Yes."

She pressed her lips together as she took a step toward me. "You just broke me out and now you want to—"

A noise outside made us turn. The shed door swung open.

It was a HARC officer.

Pointing a gun at us.

TWENTY-EIGHT

I SHOT TO MY FEET AND DOVE FOR THE OFFICER, PAINFULLY aware that I didn't have a helmet. Addie got there first, grabbing the officer's arm just as he got a shot off. The bullet sailed past her and through the shed wall.

He fired again and Addie stumbled as the bullet hit her chest. The officer whirled around to me just as I slammed into him, knocking him into the dirt. Callum scrambled across the ground and wrestled the gun from the officer's grasp.

The shouts outside meant the other officers in the area had heard the commotion. I stomped on the human's leg until I heard a crack, and he screamed and clawed at the dirt to get away from me.

I jumped over him and ran through the door, reaching my hand out for Callum's. He grabbed it and Addie dashed through the door behind him.

We ran across the yard and back to the poorly paved street. I whipped my head around to see a group of about five officers chasing us. I ducked as one fired, putting my hands over the back of my head like that would stop a bullet.

Addie's long legs made her a fast runner, and she pulled ahead of us and turned left as she approached a crossroads. Bullets flew past my ears as we sprinted after her just in time to see her take another sharp left behind a two-story building. I rounded the building and she was waiting at the far edge, back pressed against the side as she watched the street we'd just come from. The officers blew past and we waited half a second before darting back out to the street and running the opposite direction.

We got to the edge of town, where the trees were thick before giving way to the open land in front of the HARC fence. We stopped in the darkness there, and I turned to look out at the houses in the distance. The HARC officers were nowhere in sight, but shuttles hovered over the city, spotlights sweeping the streets.

"This . . . was the entirety of your plan . . . wasn't it?" Addie gasped, putting a hand against a tree as she tried to catch her breath. "Just grab me and run?"

"You have a better one?" Callum asked with a frown.

"I'm willing to bet I could come up with something."

I rolled my eyes as I pulled the map of Austin out of my pocket. We weren't far from the rebels. We could make it to their house in about ten minutes, once we were sure we'd lost HARC.

"You feel all right?" I asked Callum.

He nodded. "Okay. Still . . ." He held out his hand to show me how badly it was shaking.

"You should eat some meat," Addie said. "It helps. Especially with the whole 'wanting to eat humans' thing. It, like, tricks your system for a while or something."

"We'll get you some as soon as we get to the rebels," I said, taking another glance around before I plopped down on the grass. Callum sat beside me and laced his shaky fingers through mine. I wanted to climb in his lap and squeeze him until I'd convinced him—and myself—that everything was fine. I resisted, since Addie would probably not appreciate it.

She was still standing, reading the note from her father again. "Why'd he send you?" she asked, not looking up.

"Because I wanted a way out and made a deal."

"He helped you if you helped me," she said.

"Yes."

"You could have broken the deal. Just taken off."

"We don't get the location of the reservation until I bring you to the rebels."

She bit down on her lip and sighed. "They don't trust us at all."

"Leb was very good to me," I said, guilt invading my chest as I realized the disappointment on her face was for her father. "The best officer I worked with. And he said he had other kids, so it made sense he didn't want to risk everything."

"I guess." She glanced at Callum. "Did you leave because you were going crazy?"

"No, that happened after." He let out a humorless laugh, rubbing a hand down his face. "They were going to eliminate me because I didn't want to kill anyone."

Addie looked away, clearly uncomfortable, and I squeezed his hand. He'd found something in the distance to stare at and I wanted desperately to change the subject.

Addie slid down onto the ground and we sat in silence for a long time, listening to the distant sound of officers and shuttles. Callum's hand was warm in mine, but I was still trembling. I thought it was more from fear than from the wind whipping across my cheeks.

Callum's face was turned to the ground, and I tried not to look at him, but his distraught expression was like a magnet. I found myself opening and shutting my mouth as I tried to think of something comforting to say, but there was nothing.

I'd opened my mouth for the hundredth time when Addie stood up, brushing off her pants.

"I don't hear anything," she said, tilting her head toward the quiet city. "Want to make a run for it?"

I nodded, offering my hand to Callum as I got to my feet.

He stood and crossed his arms over his chest, letting out a big breath of air as he scanned the area in front of us. It was clear, the officers and shuttles gone.

"You all right?" I asked, lightly touching his arm.

He nodded without meeting my eyes. "I'm fine. Let's go meet these rebels."

TWENTY-NINE

THE ADDRESS LEB GAVE US FOR THE REBELS WAS PAST THE schoolhouse and in an area of town I'd known well as a child. The road curved and the houses were run-down and sad, some falling apart. It was more like Rosa in this part of the Austin slums, although many houses were painted bright, happy colors.

We half jogged, half sprinted across the town, scurrying behind buildings and trees at every noise. It was pitch-black, but the sun would start to rise any minute, and I wanted to get to the rebels before it was light out.

"That one," I said, pointing as we approached a dirt road. I slowed to a walk as we turned down it, glancing along the row of brown houses. According to the map, it was the last house on the right.

We reached the end of the street and trudged across the patchy, brown grass to the front door. This house wasn't painted. It was brown wood and windowless at the front and narrower than the houses on either side, but extended a bit farther in back. If the point was to not stand out, they had succeeded.

I glanced around the side of the house to see a short wooden fence. I gestured for Addie and Callum to follow. "Follow me," I whispered, quickly darting around. We hopped the fence and landed in the dirt of a tiny backyard. I crept up to the brown door at the back of the house and softly rapped my knuckles against the wood.

Nothing.

I knocked again, a little harder, casting a nervous glance at Callum. Dealing with humans made me fidgety. I hated relying on them for anything, and I could see by the hope in his eyes that he expected these people would have all the answers.

"What?" a man's voice said very quietly, from the other side of the door.

"It's us," I said in a low voice. "Um, Leb sent us?"

Silence followed my words, then a flurry of noise. They were whispering to one another and running around.

I dropped Callum's hand and reached to finger the gun at my hip. I wouldn't draw a weapon yet. I'd give them a chance.

It took at least a minute, but the door finally swung open to reveal a bleary-eyed boy with messy, dark curls, pointing a shotgun at my head.

Giving humans a chance was a dumb idea.

I grabbed my gun, but the human quickly held out his hand for me to stop. He was trembling.

"I don't want to use it," he said. "We're just cautious here. If you'd like to come inside, we're going to need all your weapons."

"But you get to keep yours?" Callum asked.

Callum's easy, relaxed tone unsettled the human. I could see it in the way his eyes flicked between us, swallowing hard as he looked Callum up and down. He was much shorter than Callum—almost as short as me, actually—and he looked ridiculous pointing the gun at him. We were probably about the same age, although he could have been a bit younger.

"If you want to come inside you have to give up your weapons," he repeated.

"Fine," I said, holding my gun out. I didn't need it anyway. With the way the guy was shaking, I could take his gun, break his neck, and dance on the body in two seconds flat.

I smiled as I handed it over.

"Anything else?" he asked, lowering the shotgun. He looked pointedly at Addie.

"I got nothing," she said, holding up her hands.

I slipped the knife out of my pocket and gave him that as

well. He took it, glancing over his shoulder. He shifted from foot to foot, obviously unsure of what to do next.

A man appeared behind him. He was much taller than the boy, and he gripped at the edge of the door with a massive hand. He also looked like he'd just woken up, and he ran a hand through his gray-streaked hair as he squinted at us.

"Which one is Wren?" he asked.

"Me."

"Adina, then?" he asked, and she nodded. He focused on Callum. "And you're Twenty-two."

"Callum."

"Tony," he said. He put his hand on the boy's shoulder. "This is Gabe. Leb assured us you wouldn't kill us. Are we all still good with that plan?"

The question was directed at me.

Callum actually laughed a little, and a smile twitched at the edges of my lips. "Yes."

Tony jerked his head and Gabe stepped back, keeping the gun trained on us as I crossed over the threshold. The wood floors creaked beneath my boots and I squinted in the darkness as Tony led us through a hallway and into the living room. The light came from a couple little lamps in the living room. The only window, in the kitchen to my left, was covered by dark curtains.

There was another human, this one lanky with thick brown hair to his shoulders, sitting on the plushy brown couch, his eyebrows lowered in a frown. He looked to be about the same age as Tony, and he watched my every move as I stepped inside.

My eyes darted to the kitchen, but it seemed they were the only humans in the house.

Tony took big strides across the living room and stopped at the kitchen table, picking up a piece of paper. He headed back to me and held it out. "As promised."

It was a map. I took it from him and looked from the drawing of Texas to the instructions written below. The Reboot reservation was several hundred miles north, not far from what used to be the border of Texas.

"We can help you part of the way," he said. "You can stay here until tomorrow night, then—"

He stopped. His eyes were focused intently on Callum, and I turned to see him pressed against the wall, his hand covering his nose and mouth. His whole body was shaking.

"Oh, Jesus. He's been given shots, hasn't he?" Tony asked.

"Yes. You—"

"Desmond, go get some rope," he said, and the lanky guy hopped to his feet and scurried down the hallway. He emerged a moment later with two lengths of rope and headed for Callum.

"What are you doing?" I asked, jumping in front of him.

"Sit down," Tony said to Callum. "Hands behind your back."

Callum stepped forward like he was going to listen to this human, and I grabbed his arm, pulling him closer to me.

Desmond kept coming like he intended to push past me and I gave him a look like I dared him to try. Tony put his arm out to stop him.

"It's for our safety," Tony explained. "Under-sixties can't be controlled on those crazy drugs HARC gives them."

"It's fine, Wren," Callum said, running a hand down my arm before stepping closer to Desmond and Tony. Desmond gestured for him to sit and he slid down onto the floor behind the couch. He put his hands behind his back and Desmond began looping the rope around them.

"You're in between rounds still, aren't you?" Tony asked Addie.

"Yes." She glanced at me. "I told them there might be an antidote? Or something to make him better?"

Desmond tightened the ropes on Callum's wrists and moved down to bind his ankles. "There is one. We don't have it, though."

"Who has it?" I asked. "Is it at HARC?"

"Do you want to sit?" Tony asked, gesturing to the kitchen table. "Do you want some water or coffee or something?"

I paused. What was wrong with these humans? They seriously wanted to have water and coffee with a bunch of Reboots?

Addie started toward the table but I wasn't leaving Callum tied up on the floor by himself while I had a cup of coffee. I sat down next to him and he gave me a small smile.

"I just want to know how to get the antidote." I crossed my

legs and met Tony's eyes.

He actually looked sad for a moment and his sympathy made me uncomfortable. I didn't know how to handle that look from most people, much less a human.

"It's in the medical labs at HARC. There's . . . no way. I'm sorry."

There was no way for him.

"Don't you have people on the inside?" Addie asked. "Like my dad?"

"I'm on the inside," Tony said, leaning against the wall. "I've been a HARC guard for years."

Adina gave him a confused look. "Where? I've never seen you."

"I work up on the human floors, in the control rooms." He turned to me. "But I can tell you there's no way one of our guys can get the antidote out. We don't have any people in medical and they search everyone before they leave." He gave me that awful sympathetic look again. "I'm sorry."

If he told me he was sorry one more time I'd snap his neck.

"That's fine," I said. "I'll just have to break in and get it myself."

Gabe laughed, cutting off when I turned to him. He swallowed. "Oh. You were serious."

Tony and Desmond exchanged a confused look. Tony turned to me and seemed to consider his words carefully. "Hon, you were just in HARC for five years, yes?"

"Yes. Don't call me hon."

"My apologies. So if you were just there, you know the security. You *might* get in. And that is a very big *might*. But you would never get out."

"What about in the middle of the night?" Addie asked. "Skeleton crew."

"She's still way outnumbered. And they'd just lock the doors. Cameras would see her."

"We'll find a way to cut the power," I said.

"Backup generators," Tony said. "They kick on in about a minute. You couldn't do it in time."

I clasped my hands together as a rock started to form in the bottom of my stomach. I didn't care what they said. I was finding a way to get that antidote.

"A bomb," I said. "What if we blew up a portion of the place? No one would miss it."

Desmond snorted. "I do like that idea."

"I don't," Addie said with a frown. "You might kill the Reboots."

"Not to mention we're a bit short on bombs here," Tony said. "Listen, hon—sorry, Wren—if I thought there was a way you could do it, I would tell you. But there's nothing you can do." He let out a long sigh. "I mean, maybe if you had an army of Reboots. But failing that, I've got nothing."

I froze, my eyes darting to Addie's. We had the same thought.

"How many are in there?" I asked.

"There's like a hundred and something." She looked at Tony, her eyes flashing with excitement. "Right? A little over a hundred?"

"You mean in the Austin facility? Yeah, there're about a hundred Reboots left there. But they're not an army; they're prisoners."

I glanced at Callum, who had an eyebrow cocked, his expression disbelieving. I put my hand on his knee and gave it a gentle squeeze before facing Tony.

"Then we'll go let them all out."

THIRTY

I TURNED TO THE FRONT DOOR AS ANOTHER HUMAN ENTERED. They'd been coming in a steady stream for the last hour, and the kitchen was starting to get full. They were all gathered around Tony, and I could hear snatches of conversation as they debated whether or not to help me. They seemed torn between calling the plan "idiotic" or "genius."

Tony and Desmond had stepped away as soon as I broached the idea of freeing all the Reboots in Austin. They'd had a heated argument in a back room, which ended with Desmond storming out, only to return with the first of the rebels.

The rebels were mostly men, but they varied in age. Some looked about sixteen or seventeen, like Gabe, while others were going gray. I'd thought Gabe was Tony's son, but he didn't call him Dad, and I'd heard Gabe tell Addie he grew up in the orphanage. I wasn't sure what these people had in common, besides an obvious hatred of HARC and an odd urge to help Reboots.

They were a strange bunch.

Desmond caught me staring at them and his eyebrows lowered. He leaned against the kitchen wall, crossing one black boot over the other, and didn't shy away when I met his gaze. He'd been the most vocal in his opposition to the rebels helping me—"I'm not dying for them" were his exact words—and I could see his point. Still, he was one of the humans in the room who didn't seem the least bit scared of us, and I didn't know what to make of that.

A short man stopped in front of me and Addie, planting his hands on his hips as he looked down at us.

"They took you while you were on assignment last night?" he asked Addie with half a smile.

"Yeah," she said, shooting me a wary glance.

"Were you on First Street? Or was one of your cohorts?"

"Yeah," she said in surprise. "I was sent there, but the assignment wasn't home."

The man chuckled. "Yep, that was me." He lifted his arms in victory. "Slipped by 'em again!"

"You're Henry?" Addie asked with a laugh.

"Sure am." He grinned before heading into the kitchen to

join the other rebels.

Addie watched him go. "These humans are weird." She put her elbow on her knee and propped her head up on her hand. "But we can't do it without them, you know."

"We?" I asked, raising my eyebrows at her. We were still sitting on the floor behind the couch, Callum silent and motionless beside me.

"Please don't tell me you think you can break into HARC all by yourself," she said.

"I just didn't realize you wanted to help."

"My friends are all in there. Of course I want to help." She squinted at the rebels in the kitchen. "I wish my dad had been able to come today. I would have liked to talk to him."

"I doubt he could get out of Rosa."

"Yeah." She frowned slightly. "I can't believe he works for HARC. I mean, I know he's with the rebels, but still. It's odd."

"He didn't last time you saw him?" I asked.

She snorted. "Definitely not. I haven't seen him since I died six years ago, so I guess stuff changes, but he hated HARC. I died at home of KDH and after I Rebooted he kept me. Said he wasn't letting HARC have me."

"You're kidding. For how long?" The parents who wanted to keep their Rebooted children were few and far between, although I wasn't entirely surprised Leb was one of them.

"Just a couple weeks. I eventually got all this clarity and realized he couldn't keep me hidden forever. They would have caught him. So one day when he went to work I just left. I went to the medical center and told them I was an orphan."

That explained how Leb was able to work at HARC when he had a Reboot kid. They didn't know.

A grunt from Callum made me turn. He was leaning against the back of the couch, staring vacantly at the wall. I wrapped my fingers around his arm and it took several seconds for him to blink and turn to look at me. His eyes didn't focus quite right.

"You okay?" I asked. "Do you want some food?"

He didn't respond. His eyes drifted from me to the humans and he snapped his teeth, letting out a low growl. I quickly pulled back my hand and scooted away when he began struggling against the ropes. The humans turned at the commotion and Tony stepped out of the crowd, hands on his hips.

"Why don't you take him back to the bedroom?" he suggested. "He shouldn't be in here with all of us."

Addie grabbed for Callum's bound feet and I hooked my arms under his shoulders. He twisted in our grasp and Addie took hurried steps toward the hallway at the back of the house, opening the second door on the right.

The room held nothing but a bed and a dresser. There was a small pile of clothes in the corner, and a few books on the dresser, but I didn't see much Callum could damage if he thrashed around the room in an effort to escape the ropes.

We put him on the bed and Callum stopped struggling as I ran my hand up his forehead and into his hair. He gave me a faint smile before closing his eyes, and I wished I could crawl into the bed with him.

Addie slipped out of the room and Tony appeared in the doorway, gesturing for me to follow him. I stepped into the hallway and closed the door behind us.

"Here's the thing," he said quietly, taking a quick glance behind him at the humans in the kitchen. "You've got a lot of people in there who want to help you."

I wouldn't have guessed that from the conversations I'd heard, not to mention the way everyone was looking at me.

"But this sort of thing would be most effective if we had a couple weeks to plan," he continued. "We could find the best way in and out, maybe try to get some of our people in key positions the night we do it. But . . ." He glanced at the bedroom door. "They don't want me to tell you, but I don't feel right about it."

"Tell me what?" I asked, my stomach twisting into knots.

"The antidote has a window. If you wait too long, and he's too far gone, it's going to be useless."

I swallowed down the lump in my throat, and when I spoke my voice sounded funny. "What's the window? How long do I have?"

"You definitely don't have a couple weeks," he said. "Which is why they didn't want me to tell you. I'd say you're probably within the acceptable range, but you don't have a lot of time. How long has he been like this?"

"He started feeling weird and shaking three days ago, I think. But he just started blacking out and losing it yesterday."

Tony winced, running a hand through his hair. "Yeah. You don't have a lot of time."

"How much?"

"I don't know. This is a new program; the medical team is still figuring it out themselves. They're letting some of them run the course to see what happens, and it's not good news. But I'd say . . . maybe not more than a day. You might have more, but it's risky."

I pressed a hand to the wall because the world had started to sway a little and I was worried I'd fall over. "So we'd need to go tonight."

"Yes."

I closed my eyes briefly. "What is the point of this? Is HARC trying to get rid of us?"

"Oh no. They need you guys. But they need you as aggressive, mindless soldiers. They're not getting that, particularly from the Under-sixties. This is the solution. Or it will be, if they ever get it to work right."

They needed more of me, basically. Me, with a lot less free will. I took a deep breath and nodded at Tony. "Okay. I'm going tonight, whether you help me or not. You can tell them that."

A smile twitched the edge of his mouth. "Yeah, I figured."

He turned to go and I grabbed a corner of his shirt, making him stop. I crossed my arms over my chest and tried my best not to look at him suspiciously, but I was pretty sure I failed.

"Why are you freeing Reboots?" I asked. "What's wrong with you?"

He laughed, rubbing a hand over his mouth. "What's wrong with me?"

"Yes. You've been getting Reboots out and just letting them go, right?"

"We have been, yes. It was really the only solution."

"Solution to what?"

"To getting rid of HARC. To actually have a shot at equal shares of food and medicine and everything HARC gives to the folks on the other side of the wall because they think we're a lost cause. We have no chance against HARC with all of you on their side."

"But HARC is keeping you safe," I said, the mantra I'd heard a hundred times during my five years as a Reboot. "From us, from the viruses, from criminals . . ."

"Debatable," Tony said, lifting an eyebrow. "They might have started out like that, but they're certainly not doing that anymore. Most of those criminals"—he rolled his eyes when he said the word—"you went after were one of us. Or were just people who wanted to do something crazy like, I don't know, keep their eight-year-old kid who died and came back to life. Everyone bought into this line HARC fed us about you all being these soulless creatures. Most humans have never even talked to a Reboot."

He did have a point. The majority of humans only saw us when we were on assignment, when we were hunting them down. We were rarely allowed to say one word to them.

"Come on," Tony said, jerking his head toward the kitchen. "If we're going to do this tonight we need to start planning."

I pushed open the bedroom door a sliver, but Callum was still, his eyes closed. I wanted to stay with him, but Tony was right. I couldn't just bust into HARC and hope for the best. We needed a plan.

I followed Tony into the kitchen, gesturing for Addie to come as well. The humans were at the table, sitting on the counter, standing in clumps, and they all stopped talking when we walked in.

"Tonight or not at all," Tony said. He put a hand on my shoulder and I jumped, bumping into Addie. "That's Wren's deal."

"Good," Desmond said. "No deal. Dumb idea anyway; let's all go home."

Tony shot him a look and Desmond sighed, leaning back against the wall and muttering to himself. Then they were all talking at once again, and Tony held up his hands.

"Hey!" he yelled. "Just calm down for a second. What are the absolute essentials? What has to happen for us to pull this off?"

"You have to take out the power so they can get in unseen," a short, balding man piped up.

"But you said there were backup generators," Addie said.

"There are," the human replied. "But they take a minute, and you have a much better chance of getting in while the power is out."

"Right," Tony said. "You could probably get into the building before the power kicked on again."

"We'd need to unlock the Reboots' rooms first, right?" Addie asked. "They'll all be locked in that time of night."

"Yes," Desmond said. "Control room on the fourth floor, and there will be armed guards in there. I'd suggest you go together to unlock them. Then Addie can run up to eight to get the Reboots out and Wren can go to the medical labs on seven."

"And where are we all going to go once we escape?" I asked. "Are we just running and hoping for the best?"

Desmond let out a long, exaggerated sigh to let us know how he felt about that idea.

"Suggestion, Des?" Tony asked with a half smile.

"They can't just run," he said, throwing up his arms in annoyance. "Even if some of them make it, HARC will jump in their shuttles and kill half of them from the sky."

"Good point," Addie said, chewing on her lip. "Can we disable the shuttles?"

"If we have a few volunteers willing to do that, yes," Tony said. "We could sneak in the garage and mess with the engines enough to at least delay them. We'd have to move fast, but I think we'd get most of them."

The shuttles. HARC had big shuttles, transport shuttles they usually used to move large groups of human criminals around. It was hundreds of miles to the Reboot reservation, but if we got our hands on a few of those, we'd be there in a matter of hours.

"What if we just took the shuttles?" I asked.

"Sorry?" Tony asked.

"How hard are they to drive? What if we took a couple big ones, like the transport ones, and just flew out of there?"

"Uh . . . well, you could, I suppose," Tony said. "They're not hard to pilot. I could probably draw you guys a diagram and we could have a quick lesson. I imagine you'd crash on landing, but that's not really a concern for Reboots."

"Do they have a GPS tracking system?" Addie asked.

"Yeah. Not hard to remove, though. I could do it by the time y'all were ready to go." His eyes darted around the room. "I'll need help, though."

The silence ticked by and Desmond crossed his arms over his chest with a frown. The rest of the humans seemed intent on avoiding my gaze, except for Gabe, who was lounging against the wall next to a blond guy who looked about our age.

"I'll help," Gabe said.

Tony scrunched his face up like he was going to object, but the blond boy interjected before he could. "Come on. You said we couldn't go in the building. You never said anything about the garage."

Desmond snorted. "You did say that."

Tony rolled his eyes and gave the guys an amused look. "Fine. Gabe and Zeke, you'll be with me." He turned to Desmond. "Are you up for cutting the power? You could do it from several blocks away."

"Yeah. I'll do it." He wasn't thrilled about it, though.

"Okay." Tony clapped his hands together. "Good. I've got a guy bringing us the schematic of the building, so we'll go over that when he gets here. Do you two want to rest or anything? Food, maybe?"

My stomach jumped at the mere mention of food. "Food would be great if you have any."

"Sure thing," he said, pointing to the table. "Have a seat."

Addie and I sat down at the kitchen table and most of the humans cleared out, going to sit in the living room or disappearing out the back door on errands. I kept a watch on Callum's door, but no one went near it.

Tony put sandwiches in front of Addie and me. The bread was soft and fresh, the bean spread and vegetables inside delicious. He seemed pleased as I took giant bites, and I managed a thank-you in between chewing.

"You are very welcome. That one on the counter is for Callum if you want to bring it to him later." He put a couple glasses of water on the table and headed for the humans in the living room. "Let me know if you need anything."

"Weird," Addie muttered, shooting me a confused look.

"Right?" *Let him know if we needed anything?* Bizarre. "You don't think they're up to something, do you?"

She shook her head. "No. My dad wouldn't have led us into a trap." She twisted around and frowned at the humans. "I think they actually want to help us."

I turned and followed her gaze to where Tony and Desmond were standing, heads close together as they talked.

"I think they mostly want to help themselves," I said quietly. "But I'll take it."

THIRTY-ONE

ADDIE DECIDED TO REST AFTER LUNCH, SO TONY LET HER HAVE his room and suggested I take a nap as well. I declined. There was no way I would be able to sleep, not with Callum tied up in the other room and my stomach in knots.

Instead I headed down the hallway with Callum's sandwich and peeked inside the guest room. He was on his side, his eyes fixed on the wall in front of him. His arms and legs were still bound.

"Is that uncomfortable?" I asked, crossing the room and putting the plate on the nightstand. "I can untie you while you eat if you want."

He didn't respond, so I knelt down next to the bed and ran

my fingers into his hair. "Callum."

He didn't move an inch. His eyes were empty, and when I waved my hand in front of his face he didn't even blink.

What if it was already too late? What if we'd already missed the window?

My heart was beating too loudly now. It was pounding in my ears, the only sound in the quiet room.

"Callum." My voice was desperate as I shook his shoulder. The bed creaked under his weight as I shifted him.

Nothing.

That stare that saw nothing was too awful. I shook him harder, repeating his name as the ache in my chest grew. Tears were on my cheeks before I realized I was going to cry, and I pressed my hand to my mouth to stifle a sob. It came anyway, echoing through the bedroom, followed quickly by another. I'd thought of crying as a release, but the tears were almost painful. I wanted to stuff them back inside. My body refused to listen.

I let go of his shoulder and sank down on the floor. Maybe I should have run to get Tony or Addie and ask them if he was okay, but I was too scared. I didn't want them to give me that sympathetic look again.

"Wren?"

My head popped up at the sound of Callum's voice. He blinked at me, his brow lowered as he twisted his hands against the ropes.

"What's wrong?"

I leaped onto the bed and untied his hands in seconds, pressing my head into his neck as he wrapped his arms around me. He nuzzled his cheek against my skin, his warm breath tickling my neck.

"I'm sorry," I said, taking a deep breath.

"You don't have to apologize for crying."

"No, for all of this. For letting you attack that human and for breaking you out at a really terrible time. I should have checked first. I knew they were doing this to Under-sixties and I didn't even think to check."

"Yes," he said, his voice tinged with amusement, "next time you risk your life saving me, could you please do proper planning beforehand? This is just unacceptable."

I laughed, hugging him tightly with one arm.

"You don't need to apologize," he said, his lips brushing against my ear. "If anything I should thank you."

"Please don't. It will make me feel terrible."

He chuckled, running his fingers under my chin until I turned my face up to him. He kissed me, which felt sort of like a thank-you, but it was one I didn't mind. When he pulled away he gave me a sad little smile.

"Just don't leave me like this, okay?"

I sniffled, lowering my eyes so I didn't have to look at him.

"I don't want them to make me into this . . ." He looked down at himself. "This crazy thing." He planted a soft kiss on my cheek. "It's like they won, you know?"

It was exactly like they'd won.

"I don't want to kill more people." He scrunched up his face. "Or worse, eat anyone. So, if it doesn't work out, don't just let me be like this, okay?"

I nodded, pressing my lips together to stop the tears. "Okay."

Callum was quiet for a moment, his eyebrows lowered in thought. "And even if we don't get the antidote, you should help them." He nodded at the door. "Go to the reservation and get the other Reboots to help them, too."

"The humans?"

"Yeah. You can't let HARC win. Not after everything they've done. So even if I don't . . . if I don't make it, I think you should help them."

He knew I had very little interest in helping the humans. All I wanted was for him to be better so we could get away from them and never come back. And I didn't want to think about what I would do if Callum didn't make it, but sticking around to join forces with humans was not on the top of my list.

"That won't be an issue. You'll be fine."

"Wren, think about it at least. You shouldn't let the fact that you're a badass go to waste."

I managed a laugh. "I will think about it."

It was a lie. I wasn't going to think about any scenario that didn't include him.

Callum eventually faded away again, even though I could

see him trying to fight it. I sat on the floor for a long time, until I couldn't take those vacant eyes anymore. I refused to panic about it, so I tied him up and moved to the living room, where I spent the afternoon and early evening pacing back and forth.

The sun had just set, and I was anxious to head over to the facility, but Tony insisted the best time was very early morning. The facility had the least guards on duty between the hours of four and six a.m., and it was best to go near six, since a few lab personnel would be on duty by then. No one could tell me what the antidote looked like, so I might need a human to point it out.

Tony was at the kitchen table with about ten other humans, poring over the schematic of the Austin HARC facility. A larger group than I had expected had agreed to help us. A few had left, saying they were certain we'd all be dead by morning, but the rest seemed thrilled to have such an ambitious plan after years of trying to defeat HARC.

Gabe slipped through the front door with Zeke, the blond boy from earlier. Gabe was holding a black canvas bag against his chest, and he nodded at Tony.

"I got them," he said, dropping the bag on the couch and reaching inside. He pulled out several black guns and dumped odd-shaped yellow bullets onto the table. I frowned, leaning over to grab one of them.

"What is this?" I asked, turning the yellow plastic bullet

around in my fingers. It had a tiny needle coming out of it.

"Tranquilizer darts," Gabe said. "Tony doesn't want you killing humans while you're in there."

I turned to Tony with raised eyebrows, and he leaned back in his chair to meet my gaze. I held up the yellow dart. "These things actually work? Quickly?"

"Within a couple seconds. Aim for the chest or arm or leg."

"How long will they be out?" I asked.

"Hours. You don't have to worry about that. I'll give you your real gun back, but I don't want you to use it in there. Most of those guys are just doing their job. And some of them are with us."

I nodded, dropping the dart on the table. "Fine."

"Did you find some helmets?" Tony asked.

"Yeah, Henry will be by soon with them," Gabe replied.

Addie grabbed one of the tranq guns off the table and stuck a dart inside, studying the gun curiously. Gabe darted behind the couch and she snorted. "Oh, relax, human. I know how to use a gun."

"Gabe," he corrected, wincing as she pointed it at the wall behind Zeke.

"Come out from behind the couch, *Gabe*. I'm not going to shoot you. Unless you deserve it."

He crept out of hiding, cautiously reaching for the gun. "I'll just take that."

Addie rolled her eyes as she handed it over, and I shot her an amused look.

"Hey." I turned at the sound of Desmond's voice. He plopped a ladle of something into a bowl. "Do you want dinner?"

"Yes, thank you."

"Then come and eat."

I scurried into the kitchen, peering into the bowl. It was some sort of stew. I gave him a grateful look as I spooned some into my mouth. I hadn't expected to be fed again.

"I thought the lower numbers were supposed to be nicer!" I heard Gabe exclaim from the living room, and I glanced over to see Addie holding a tranq gun to his chest.

"Adina, stop torturing Gabe," Tony called with a chuckle.

I almost laughed, but Desmond was staring at me like he was plotting my demise. I swallowed my food and wiped at my mouth. He'd been quiet and moody all evening, obviously not in favor of the plan.

"Why are you helping if you don't want to?" I asked.

"I said I would, didn't I?" he asked. He'd pulled his brown hair back into a short ponytail, and the sharp edges of his face looked harsh. He wasn't an attractive man, even when he was happy.

"And you seem so pleased about it."

All I got in response was a glare. I considered taking my food in the other room, but I had too many questions. While he didn't seem scared of me, he appeared to hate me only slightly less than the average human did.

"But why help us at all if you hate us?" I pressed.

He let out a long sigh and leaned against the counter. "I don't hate you. I just don't trust you're not going to come back and kill us all."

Valid concern, in my opinion. "So you decided to free us and take your chances?"

He paused, sliding his hands into the pockets of his jeans. "There was a discussion a few years ago. When we decided we needed the Reboots gone to have any sort of success against HARC, some people thought we should kill you."

"Ah. And you saw their point."

He cleared his throat. "Maybe a little. But then Tony was like, 'Let's just meet one. Let's go rescue one and talk to them without HARC watching and see what they think.' So we did."

"And the Reboot was . . . what? Nice?"

"No. Or hell, I don't know. She sat in the living room and sobbed. Wouldn't say one word to us."

"She probably thought you were going to kill her."

"Yeah. None of us really expected that reaction, though. We thought she'd fight back, attack us. When she didn't and it came down to it, we couldn't kill her. We'd heard rumors of Reboots up north, so we got her as far as we could and let her go. Asked her to talk to any Reboots she found about the possibility of them taking in any others we rescued. You know, see if they'd be willing to work with us. And they were."

"Why couldn't you kill her?" I asked. "HARC eliminates us all the time. Tony must have seen it."

"I'm sure he has. But it's different, when you're sitting with a fifteen-year-old who doesn't really seem all that different from you." He shrugged. "I've always thought we were taking a terrible risk, freeing you, but it was the best of two shitty options. So here I am. Hoping you lot will be grateful enough to not come back and destroy us all."

"If it helps, I have no interest in coming back to kill any of you."

A hint of a smile crossed his face. "I appreciate that."

"Des, stop it; they're not murderers." Tony put his hands on my shoulders and I jumped, almost dropping my spoon. It was weird he didn't mind touching me.

I minded it, though, so I sidestepped his hands and frowned at him. He either didn't notice or didn't care, because he just smiled at me. I glanced at Desmond again. Maybe he was the only sane one here.

"Wren, you want to come map this out again with me?" Tony asked. "I want to make sure my guys know where they're going, but they'll be following you."

I nodded and joined him at the table, standing behind the humans while Tony again outlined the route we'd take to get inside. It was dark now, and he had to move a lamp closer to the table for us to see it.

"And then you'll come out here," Tony finished, running

his finger through the HARC lobby. "Or wherever you want, I guess. After you release a hundred Reboots I think you can probably take your pick of exits."

A smile tugged at the edges of my lips.

He had no idea.

THIRTY-TWO

I HUGGED MY ARMS AGAINST MY CHEST, SHIVERING IN THE cool night air as I stared up at HARC from the shelter of the trees that surrounded the building. It stood tall and black at the edge of the Austin slums—fifteen or twenty stories high. I'd never come out far enough to see it as a kid.

A group of about ten rebels stood several yards to my left, dressed in what looked like black HARC uniforms. They were fakes, but we were hoping no one would notice in the chaos, and the rebels would be able to get upstairs to steal the weapons and medicine HARC had been hoarding. It was a huge risk, and I could see the fear in their tight, blank expressions.

Callum grunted behind me and I looked down to see Tony

and Addie tightening his ropes to a boulder. We'd dug a hole next to it, only a few feet deep, but enough to keep him hidden while we were inside. His legs were securely bound, the cloth around his mouth muffled his occasional growls, and he could barely move.

Addie replaced a couple of the tree branches over the hole as she and Tony crawled out of it. It was barely visible through the thick bushes, but I could see Callum's dead eyes glinting as he looked up at us. He'd never come back.

I was terrified it was too late.

I turned away and walked a few feet until I could see the sky. The sun was just beginning to rise and the horizon was bathed in red and orange and blue.

"I went up north once when I was kid, just before the virus hit." I closed my eyes as my mom's voice filled my ears. *"We drove for three days from Austin, and when we got there I remember looking up at the sky and wondering where the rest of it went. There's more sky in Texas, darlin'. You ain't ever gonna know anything else, but look up and appreciate it occasionally anyway."*

"Wren."

I opened my eyes, and they followed the streaks of color until they disappeared in the distance.

"Wren, let's go. Desmond should have the power off in a few minutes," Addie said.

I turned and took the helmet she held out to me. I secured it around my chin as Tony looked down at Callum.

"He should be fine there until you get back," he said with a nod. "No one will be out here; they'll be chasing y'all in the opposite direction."

"Do you know how long it will take for the antidote to work?" I asked. "Will we be able to run right away?"

"Should be really fast. The lower the number, the faster it works, in my experience." He paused, clearing his throat. "What do you want me to do with him if you don't come back?"

I avoided looking at Callum. I needed to be focused, and every time I caught a glimpse of him I started to panic. "I'll come back." There were no other options.

He opened his mouth, seemed to think better of it, and gave me a sad smile. It was not the most encouraging expression. "Okay, hon." He turned to join Gabe and Zeke with the other humans.

Addie and I headed closer to the chain-link fence that surrounded the HARC property. It wasn't electrified, but we were to wait until after they shut off the power so the cameras wouldn't catch us.

We stood in the shadows, the only sound the chirping of the crickets and the breeze blowing through the trees. My heart beat so loudly I was sure Addie could hear it, but she just stood there stoically, staring at the building and the one security guard in sight. I pushed away the screaming fear in my chest, pushed away the little nagging voice that was reminding me this was my only chance to save Callum. I didn't need fear or doubt right now.

I just needed to focus.

The lights clicked off and I ran, the sound of boots hitting the grass all around me. I wrapped my fingers around the metal and jumped up, flying over and landing a few seconds before Addie. The humans trailed behind us.

I held my hand out as we approached the building and everyone behind me stopped. Pulling my tranq gun from my pants, I crept across the grass and onto the slab of concrete. My boot squeaked as I stepped forward and the officer on duty whirled around, mouth wide open as I squeezed the trigger.

The dart lodged in his chest. He took one step before his head began to droop, and I caught him as he fell, hauling him against the building in hopes that the camera wouldn't spot him right away.

I grabbed the key and access card off the guard's belt and stuck the key in the lock, throwing the door open and motioning for Addie to hurry. She darted through and I followed, holding it open for the rebels as well.

The lobby was dark and deserted, the round desk in the center of the room empty. I'd never seen a HARC lobby before. Reboots were always dropped off on the roof by shuttle.

They had posters on the walls. Signs advertising their brilliance.

Count on HARC for the cure! The woman in the poster smiled, apparently completely cured of whatever had ailed her.

HARC protects! That poster had a picture of Reboots on it, although they were in the distance and blurry next to a shuttle.

Addie turned and gave the posters a baffled look as we passed.

"Are they serious?" she muttered.

The black tile looked like a dark river as we hurried across it to the stairwell. We stepped aside and let the humans go up first, since they were headed to the top floors with the food storage, human meds, and the armory. I was almost sad as I watched them lumber up the stairs. It was a suicide mission for at least half of them, if not all, and they knew it.

I let the door close softly behind me. We sped up the pitch-black stairs, taking them two at a time until we reached the fourth floor. Dim lights clicked on in the stairwell. The generators were on.

Addie looked back at me as she gripped the door handle. I nodded.

She opened it just enough to peek through. "Two guards at the end of the hallway," she whispered. "At least two in the room, as far as I can tell." She inched the door open a bit wider. "See where we're going?"

The white hallway stretched out in front of me. The guards at the end were bored, leaning against the wall and talking quietly to each other, despite the momentary blackout.

To the left was the control room. The doors were open, and one officer sat in front of a large computer as another peered over his shoulder. Judging from their relaxed expressions (and the fact that neither of them had their guns out), they hadn't spotted us on the camera feeds yet.

Good news.

I nodded to Addie. "I'll take the two in the room."

She threw open the door. I crouched down and darted around her toward the control room as gunfire exploded from the end of the hall. The guards whirled from the computer, reaching for their guns. But they were too slow.

I fired twice, hitting the chest of one and the neck of the other. They hit the ground in seconds, just before I heard the thuds of the two humans in the hall.

I let out a slow breath. Step one down.

I turned to give Addie a victorious smile, but it faltered at her dazed expression. She blinked and raised her fingers to her temple.

There was blood.

I jumped over one of the officers and pushed her helmet back. The blood soaked her hair, covering my fingers as I searched for the bullet hole.

"No, it's okay," she said. She trembled as she nudged my hand away and pulled her helmet back into place. "It just grazed me."

I nodded, even though my stomach had twisted into knots. It looked like it had more than grazed her.

Addie swiped her fingers across her bloody forehead and

stepped past me into the control room, shoving the closest human away with her foot. She sat down at the computer. She tapped the screen a few times as I paced behind her, nervously glancing out into the hallway as I waited for more guards to barrel through the doors.

I was incredibly lucky that bullet hadn't hit her more directly. I didn't think I could get to medical and free the Reboots. I would be stuck in here without her, and Callum would be stuck in that hole until HARC found him.

I gripped the edge of the doorframe, watching as Addie touched the screen again. She stopped suddenly, leaning back, and I opened my mouth to ask what was wrong.

Doors Unlocked flashed across the screen in bright red letters.

"Got it," she said, jumping up from the chair.

We ran through the hallway and back into the stairwell, a burst of energy exploding in my body as my brain realized we might actually make it.

"How long do you want me to wait?" Addie called as we flew up the stairs. "I'll probably make it to the shuttles first."

"As long as you can," I said as I passed the sixth floor. "But if HARC starts closing in, just take off. Find someone else to fly the second shuttle."

"Okay."

I stopped in front of the seventh-floor door and glanced at Addie as she continued up to eight. She gave me an encouraging smile, but I could see the blood still trickling out of her helmet. She had to wipe it away again as she darted up the steps.

"Good luck," I called.

She laughed. "I think you need it more than me. I'm about to get backup from a hundred Reboots."

She disappeared around the corner and I tightened my grip on the tranq gun as I turned to face the door again. This was it. If I didn't get to the medical lab there was no hope for Callum.

I reached for the handle and wrapped my fingers around the cool metal.

The door swung open from the other side and I leaped back, grabbing on to the railing before I tumbled down the stairs.

Three officers poured into the stairwell, guns raised.

I ducked as the first officer pulled his trigger. I aimed my gun at his leg and sunk a dart into it, leaping back as he fell headfirst for the stairs.

I got off another shot, hitting the second officer in the stomach as a bullet from the third guard rocketed into my shoulder. I grabbed his arm as he tried to fire again and twisted it behind his back, pressing the tranq gun directly into his back. I let him go as he slumped forward.

The excitement of a fight crept in over my fear, and I almost smiled as I jumped over the officers' bodies and reached for the door. I threw it open to see a long, white hallway, deserted except for one lone human running away from me. A human in a white lab coat.

My eyes widened as I reached for the real gun at my hip. I needed that human.

"Stop!" I yelled, purposefully angling the gun too far to the left as I fired.

But he kept running. His shoes squeaked on the tile as he headed for the exit door at the other end of the hallway. I took off after him, aiming my gun at his right shoulder. I pulled the trigger.

He let out a scream and stumbled, grunting as his knees hit the floor. He whipped his head around and his eyes widened when he saw me coming.

He pressed a bloody hand to the floor as he tried to get to his feet, but I was there first. I hauled him up by the back of his lab coat and wrapped my arm around his neck. I glanced down at the name on his coat. Bishop.

"Bishop," I said, squeezing my arm tighter to his neck as he squirmed. "I'll make you a deal. You help me into that room"—I pointed to the medical lab, behind clear glass to our left—"and I won't kill you."

Bishop said nothing. He continued to wriggle and choke in my grasp, tears running down his cheeks. He was young, in his early twenties perhaps, with a round, cute face. He was on the short side for a man, but I still had to stand on my tiptoes to hold him.

"Hey," I said, loosening my grip against his neck just slightly. "Deal?"

He nodded. A strangled sob escaped his mouth and he opened it wider. Preparing to scream.

I pressed the gun to his temple as I pulled him down the deserted white hallway. "Screaming is my very least favorite thing."

His mouth snapped shut.

I stopped in front of the lab door and reached down for Bishop's key card. I swiped it across the lock and the door slid open. Bishop staggered forward as I dragged him into the room.

The narrow space stretched out almost the whole length of the hallway. Computer screens lined the walls and lab tables ran down the center. It smelled like disinfectant and Reboot. Someone had tried to erase the smell of death and failed.

Tony had said the antidote would be at the back of the lab, locked up tight in a large glass room. I lugged the human down the center of the lab, past the computers and long tables and thick books.

The vials were lined up in neat rows in cases, just like Tony had said. They were also labeled just as Tony had suspected, with random letters and numbers I didn't understand. There was no way for me to know which one I needed.

I swiped Bishop's card against the lock and the doors opened. I stepped into the cool room and released my arm from the human's neck, poking my gun into his good shoulder.

"Which one is the antidote?"

He blinked at me. There were tears on his eyelashes as he

squinted down at my bar code.

"One-seventy-eight," I said. "It's not for me."

He hesitated, looking from the vials to me. He must have known he could lie to me. He could point me to some awful drug that would do terrible things to Callum. I was relying very much on this human's fear of me.

"I just told you I'm One-seventy-eight," I said, pressing the gun harder into his shoulder. "It doesn't bother me in the least to kill you."

He took in a shaky breath and pointed down to the cases on the bottom shelf. There were three of them, with about fifty vials per case. The liquid inside was murky, almost gray.

"Pull them out," I said. "All of them."

A sound above me made me pause, glance up at the ceiling. Running. The sound of a hundred Reboots running. The ceiling was shaking, laughing and shouting filling the air.

Addie had done it.

I smiled before focusing on the human again, who was still standing there staring at me. I jerked my head at him and he got down on his knees and pulled the first case off the shelf, stealing a glance in my direction.

"You've killed us all," he whispered.

"How do you figure?" I gestured to the vials around me. "I'd say you're the guilty ones, injecting us with this crap."

"We're trying to protect ourselves from you," he said, wiping his hand across his nose and setting the second case on top of the first. "Now you've . . ." He pointed to the ceiling, to the eighth floor, where he must have also recognized the sound of Reboots running. "You've let them all out."

"We saved them."

Bishop grunted his disagreement and placed a third case on top of the stack. "There. That's it."

"You sure those are the right ones? Because I'm going to go out there and test it right away. I'll come back for you if it's wrong. Trust me, you don't want me to come back."

He nodded. "That's it."

I wanted to smile and scream and jump up and down, but I held it back. I was so close. All I had to do was get out of the building.

I leaned down to grab the vials.

I realized my mistake as soon as I took my eyes off Bishop.

He sprinted out of the glass room. I whirled around and stumbled after him.

Too late. My hands hit the glass.

I was locked inside.

THIRTY-THREE

BISHOP'S FACE BROKE INTO A GRIN AS HE STARED AT ME FROM the other side of the glass. He fumbled around in his pocket and produced a com, almost dropping it as he held it up to his mouth.

"Bishop," he said into it. "Medical lab on the seventh floor. Tell Officer Mayer and Ms. Palm to get to Austin right away. I've got One-seventy-eight."

I've got One-seventy-eight. The words rang in my ears, caused my throat to close up. He couldn't have me. I wasn't failing because of this one little human.

I pulled the gun out of my pocket. The glass couldn't be bulletproof.

It couldn't be.

I fired one shot. The bullet flew straight through, leaving a spiderweb of cracks around the hole. Bishop's eyes widened, and he took several steps back, slamming into a lab table.

I grinned, lifting the gun again.

Nothing.

I was out of bullets. I reached for my tranq gun, which had plenty of shots left, but that was useless with the human on the other side of the glass.

Bishop let out a visible sigh and spoke into his com again. "No, it's fine. Come quick, though."

"Don't move," I heard a voice on the other end of the com say. *"Keep her in your sights."*

Bishop swallowed and nodded, taking a few more steps back from the glass.

I looked down at the vials at my feet. No. I wasn't letting Callum die a blank, emotionless HARC robot.

I was getting out of here.

I lifted my boot and kicked the glass as hard as I could.

A crack snaked up from the bullet hole to the ceiling.

I kicked it again. Another crack.

Bishop stumbled as he scrambled to the other side of the lab. "Hey!" he yelled into the com. "Hurry! She's—"

The glass shattered. I let out a whoop and launched myself across the lab, leaving the vials for now. Bishop was headed for the door and I wasn't going to make the same mistake twice.

I grabbed him by the hair and he yelled as I jerked his head back. He gasped, strangled noises escaping his mouth.

"Please don't kill me," he sobbed.

I didn't want to prove him right, so I punched him instead. I hit him so hard I heard a crack and he sunk to the ground. I fired a dart into his neck for good measure and his body sagged.

Racing back to the vials, I scooped them up in my arms and bolted out of the lab and through the hallway. It was still empty, and I threw open the door to the stairwell.

Reboots streamed down the stairs, running and jumping and laughing. They all had on their helmets and field gear and I didn't see a single guard among the crowd.

I stepped into the crowd and let them carry me along down the stairs. Explosions and gunshots rocked the building but the cheers and excitement didn't fade in the least. I couldn't help grinning.

We were almost free.

As we poured through the door on the ground floor, I saw the lobby was full of smoke and dead or unconscious HARC officers. I clutched the cases of vials close to my chest as we burst through the back door. The early morning sun burned my eyes and I squinted as I sprinted across the grass to the trees where I'd left Callum.

Two big HARC shuttles were parked immediately to my left. Addie stood in front of one, directing Reboots. She beamed at the sight of me. The blood was gone from her forehead, and

I felt a tiny burst of relief that she was okay.

"I'll take those!" she called, rushing over. I dumped the cases in her outstretched arms and plucked out one vial for Callum. "Get him quick. We've got to go!"

Addie turned back to the shuttles and I raced to the fence, wrapping my fingers around the metal and hurling my body over. My momentum carried me into the trees, where I vaulted a fallen log, clutching the antidote. The hole was just ahead of me and I quickly tossed the leaves and branches covering it aside.

Callum was curled up in a ball in the dirt, his eyes half-open. He didn't move or make any indication he'd heard me approach.

I lowered myself down in the hole and tugged him up to a sitting position. He was limp, an empty shell.

I jabbed the needle into his arm and pushed the liquid in.

Nothing happened.

It would take a minute. That was all it was. I balked at the alternatives as I untied his legs and arms and plopped down in his lap. I put my hands on his cheeks, my panicked attempts at breathing filling the silence. His head swung back and forth as he looked beyond me at nothing in the distance.

"Callum," I whispered, my fingers inching up into his hair.

What if it was too late? What if it wasn't the right one? My throat closed and I pressed my lips together to keep in the scream. What if that human had given me something else? What if—

Callum took in a sharp breath and his head jerked up. He blinked a few times and color bled back into his face.

The laugh escaped my chest as a strange sort of gasp and I wrapped my arms around his neck and pressed my lips to his. I trailed kisses across his cheeks until he laughed, too.

I ran my hands up to his neck and stared into his eyes. "You feel okay? You feel normal again?"

A smile spread across his face. The big, happy, hopeful smile I loved. He nodded, leaning forward until his lips brushed my cheek. "You're shockingly good sometimes, you know that?"

I laughed and gave him another quick kiss and hopped up. "We've got to get out of here." I dug my fingers into the dirt and scrambled up from the hole, turning to help Callum. He'd already climbed out behind me and was on his feet, staring at the scene in front of him with wide eyes.

Reboots ran across the lawn and officers lay unconscious on the ground. The back of the HARC building was riddled with bullet holes. Smoke poured from several windows on the upper levels.

I reached for Callum's hand we ran out of the trees and launched ourselves over the fence and across the grass. "In! In!" Addie yelled. "Everyone, now!"

I didn't see Tony or any of the other rebels anywhere, and I paused near Addie on my way to the second shuttle. "Tony?" I yelled.

"Gone. They made it out." She slammed shut the back door

to her shuttle and tossed me the tracker locator. "I got another one inside for my shuttle."

"Thanks." I passed the locator to Callum as I threw open the driver's door to the second shuttle. I gestured for him to get in, and he raised his eyebrow.

"You're driving?"

"Just get in," I said with a laugh. He climbed into the passenger's seat and I followed, clicking the door shut behind me. The dash in front of me looked very much like the diagram Tony had drawn. The lever in the center took us up or down; the buttons on either side were for landing gear and communications. Someone had already started the shuttle, so everything in front of me was lit up, ready for takeoff.

Bullets pinged the door and I squinted out the window to see a few straggler HARC officers staggering across the lawn. I quickly grasped the center lever, like Tony had taught me, and pushed it up.

We were off the ground. I pushed it higher and we lurched. I could hear people in the back yelling and crashing into one another, and Callum was gripping the dashboard in front of him, but I focused on flying, pushing the lever forward to increase our speed.

"Here," I said, pulling out my knife. "Give them the locator. They all need to get their trackers out as fast as possible."

He nodded and disappeared into the back of the shuttle. I pushed the lever to the right until I could see the other shuttle hovering not far from us. I followed its lead as it swung north.

A hand brushed under my chin and I jumped, turning to see Callum. He grinned as he unhooked my helmet and kissed my cheek.

"I'm driving here," I said with a laugh as he kissed me again.

"I noticed. What a show-off," he said with a chuckle. "Saving just me wasn't enough for you?"

I grinned as he kissed me again. He plopped down in the seat next to me, both our helmets in his lap. Behind me, I could hear the clinks as trackers hit the floor of the shuttle and the Reboots celebrated.

"Do we know where we're going?" Callum asked, leaning forward to look out the window. The slums were below us, and a few humans were beginning to mill around.

"Addie has the map; we're following her," I said. "But I know the general direction if we get separated."

As we watched, the side door of Addie's shuttle opened a crack and tiny pieces of silver caught the sunlight as they rained down. Trackers.

"Hey!" I called, twisting around in my seat. "Toss your trackers out the door!" A few Reboots nodded, and I turned to face forward.

We passed over the HARC fence at the edge of Austin and I leaned sideways to look out the window to my right. The sky was clear behind me, the HARC building growing smaller and smaller in the distance.

I let out a long sigh as I turned to look at Callum, a smile spreading across my face at his excited expression. I focused on the sky in front of me again, gripping the lever and pushing it forward just a little. We were a few shuttle lengths behind Addie, and I pushed the button marked *cruise*. The shuttle continued forward as I let go of the lever.

"Soooooo . . ."

I turned around to see a girl about my age gripping the edges of the pilot's door, a crooked smile on her face. She tilted her head to one side, her dark ponytail swinging.

"We're sort of wondering where we're going." She looked from me to Callum. "And who you guys are."

A younger Reboot stood on his toes to peek over her shoulder. "I heard Addie say she was One-seventy-eight."

"Yeah," I said, holding my hand out. "Wren. One-seventy-eight."

She raised her eyebrows as she shook my hand. "Beth. One-forty-two."

"Callum," he said. He didn't offer his number, but I saw her glance at his wrist and frown in confusion.

"We're headed north," I said. "Toward the old Texas border. There's supposedly a Reboot reservation there."

The Reboots behind her got quieter, several of them shuffling closer to hear.

"Where Reboots are living by themselves?" Beth asked.

"Yes. That's what we've heard, anyway. We have a map."

Beth's eyes bounced around the shuttle. "Don't you think you might scare the crap out of them, arriving in a couple HARC shuttles?"

"We're landing several miles from the reservation and we'll walk in." I left out the part where the human rebels suggested we do that, to avoid getting shot down. We could fill them in about the rebels later.

Beth looked from me to Callum. The way everyone stood behind her quietly made me think she was one of the highest numbers in the Austin facility, if not the very highest.

She let out a soft laugh, taking a few steps back. "Interesting plan. I hope it works." She jerked her head toward the front window. "Some of you guys should take a look."

I turned my attention forward as a few Reboots stepped into the pilot's area. The shuttles weren't meant to fly too far off the ground, so we weren't high above the trees. Open land spread out in front of us, a lake sparkling in the distance. I could see pieces of old, deserted highways where greenery was poking through the black asphalt.

Callum leaned forward in his chair, blinking at the scene around him. He was still a little pale, but otherwise looked like himself.

"Do you feel okay?" I asked softly, scooting sideways until I could put my hand on his leg.

He turned, taking my hand and pressing his lips against it. "I'm fine."

He slid one hand up my neck and inched forward until he could press his lips to mine. I reached for his hand, melting into the kiss. Behind me, someone cleared her throat.

"Are we kissing or flying?" Beth asked, her annoyance tinged with amusement.

I pulled away from Callum with a grin. "Right. Flying."

The shuttle quieted some as we continued north, the occasional Reboot wandering up front to check out the view. The land was mostly trees and grass, but there was an occasional animal or two. We flew over a big group of cows at one point, and I wondered how the Reboots in the reservation got food. Did they hunt? Farm?

The Austin Reboots didn't spend too much time up front with me and Callum. They mostly spoke in hushed whispers behind us, casting suspicious glances our way. I couldn't really blame them.

Many of the Reboots stared at me but didn't come over to talk, and I ran my finger over the *178* printed on my wrist.

"You think the numbers will matter there?" I asked quietly.

"I hope not," Callum said, leaning back with a sigh. "I mean, I don't think so. HARC is the one who started all that."

But we bought into it. We separated ourselves into groups and acted accordingly. I glanced back at Beth, who was standing with two girls and a guy. I didn't even need to ask to know they were the One-twenties of the Austin facility. Their faces were serious, the guy's eyebrows knitted together as he listened to Beth. The other Reboots milled around them, but no one came too close.

I had no idea how Reboots would divide themselves up when left to their own devices. Maybe they wouldn't. Maybe Callum was right, and the numbers wouldn't matter without HARC around.

I looked up at him and smiled, turning my wrist over so I couldn't see my number. I hoped so.

Callum straightened suddenly, pointing in front of him. "Look."

I turned to his window to see the remains of a city. It was bigger than any one I'd known and lay smack in the middle of a circle of highways. Parts of the city looked untouched from this distance, but as we flew closer I could see destroyed buildings.

"Which city was that?" I asked.

"I don't know. I think we're too far west for the original Dallas or Fort Worth." He looked at me with a smile. "We should go see those sometime. I heard they're huge."

I'd never considered going to any of the old cities. I wouldn't have guessed it would be appealing, but I felt a spark of excitement at the prospect. "We should."

Addie's shuttle started to descend about twenty minutes later, and I held my hand out to Callum. "Helmet. Put yours on, too." I glanced at the Reboots in back. "Everyone put your helmets on and brace yourselves!"

"But I don't see anything," Callum said worriedly as he

handed my helmet over and strapped on his own.

I scanned the area in front of us. The land was pretty flat, but I couldn't see that far at this height.

"We're landing a few miles out," I said. "We still have to walk a ways."

He nodded, taking one more glance around as we headed for the earth. "We're totally going to crash, aren't we?"

I grinned at him. "Probably."

I pushed the lever down and tried to lower the shuttle slowly, but the ground was suddenly right there and we were smashing into it. I locked my arms against the dash as we flipped once, twice, three times. We ended up on our sides, Callum crumpled against the window, and when I pulled off my seat belt I tumbled on top of him.

"Sorry," I said with a laugh, grabbing the edge of the driver's seat to pull my way to the door. I shoved it open and crawled out, landing in orange-red dirt. Addie's shuttle skidded to a stop a few yards away, and I squinted at it in the sun. She'd had a rough landing, too, but at least they didn't flip. The land beyond her shuttle was flat and dry, the sky stretching out massively above the red dirt.

A strong wind whipped across my face as I offered my hand to Callum and he climbed out beside me. I opened the back door of the shuttle to see the Reboots were all piled on top of one another but grinning, their eyes wide as they took in the scene behind me. They chatted happily as they emerged.

"Hey, nice landing!" Addie called, and I turned to see her standing next to her shuttle, grinning.

I laughed and shrugged my shoulders. "They're all still alive!"

"Sort of a low bar you set for yourself, huh?" Beth asked, playfully punching my shoulder as I helped her out of the shuttle.

I laughed again, the sound echoing in the sudden silence. The chatter and giggles around me stopped all at once. Everyone went quiet.

Callum touched my arm, and I turned to see a grin spreading across his face.

He pointed in front of him at a large wooden sign.

REBOOT TERRITORY
ALL HUMANS TURN BACK

ACKNOWLEDGMENTS

SO MANY PEOPLE HELPED TO GET *REBOOT* INTO READERS' HANDS, and I am forever grateful to all of you. Thank you to:

My agent, Emmanuelle Morgen, who had incredible faith in *Reboot* and worked so hard to make sure Wren and Callum found a good publishing home. And thank you to Alison, Ellen, Judy, and Sarah at Stonesong for your enthusiasm and support!

My editor, Kari Sutherland, for your editorial insight and amazing attention to detail. This book truly became so much better in your hands. And thank you to Farrin Jacobs, Alice Jerman, and the whole team at Harper for taking such good care of me and *Reboot*.

Lucy Stille and Lane Shefter-Bishop, for the amazing work you did with the book's film rights, and everyone at Paradigm, from my mailroom buddies to the chairman, who reached out to celebrate with me. And thank you, Lindsey and Peggy, for providing me with happy days at work so I was refreshed and ready to write this story at night.

To all the other writers who took this journey with me: the Lucky 13s, for answering all my questions (even the dumb ones) and being so wonderfully supportive. Natalie, Kim, Michelle, Amy, Ruth, Corinne, L.J., Deborah, Gemma, Lori, and Stephanie—thank you for sharing your stories with me and listening to mine.

John T., Sara, and Sean, for offering to read and crit not just *Reboot* but the last book; Vong and Hannah R., for your feedback on the first part of the manuscript; and Hannah P., for being *Reboot*'s first fan and pointing out that I was using the wrong "its" (you were right). All my friends who read my work, celebrated with me, and didn't get mad when I wouldn't hang out on Sundays—Michelle and Josh, Sara and Sean, Mely and JP—thank you for putting up with my weirdness!

My family, for always encouraging my writing, even when I was scribbling out novels by hand. Thank you to my mom and dad, for sharing your love of reading with me and allowing me to chase my dreams.

Mike, thank you for your unfailing optimism and

enthusiasm, and for never getting mad when I ignored you to spend time with imaginary people.

And my sister, Laura, the first person to tell me she loved *Reboot* and the only person to have read every single bad book that came before it. Thank you for being my first and best crit partner.

READ ON FOR A SNEAK PEEK AT

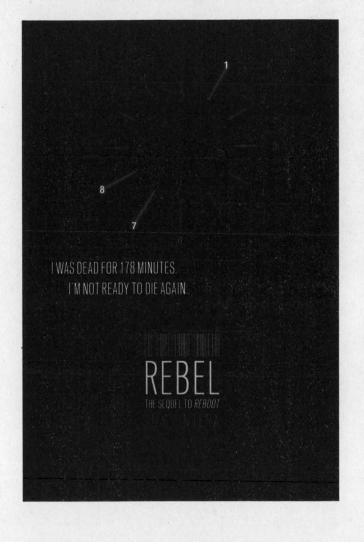

I WAS DEAD FOR 178 MINUTES.

I'M NOT READY TO DIE AGAIN.

REBEL

THE SEQUEL TO *REBOOT*

ONE

CALLUM

WREN WAS SILENT.

She stood completely still next to me, staring straight ahead with that look she got sometimes, like she was either happy or plotting to kill someone. Either way, I loved that look.

The other Reboots around us started jumping up and down and yelling in celebration, but Wren just stared. I followed her gaze.

The wooden sign must have been hammered deep into the orange earth, because it didn't move even though the wind was brutal. The sign was at least a few years old, the words slightly faded. But still, I could make out every one:

REBOOT TERRITORY
ALL HUMANS TURN BACK

But "Reboot Territory" appeared to be nothing but flat, dry land and powerful, gusting wind. I was sort of bummed, to be honest. The Texas I knew was lush and hilly and green. This Texas was flat and orange. Who'd ever heard of orange dirt?

"It should be a couple miles that way!"

I turned at the sound of Addie's voice. She brushed her long, dark hair out of her face as she studied the map to the reservation that the rebels had given us. She glanced back at the two crashed shuttles behind her, then turned and pointed straight ahead to empty space. The flat land gave way to a small hill in the distance, so perhaps there was something over there we couldn't see yet. I certainly hoped so, otherwise Reboot territory was looking pretty pathetic.

Wren held out her hand and I laced my fingers through hers. I caught her eye and smiled and she attempted one in return, the way she did when her thoughts were elsewhere. A strand of blond hair escaped from her ponytail and she pushed it back, as usual not appearing to care where it landed or how messy her hair looked.

We started walking and the Reboots around us stole occasional glances at Wren. They all slowed until they were slightly behind us, letting her lead, but I didn't think she noticed. I was pretty sure Wren was proud of her One-seventy-eight—her impressive number of minutes dead before the KDH virus caused her to Reboot—but she often seemed oblivious to the way people treated her because of it. Or maybe she was just so used to it that it didn't faze her anymore.

Personally I would have been freaked out if everyone stared at me like that.

We walked in silence for almost half an hour as the Reboots behind us chattered, but now didn't seem like the time for conversation. My stomach was in knots, my mind buzzing with what we were supposed to do if the reservation wasn't here. How much fuel was left in those shuttles we just abandoned? Would Wren's even work after that crash landing? It had only been hours since we escaped HARC. What if they were on their way to find us right now?

I held Wren's hand tighter as we approached the hill. It wasn't terribly steep, and we climbed to the top quickly.

I stopped, my breath catching in my throat.

If that was the reservation, then someone hadn't explained it right. Someone should have piped up and said: *"Oh, it's not really a reservation. It's more like a huge compound in the middle of some ugly orange dirt."*

They'd built a fence all the way around the compound, not unlike the HARC fences that surrounded the cities of Texas. Except this fence was made of wood and stretched at least fifteen feet high, hiding the interior from our view. Towers even taller than the fence were at either end, and there was a person standing at the top of both of them. The towers were simple wooden buildings that seemed to only function as lookouts. On each one, long blocks of wood crisscrossed in between the four beams of the tower, and a ladder ran up one side. At the top was a bare slab of wood with a roof, but it was open on all four sides.

Beyond the reservation was a lake and large patches of trees, and past that more flat, orange dirt. I couldn't get over how big it was. *That* was a Reboot city? It had to be almost the size of Rosa.

Wren took in a sharp breath and quickly pulled her hand from mine. "They have guns," she said, pointing. "Look at them. They all have guns." She glanced around at the other Reboots. "Put your helmets on if you took them off. Raise your hands!"

I squinted at where she was pointing and took in a sharp breath. In front of the compound, lining the gate, was an army. There were maybe seventy-five or a hundred people, and it was impossible to tell if they were Reboot or human from this distance.

I tightened my helmet strap and raised my hands. "They could be humans, couldn't they?" We had a hundred near-invincible Reboots, but if those were armed humans we could be in a lot of trouble. Only a shot to the head could kill a Reboot, but a few of us didn't have helmets, and we hardly had any weapons at all. I swallowed as I looked at them again.

"They could." She squinted as she raised her hands. "We're too far to tell."

If it turned out we escaped from HARC—the Human Advancement and Repopulation Corporation, which enslaved Reboots and made us do their dirty work—only to get killed by a bunch of humans living in the middle of nowhere, I was going to be pissed. If they killed me, I was coming back from the dead (again) to hunt down the human rebels who told us about this reservation.

One of the men pulled away from the group and strode across the dirt, his black hair shiny in the morning sunlight. A gun swung from one of his hands and he had another tucked into the waist of his pants.

"Reboot," Wren said quietly.

I looked from her to the man. How could she tell from this distance? I couldn't even see his eyes yet.

"The way he walks," she clarified.

I turned to the man. He walked quickly, but evenly, like he knew where he was going but he wasn't going to panic about it. I didn't see how any of that said "Reboot," but I wasn't a badass five-year veteran Reboot who could take down nine men by myself. So what did I know?

The Reboots around us slowed as the man got closer, and many of them were watching Wren. I lowered my hands, nudging her back, and she looked at me as I tilted my head toward the man.

"What?" She took a quick glance around at the other Reboots, then turned back to me with a slightly exasperated expression. "Am I elected to talk to him or something?"

I tried not to grin, but I failed. Wren was so oblivious sometimes to how other people saw her, interacted with her, looked up to her. She'd been elected to talk to him miles back, before we ever saw anyone.

"Go," I said, giving her another gentle nudge on the back.

She sighed that "What do you people want from me?" sigh and I bit back a chuckle.

Wren stepped forward and the man stopped, lowering the gun slightly. He was in his mid to late twenties, but his eyes were calm and steady.

"Hello," the stranger said. He crossed his arms over his chest and cocked his head to one side. He scanned the crowd briefly and settled on Wren.

"Hi." Wren glanced back at me for a moment before turning to the man. "Um . . . I'm Wren. One-seventy-eight."

He had the same reaction as everyone else. His eyes widened. He stood up straighter. Wren's number earned her extra respect, even here. The reaction bugged me every time. Like she didn't matter without that number.

Wren lifted her wrist, and the man stepped closer to examine the number and bar code printed there. I closed my fingers over my own *22* and wished I could scrub both numbers off our arms. A higher number supposedly meant a Reboot was faster, stronger, less emotional, but I thought that was just a line HARC fed us that the Reboots bought into. We all used to be humans, before we died and came back to life as Reboots. I didn't see why the number of minutes dead mattered so much.

"Micah," the man said. "One-sixty-three."

One-sixty-three seemed very high to me. Wren had been the highest number in the Rosa facility, but I didn't think any of the other Reboots had been that close to her. A guy named Hugo was the closest and he was, what, One-fifty?

Micah held up his arm. His ink was more faded than Wren's, and I couldn't make out the numbers from this distance. But Wren tilted her head and stared at him blankly. She gave people that look when she didn't want them to know what she was thinking. It worked.

"I see you brought a few friends," Micah said, a smile spreading across his face.

"We . . ." She turned and found Addie in the crowd and pointed. "Me and Addie broke into the Austin facility and released all the Reboots."

Addie unhooked her helmet, her dark hair blowing in the wind. She ducked her head behind the taller Reboot in front of her, like she didn't want to be recognized for this feat. I couldn't really blame her. She hadn't really asked for any of this. Wren came to rescue her as part of a deal made with Addie's father, Leb—one of the HARC officers at Rosa—in exchange for helping Wren and me escape. Addie had just gotten caught up in the whirlwind.

Micah's smile disappeared. His face was expressionless, his mouth open a tiny bit. His eyes flicked over the crowd again.

"That"—he pointed—"is the entire Austin facility?"

"Yes."

"You released all of them?"

"Yes."

He stared a moment longer before taking a step closer to Wren. He put his hands on her face and I saw her body jolt. I resisted the urge to tell him only a dumbass would touch Wren without her permission. He'd discover that one for himself if she decided she didn't like it.

His hands covered most of her cheeks as he gazed down at her. "You. Are my new favorite person."

Yeah, get in line, dude.

Wren laughed and stepped away from his grasp. She tossed a look back in my direction like, *"Really? You made me deal with this guy?"* I grinned, stepping forward and offering her my hand. She slid her fingers between mine.

Micah stepped back to address the group. "Well, come on then. Welcome."

A few cheers erupted, and people began talking excitedly all around us.

"We already took their trackers out," Wren said to Micah. "Way back near Austin."

"Oh, that doesn't matter," he said with a chortle.

It doesn't? I frowned in confusion and saw a matching expression on Wren's face, but Micah had already turned away to talk to a cluster of eager young Reboots. He began leading the way to the reservation and I started to follow, but I felt a tug on my hand as Wren stood her ground, watching the Reboots stream after Micah.

She was nervous, although it had taken me a while to learn what that particular expression looked like. She took in a small breath, her eyes darting over the scene in front of us.

"Everything okay?" I asked. I was nervous, too. When Wren was nervous, I was nervous.

"Yeah," she said softly like it wasn't. I knew she wasn't as excited to go to the reservation as I was. She'd told me she would have stayed at HARC if it weren't for me. I couldn't begin to understand that, and it occurred to me for the first time that maybe she hadn't just convinced herself she was happy as a HARC slave. Maybe she really was.

I wanted to think that she'd adjust and be happy here, too, but it was hard to say. I wasn't even entirely sure what made Wren happy, besides beating people up. Of course, if I were as good at that as she was, it might make me pretty happy, too.

She barely nodded, as if convincing herself of something, and began walking in the direction of the reservation. The Reboots lining the gate were still as we approached, their guns all pointed at us.

Micah stepped away from the group, holding one hand up to his troops. "Weapons down! Hold your positions!"

As soon as he shouted the command, every Reboot lowered their gun. Their bright eyes were glued to us, and I took in a breath as I glanced down the line. There were so many. Most of them were about my age, but I spotted a few who seemed closer to thirty or forty.

The reservation Reboots were dressed in loose, light-colored cotton clothes, nothing like the black uniforms HARC made us wear, with the exception of the helmets on their heads. They were strong and well fed, and even though they were positioned for what they thought was an attack, no one seemed scared. If anything they were . . . excited?

Micah lifted a black box to his mouth that looked like one of the coms HARC used. He spoke into it, glancing up at the tower to our right. He listened for a moment, nodded, and said a few more words into it before sliding it into his pocket.

He took a step backward and beckoned in our direction with two fingers. "Wren."

She stood still next to me, her shoulders tense. Micah gestured with his head for her to come, and she let out a tiny sigh as she slipped her fingers from mine. People moved aside as she walked toward him, and I felt uncomfortable on her behalf. They were all staring.

Micah beamed as she stopped next to him. He reached down and grabbed her hand, making her jump. He had an expression of such pure adoration on his face that I would have been jealous if she weren't looking at him like he was an alien.

Okay, maybe I was slightly jealous. She'd looked at me like I was an alien at first, too, but now I was pretty sure she liked me.

Well, more than pretty sure. Mostly sure. As close as you can get to sure without being totally sure. She had left her "home" (prison) for me, and then risked her life and took down an entire HARC facility to save me. I thought that was like Wren's version of "I'm totally into you." I'd take it.

Wren yanked her hand from his, but Micah seemed oblivious, beaming as he faced the reservation Reboots.

"Guys, this is Wren One-seventy-eight."

A few of them gasped and I sighed inwardly. Any hopes I'd had of our numbers not mattering here were being further dashed by the second. Some of the Reboots were gazing at her with such awe and excitement that I wanted to slap them and tell them to stop being weird.

"She brings with her the entire Austin facility," Micah continued.

More gasps. At least they were excited to see us.

"I didn't do it by myself." Wren scanned the crowd, but didn't seem to find Addie. "Addie Thirty-nine and I did it together."

Micah sort of nodded in that way people did when they weren't really listening. He was grinning at the crowd of reservation Reboots. They were whispering, their faces cautiously optimistic.

Wren cast a confused look at me as Micah raised his hand. The crowd went silent.

"All right then," he said. "I have good news."

Thank goodness. I needed good news. I hoped it was something along the lines of "I have food and beds for all of you right now."

Micah gestured to the tower. "I just got word that there are more HARC shuttles coming. They're on their way right now."

Wait. What?

"About a hundred miles out," Micah continued. "At least seven confirmed."

Which part was the good news?

"So." Micah grinned as he lifted one fist in the air. "Ready?"

Every reservation Reboot responded together in one loud yell.

"ATTACK!"

TWO

WREN

I FROZE AS CALLUM CAST A HORRIFIED LOOK IN MY DIRECTION.

Attack?

"Wren." Micah put his hand on my shoulder. I shrugged it off. "You came in HARC shuttles, didn't you? Where are they?"

I blinked. How did he know that? How did he know there were more HARC shuttles on the way?

"We left them a couple miles back," I said. "We didn't want to alarm you by getting too close in them."

"We were alarmed, obviously," Micah said with a laugh, gesturing to the army of Reboots behind him. He stuck his fingers in his mouth and whistled. "Jules!"

A girl a few years older than me joined us. Her red hair was in a braid, and she had a HARC bar code stamped on her wrist, but I couldn't make out the number.

"Go fetch those shuttles." Micah lifted his hand, made a sort of circular motion with his finger, and the massive wooden gate immediately began to creak open. The Reboots in front of it scrambled away.

I felt a hand on my back and turned to see Callum behind me. "What's going on?" he asked quietly.

"I don't know."

The gate swung open the rest of the way to reveal about ten Reboots sitting on contraptions I'd never seen before. They had two big wheels—one in back and one in front—and looked sort of like one of those motorcycle things I'd seen pictures of, but bigger. Three people could probably fit on the wide, black seat stretched between the two tires, and a loud rumbling noise came from each one.

"Kyle!" Micah said, waving. A tall, beefy Reboot inched his bike away from the others. "Take Jules and—" He stopped and turned to me. "Who flew those here?"

"Me and Addie."

"The Thirty-nine?"

"Yes."

He nodded and turned back to Kyle. "Take Jules and Thirty-nine to the shuttles. Quick. No more than twenty minutes round-trip."

Kyle twisted his hand around one of the handlebars and the

bike roared forward, coming to a screeching stop next to Jules. She hopped on and eyed the crowd of Austin Reboots expectantly.

"Thirty-nine!" Micah yelled.

Addie stepped out from the crowd, arms crossed over her chest. She ignored Micah completely and stared at me like she was waiting for something. I wasn't sure what it was. Did she want me to tell her it was okay to go?

I avoided Micah's gaze as I strode across the dirt and stopped in front of her.

"They want you to take them to the shuttles," I said. "And probably fly one over here."

Her eyes darted behind me. "And you think we should trust them?"

I paused. Of course I didn't think we should trust them. I'd just met them, and so far, they seemed weird. But we'd strolled up to their home and asked to be let in, so maybe it was too late to think about trust.

"No," I said quietly.

She looked taken aback by my answer. "No?"

"No."

She blinked as if waiting for more, and a smile began to appear on her face. "Okay then. I feel better." She took a deep breath. "Right. Ride off with the strangers. Hope for the best. Got it."

She nodded her head as she finished, and I blinked, suddenly realizing what I was asking.

"I can go instead—"

She laughed as she stepped back. "That's all right. Can't fault you for being honest." She jogged across the dirt and hopped on the back of the bike, pointing in the direction we'd come from. Kyle peeled out, the bike spitting dirt as they disappeared.

"One-twenties and over with me!" Micah called to the Austin Reboots. "Let's do this!" He was practically jumping up and down, he was so excited.

I didn't understand.

I took a glance behind me at the Austin Reboots to see similar confused expressions on their faces. Beth One-forty-two, a couple girls, and two guys who I assumed were Over-one-twenties broke off from the group and slowly headed in Micah's direction, but they kept turning puzzled faces my way. There were less Over-one-twenties in Austin than there had been in Rosa, but I'd been stationed in the toughest city in Texas. More assignments meant they needed more skilled Reboots.

"Micah!" I called, following him as he darted for the gate. "What's going on? How do you know HARC is coming? How did you know we were coming?"

He stopped. "We have people stationed in strategic places, and equipment that monitors air traffic in the area."

I raised my eyebrows, surprised. I hadn't expected them to be so advanced.

Micah spread his arms wide, beaming at the Austin Reboots. "Guys! Let's see some excitement!"

We just stared.

He raised his fist. "Whoop!"

"Whoop whoop!" a hundred reservation Reboots yelled at once, and I jumped. What the hell?

"Oh, come on," he said with a chuckle. "Who wants to kick some HARC ass?"

That produced a few laughs. Someone at the back of the crowd of Austin Reboots raised his hand. "I'm in!"

I'd actually kicked enough HARC ass this past week to last me a very long time. I glanced at Callum. He'd never wanted to fight anyone, human or Reboot.

Micah chuckled as he caught my expression. "I know you're probably tired. And you're going to have to tell me the story soon about how you got out of Rosa, ended up in Austin, and stole two shuttles filled with every Reboot in that facility. But right now, we've got a bunch of HARC officers on their way here to attack us. So we don't have much choice."

I looked at Callum and he lifted his shoulders, like he wasn't sure what to do.

I knew what I wanted to do. I wanted to hightail it out of here before HARC arrived. I didn't know where we'd go, but we certainly didn't have to stay and fight.

Or maybe we did. I regarded the group of Reboots I'd brought here and saw several faces turned in my direction, watching to see how I'd react. I'd busted into the Austin facility and ushered them all into shuttles and dumped them into this situation. If I asked Callum to make a run for it, he would tell me they needed my help. And he would be right, unfortunately.

But this was the last time. If it seemed like there were going to be more attacks from HARC, I'd grab Callum and go. I didn't want to spend the rest of my life fighting off the humans. I'd be perfectly content never to see them again, actually.

I sighed and barely nodded at Micah. He clapped his hand on my back like he approved.

"Under-sixties with me!" a thin guy yelled.

I shook my head at Callum and held out my hand. We weren't doing that. A corner of his mouth turned up as he walked toward me.

Micah glanced down at Callum's wrist. "One-twenty-two?" he asked, squinting.

"Twenty-two," Callum corrected.

Micah pointed to the crowd gathering around the thin man. "Under-sixties with Jeff."

"Callum's with me." I held his hand tighter.

Micah opened his mouth, but closed it with a hint of a smile. "Fine." He turned to the reservation entrance, gesturing for us to follow him.